Toni's Smile

A novel about power and
the first Blatina President

By Jeff Stilwell

She smiled.

And wondered.

What is left after we are gone?

Isn't that the point of life, after all? To answer that question?

Look at Alexander, the Great Thug of Macedonia. What did he do? Lay waste to all the world that he could compass. All the world that he could imagine. Take a city. Rape it. Slaughter it. Rebuild it. Rename it. After himself of course. And move on to the next one.
A series of smoking monuments to himself, one after another, each bearing his name stamped in gold in all too large letters.
It must have sounded like a good plan.
At the time.
No.
For they all wound up deriding into dust. Eventually.
To be forgotten.

Or misremembered.

Take Iskandar. The medieval corruption of his original naming of the city and its surrounding environs after himself.

Hell, Toni thought to herself as she took one last sip and set down the Delft (ohh!) porcelain cup with its presidential seal and sleepily nestled into the high-thread cotton sheets of this largest bed she had ever slept in with its ever-vigilant, if a bit too tight-assed and too tightly buttoned, Secret Service protection right outside the door.

(Was she already asleep, she wondered. Was she dreaming? Did it matter?)

That monument to Alexander the Great's glory, which was designed by the Fearless Leader of his time to last for all eternity as a testament to his greatness, his own twin tablets honoring his mercy, his beneficence, his divinity – that name, instead, had come down to modern ears with the sobriquet as the outhouse of humanity.

Kandahar.

Factory of gravestones.

Crucible of sorrow.

Like any shithole. Oh, and of terrorists, too.

So much for monuments.

What is left after we pass, she wondered?

She smiled.

I

She woke with the smell of Mama's fried chicken in her nose. "Best in the world, child!" The memory of Mama's wide beam, so bright as to blind the whole community, sparked an exhausted grin on her own cheeks.

Mama had lived in the row apartment on the corner, just a few doors down in Trumbull Village. When her own mother, soused as usual, had simply walked without explanation into a SunTran city bus on Zuni Road, Toni had shrugged her sixteen year old shoulders and gone straight to Mama.

She blinked the fuzzy sleep out of her eyes, reflexively tamping down any thoughts of her mother, and wondered what had awakened her.

The sharp rap came on her door again.

Oh.

The "Witch of the White House" was calling.

On better days, Beatie – her handler, minder, chief strategist, best gossip, and closest thing to a real friend – termed herself "the Oracle of the Oval Office." If Warren, the Chief of Staff, kept the trains running, Beatie pointed out the ones about to crash days before anyone else saw them coming.

At any rate, on those days when the Oracle was coming to join her for muffins and coffee in the West Sitting Hall before the Tiffany lunette window that Toni loved so much, on those quieter mornings, Rod's softer tap on the door awoke her with a smile.

When the Witch came to breakfast, however, Toni was awakened by Beatie's sharp rap.

She sighed, wondering what it was all about. Something.

God, why was she always so exhausted?

Grumbling, throwing back the heavy comforter and rich golden amber sheets, she slipped out, sliding her feet into her fuzzy slippers and picked up her bathrobe.

Stopping before a mirror of the Master Bedroom, redone for Hap McDougal in imperial golds and ivories by his wife, Toni spared a thought for the sad woman as she ran some fingers through her messy tangle of a 'fro.

Harold "Hap" McDougal, patrician of Massachusetts, with Boston Brahmin blood bluer than the Kennedys, had connected with the masses through large plates of Boston Baked Beans and Massachusetts Bay Shrimp, both served with large hunks of salt pork, his fiery rhetoric of "standing up for the little guy," and the long string of mistresses that seemed to surround him like an entourage. No small feat in the #MeToo era.

His wife? She was an afterthought.

Toni had often considered that, had she found herself married to such a serial philanderer, she would have gelded him after the first affair. Not his wife.

His large appetites had gotten Hap in the end, though. Not ten hours after being sworn in at noon on January 20th, Hap had disappeared out a side door of the Commander-in-Chief's Inaugural Ball at the National Building Museum to bang a campaign intern with big tits and bigger blonde hair on the antiquated desk of some revered Pension Bureau official dating back to the 1850s. His orgasm – or his excitement – was apparently too much for his ticker, which had exploded.

The intern screamed.

Which made a cover up impossible.

Thus, Toni had found herself yanked without warning into a side room of her own Vice President's Home State Ball at the convention center by an uncharacteristically freaked out Warren and being administered the Oath of Office for the second time that day. This one – administered by an equally unnerved Chief Justice of the United States Supreme Court – was shorter.

I do solemnly swear that I will faithfully execute the Office of President of the United States, and will to the best of my Ability, preserve, protect and defend the Constitution of the United States.

Thus, because a White patrician elder statesman – graduate of Groton and member of the Porcellian Club at Harvard, a feat that even FDR didn't manage – couldn't keep his dick in his pants,

Antonia Camila Madison became the first Blatina President of the United States.

And every one of those thousand or so days since, she had been reminded in ways large and small, that it wasn't supposed to have been this way. Wags had even invented a nickname for her. Well, not invented. Not really. The old pejorative for veep John Tyler – "His Accidency" – awarded after President William Henry Harrison had unexpectedly died a month into his term – had been revived, just for her.

Hap had chosen the unknown fifth-termer from the New Mexico 1st (Albuquerque, or ABQ to the locals) because the electoral math worked. She balanced the ticket, being all things he was not – a she, a southwesterner, a brownie or a blackie, depending on who was counting. Even better, with her gun-slinging Billy the Kid persona, earned taking on street gangs in ABQ, she was just Tex-Mex enough to pull it off with the NRA crowd. Best of all, as far as he was concerned, she was easy on the eyes. She had knockers that would have been the pride of any Hooters Restaurant.

Besides, everybody knew that the job of vice president wasn't worth a bucket of warm spit. Nobody expected her to do anything. Not really.

And she hadn't, she mused, continuing to untangle her fro on this day. Deciding, again, as always, to wrap it in a scarf. Every morning, the same argument, ending the same way. Michelle Obama might have conscientiously had her hair regularly straightened to make her husband more presentable to White voters. Toni just didn't have the time. (Except for State Dinners.)

What *had* she accomplished with her all too busy days? The question nagged. As far as she was concerned, she had done almost nothing. Nothing exciting. Nothing of any consequence. Beatie liked to say that she had done the most important thing – she had survived.

In that first year, after the Inaugural *Balls* Scandal (a popular FOX News zinger, that one) finally died down, she had calmed the troubled waters. She kept Hap's Cabinet, losing only a handful that refused to take orders from a woman. Of color. She kept as many of his White House staff that would stay, letting her own go almost completely. She met repeatedly with the House Speaker, the Senate Majority Leader, the Gang of Eight Congressional Leaders, the heads of the AFL-CIO, SEIU and other major unions, the heads of the US Chamber of Congress and National Association of Manufacturers, Wall Street and other denizens. She even had coffee with the Koch Brothers, in the Oval one morning in May, which turned out to be surprisingly genteel.

To all, she sang the same tune. This is Hap's administration. We are sticking with his plan.

And she had. *To the best of her Ability.*

The last three years had seen the national coffers fill again, no small feat after the rampant profligacy of the previous administration. They were also remarkably scandal free. But then, given that the previous administration had made Warren G. Harding's Teapot Dome presidency look like a bunch of choir boys, nobody was too impressed by that feat.

After a bit of hemming and hawing, Wall Street finally came around, deciding fatalistically that she was too powerless to do anything seriously wrong. Main Street came around, too. Kinda. The economy rebounded. Sorta. Jobs started coming back. A bit.

Slowly.

Overseas, she pretty much let the Joint Chiefs have their sway. As such, US military policy stopped being so adventurous and retreated to its historical role of silently waving a big stick at any who got seriously out of line. Not really doing anything with the eleven aircraft carrier strike groups other than ceaselessly patrolling, reminding would-be baddies, such as the Strait of Hormuz pirates, that the US Navy was always there.

At home, budgets were planned and passed. Appropriations were planned, passed. Taxes collected. Even the characteristically cantankerous House Freedom Caucus was known to take the occasional quiet nap. The mid-terms came and went with hardly a murmur. (She would have campaigned for her party, but no one asked. As a result, the balance of power in House and Senate had shifted, largely, to the other side. Not that it mattered.)

For three years, the dull machinery of national government – basically one large retirement fund with an army attached – kept quietly grinding along.

If anything, the only danger she could see was that she was boring everyone to death.

But, now, entering her fourth spring as chief executive, she had noticed that that troubling, trickling thought had been springing up in the back of her mind more and more lately.

She was failing the people. They deserved better.

Enough was enough. It was time to meet her Witch.

Stepping outside the door into the bright sunshine of the sitting room, she smiled at Beatie. Who was already fuming.

"Do you know what that rat-fucker did last night?"

Malcolm, the First Family Steward, thankfully, was in the kitchen opposite. She could hear him opening a cabinet. As for Rod? Toni darted a glance at him, standing a discrete twenty feet down the wall, only to see precisely what she expected. A face set in stone. Only one thought running through that Praetorian mind – who wants to hurt the President? Nothing else mattered.

His all too muscular frame, as usual, was tucked neatly into his suit. Tie tied off sharply in a half windsor. Hair briskly clipped in a high and tight just going gray. Shoulders cut with a fine edge. Just like that lantern jaw of his.

She sighed. This was not the time to daydream over her primary bodyguard.

Instead, she smiled more brightly as she stepped over to the couch facing her strategist. Between the couches, just at knee level, was a small tray festooned with the usual china containing coffee, flanked by a croissant (the White House Chef insisted on making them so rich she could only handle one) neatly tucked on one tray and a small hill of Beatie Cakes on another. Beatie couldn't get enough of the treat. She ate them all day long, ever since the chef had created them – fluffy white sweet cream inside a dark chocolate muffin, with the initials BC in lighter colored chocolate frosting on the top – and named them in her honor. Indeed, she was holding one with a large bite taken out of it now.

"And which one are we discussing this morning?"

Her John Lennon glasses with their lilac lenses (today) almost steaming over with indignation on her plump Black cheeks that so often reminded Toni with a pang of Mama, Beatie rapped out, "Langton."

Ah.

Her veep.

Edward Langton was almost as Hap as Hap. Almost. Just without the spine, the vision, or the damn-the-torpedoes attitude that had won a very skeptical Toni to Hap's side in the early days. Ed had been forced on her by the DNC, the national party organ of the Dems, almost the moment she had been sworn in. Still too dazed to think at the time of Warren's entreaties right there at the Ball, she had numbly agreed. It had made sense, even to her. In the age of YouTube, Ed looked as presidential as she did not.

"Do you know what that scrawny-assed, self-entitled, silver spoon in his mouth, frat boy said?"

Malcolm entered now. As he bent to pour out her cup of steaming black hope, Toni forced herself not to answer, watching him instead, wondering if the pause would make Beatie take another huge gulp of her breakfast.

It did.

Those adorably chubby cheeks were clearly working on it furiously, however. Toni ignored them and took a long, luxurious sip of her favorite morning joy and looked out the window. Tiffany's large wonder, it was easily the length and a half of a couch. Just white arches within one another, holding large splashes of glass, with a delicate web of frames making up the whole, she found it comforting. In a world gone mad, it was a symbol to her of simple beauty. Comprehensible, even though she knew she barely had a clue how he and his designers had wrought it. A contemporary of them, Teddy Roosevelt – whom she privately called T-Rex, thinking of his flashing teeth and need to hunt down big animals with big guns, as if he were compensating for some other lack – hated Tiffany glass, thinking it effeminate. He had ordered all Tiffany glass possible packed up and hidden away in storage during his White House years. He probably would have preferred hanging all his lion and elk heads up, instead, like he had had at home. Knowing this only further endeared the window to her. Some days, particularly after yet one more awful high school shooting, her window, and T-Rex's hatred of it, reminded her of everything she did not want to be as President.

Beatie was already snatching another BC and greedily taking a huge bite. She mumbled something that sounded like "primary," but Toni wasn't sure.

She waited.

Beatie swallowed, wiping some sweat off her brow. "We must stand with the President in her time of travail," she intoned. "That rat-faced fucker!"

Toni took another sip, then took a delicate bite off one end of the croissant. Flaky, buttery, rich. Heaven.

Travail didn't sound bad. It pretty much summed up her state of mind. Not that Ed meant it that way.

Beatie growled.

Toni was distracted for an instant by the thought of how Rod took her strategist's growls. From appearance, he clearly was not bothered by them, much less ever considering them a threat to her person. He barely seemed to even notice them. Yet, Rod caught everything. She knew that from experience. She darted a glance at him. Oh, to be the woman who got to run her hand down that backside.

She almost growled herself at that thought, shushing it out of existence and forcing herself to focus on her friend. Who was just taking another large bite of another treat.

She was speaking around the chocolate, white cream poking out at the corners of her lips. "That two-faced son-of-a-bitch is gonna primary your Black ass!"

Oh. That.

During the mid-terms a year and a half – and a lifetime – ago, when she had reached out to those House members and Senators the polling showed most vulnerable, offering her services to campaign for them, the answer had been largely unequivocal. No. Don't come. You will hurt more than help. Beatie had made her do a face-saving whistle-stop tour of the few districts that had answered ambiguously. Almost pushing her on them. It had been uncomfortable. And eye-opening. Even metropolitan areas with large Hispanic and Black neighborhoods had been ambivalent about her visit. The truth was brought home to her. Hispanic and Black communities did not like women in power, no matter their color. That she sat behind the Resolute Desk in the Oval Office made not one bit of difference. Paradoxically, it was the White communities that would have been more open to her visits, except for the fact that she wasn't White. So, she had pretty much sat it out, asking Ed to take up the slack. And he had. Manfully. He wasn't all that great a speaker. He didn't have Hap's animal magnetism that made women a little crazy and men want to crowd around slapping him on the back. No matter. It was something.

Later, just before Election Day, Beatie had begun fuming that she was hearing things. Bad things. Troubling whispers about

"Fast Eddie" making promises about "big changes in two years." That sort of thing.

Toni had tried to shut it all out. She was struggling with her own depression about feeling utterly useless at the time and the maddening amount of energy that it took to put on a bright smile each morning.

Finally, after the mid-terms were safely over – and, therefore, no longer clickable material, worth leaking – mostly just to shut Beatie up, she had asked Ed to the Oval.

And she asked him straight out. "Ed, are you planning to primary me in a year?"

He had been shocked. Horrified. And not a little offended. She was still getting used to his rhetorical flourishes – mostly because she had largely ignored him those first two years, letting Warren handle him – but as he took a deep breath, she easily recognized the wind-up that every politician she had ever known did when about to launch forth on a litany of abuses, mischaracterizations, and misunderstandings that could make the sky fall, she had quickly decided that she believed him, shaken his hand, and nodded at Warren to get rid of him.

Travail.

Beatie was intoning again, in mimicry of Ed's Georgia twang. From memory. Toni had only rarely ever seen her need to consult any tablet, piece of paper, whatever. Her mind just worked like that.

"We saw during the midterm elections how the great burdens of office occupied President Madison to the point that she could barely leave the building. Others had to come forward to rally the troops, to carry the party standard. They rallied to the cause. They stood by her, knowing that her heart was in the trim. As it always is. She wanted to be there. It grieved her not to be there. I know that for a fact. With the heavy burdens of the office, however, it simply was not possible. Make no mistake. Other presidents may find themselves free enough to golf most weekends. Not this one. This one has her hands full with a troublesome world. And it is only going to get harder for her. We must stand with the President in her time of travail."

Well...Toni thought.

"Translation?" Beatie fumed. "Those sweet, delicate Blatina shoulders can't lift the weight. But, hey, don't worry your pretty little head over it. You won't be here all that long, anyway." She took another huge gulp.

Toni found herself frowning, considering.

Her eye wandered to the door of the Prince of Wales Room opposite, also known as the Family Residence Dining Room. When she had first arrived, she had hidden in the Master Bedroom each morning. Her breakfast tray dutifully brought to her by Malcolm. Rod, as always, at Malcolm's side. This went on for the first few months, until she realized that she was probably supposed to eat in the Family Residence Dining Room. At least it might make her look more presidential, which

13

couldn't hurt. Mightily confused at the names of rooms those first days, however, she kept mixing up references to this room with the more formal Family Dining Room on the first floor where she would wind up entertaining the Gang of Eight congressional leaders in the days when she believed they truly would work with her instead of waiting out her eighteen months. Eventually, exasperated, one day she worked up the nerve to ask Malcolm the difference. He had – in his quiet, conscientious way – explained that people often referred to the dining room on the second floor as the Prince of Wales room, since the future king had stayed there, when it was still a bedroom, upon his visit during Buchanan's years on the eve of the Civil War.

That suited Toni just fine. Everybody in the Southwest knew that the randy Prince of Wales – likely to piss off his mother, embodiment of the strictest personal morality ever to sit on the throne in the UK – had whored his way through his visit to the United States, adding to his already fabled roster of fifty-odd mistresses in his lifetime. Local lore had it that he had even hooked up at some point with "Little Egypt," one of the first belly dancers to achieve an international following. Fatima, as she was also known, had gotten her start at the Birdcage Theatre in Tombstone, Arizona, in Wyatt Earp's time. The gunfighter's legendary companions Doc Holliday and Bat Masterson used to play cards in all night poker games down in the muddy basement of the Birdcage, probably while Little Egypt was dancing upstairs on the dinky stage.

Feeling all at once at home, even with such a tenuous connection, the second President Madison thereupon informed the First Family Steward that she would begin each day with breakfast in the Prince of Wales Room.

Malcolm, true to form, pulled out all the stops. He served her such delicious pancakes, omelettes, crepes, frittatas, parathas (the Indian "tortilla" for lack of a better term, with its characteristic chopped green onions folded, pastry flour style, into the dough), bacon, sausages of a bewildering variety, eggs served in a myriad of styles, potatoes fried in a bemusing array of presentations that she began to gain weight. At an alarming rate. She also quickly felt the need to get up, shower, makeup, do her hair in something other than a mess, wear the nicest blouses and skirts and belts with matching shoes, coats and scarves she could find, just to do honor to his efforts. Oddly, the more ornate her preparations, the more elaborate Malcolm's breakfasts became, almost in some sort of good-natured arms race that only made sense to him. He added servers, then put them in waist-coated tuxedos with bow ties. He added freshly cut flowers, then changed them out daily, then scoured the city for the most fragrant ones available after she had made the mistake of complimenting the scent of some Imperial roses one morning that first summer. He even brought in a harpist a few times, then a handsome Spanish lutist with soulful eyes, then a soft flautist, then a cellist. Since she knew he took his job, his place as First Family Steward, and the august history of the museum that she currently lived in, so seriously, she didn't even bother considering that it might be some kind of oneupmanship, or a subtle hazing of the new President. Others might love to remind her how she didn't belong there. Malcolm wasn't the type. He would faint at the mere suggestion, from sheer stress.

In any case, when she found herself about to tell Janice to bring in the stylist who stretched her hair in the days prior to state dinners, she realized that things had gone too far. A state dinner with the British PM or German Chancellor was one thing. But breakfast? No. How to change things – since ending them was out of the question for Malcolm would be deeply wounded – would take some tact.

One day, when the Witch had cometh first thing in the morning, ready to burn down the Speaker of the House's suite of offices in the Longworth Building because of....because of something. Toni couldn't remember. She had decided on the spur of the moment to ask Malcolm to serve them in the West Sitting Hall, on the facing couches in front of her window. Mostly, she hadn't wanted Beatie to start making fun of whatever musician Malcolm had lined up that morning. Her steward had responded without turning a hair, she noticed with surprised pleasure. Something about meetings with the President, she guessed? A personal pride that any occasion involving matters of State, no matter how precipitous or unexpected, would be met without a murmur? It was a thought.

Regardless, the tray had appeared, complete with – another surprise – Beatie's small hill of cakes and a berry crepe for her. When Beatie made a comment about "why we eating out here?" Malcolm had smoothly replied that President and First Lady Eisenhower had often eaten in the West Sitting Hall on tv trays while they watched television, each with their own tv set.

That was enough for Toni. Eisenhower was a personal icon, only recently discovered, because of his smooth handling of international bad boys. If it was good enough for him, it was good enough for her. The pattern had stuck.

A couple of years later, here they were still. Her first meeting of the day, each day, in pajamas and bathrobe no less, Malcolm as ornately pouring her coffee as if she were wearing a Chanel gown.

"Madame President?"

Beatie's harsh question grated in her ears.

Toni came back to the moment. Ed had promised her. Besides, he didn't have the stones to go out on the limb by himself. She knew that.

She sighed, taking another look at Beatie's furious gaze. But her stomach turned to water as she abruptly realized that her chief strategist knew that, too.

Catching a sob of exhaustion, carefully keeping it inward, she retreated in her mind to the smell of Mama's fried chicken. "Best in the world, child!"

***

At the funeral for Rosa Madison, after she tossed a handful of
dirt onto the cheapest coffin that Mama had been able to find –
her mother's new home for all eternity – Toni had stiffly walked
back to Cesar. Mama was too fat to attend, so she had sent one
of her boys to look after Toni. Cesar was gang. Every boy was
gang in Trumbull Village. But he was also good-looking, so
Toni didn't mind. Besides, he wouldn't dare hurt her now that
she had Mama's stamp on her.

Mama ran their little corner of the world as if she were the
Queen of England, herself. To live in Mama's world meant to sit
in her kitchen all day long, at the table, surrounded by the smell
of breaded chicken fried in her 21 cup deep fat fryer that took
one and a third gallons of oil at a gulp. Toni knew. She had
filled that fryer many a time. Had been burned by it, too. But
then Mama would grab her up with the cry, "Child, what mess
you got yoself into?" and mash Toni's face into her huge boobs.
It was the safest place on the planet, Toni always thought. Then,
Mama would bark out the commands to "Get that lovin' hand
under some cold water!" and after a few moments, in softer
tones, "Now break off a nub of that aloe vera and bring it to me"
for Mama had just such a plant sitting in the kitchen window, a
huge one, with long, thick spiny leaves in soft green reaching out
to the sun. Toni used to wonder how many burns that plant had
healed over the decades as Mama would squeeze out a little of
the green gel from the end of the nub she had broken off, and
smear it gently on the burn. The gel always felt wonderful,

immediately. Like Mama's hugs. And it was cool, too. Every time, no matter how hot the summer ABQ day. Mama's hugs were not. Nor was her kitchen. It was always steaming hot, every day of the year. To sit in Mama's kitchen at her table was to sweat. Surrounded by fried chicken resting on cooling racks, dripping oil onto the paper towels underneath.

And to smoke. Second-hand, anyway. For Mama would bat your hand if she caught you with a cigarette in it. Toni knew. The only time Mama had ever struck her.

And to listen. For Mama had an opinion on just about every question of this world – from the true shape of Michael Jackson's nose to whether Jesus was our Savior to whether the North Vietnamese had been winning the war when her Elijah had forgotten to come home from the jungle. That was how she had come to live there, in Trumbull Village, at the row apartments. For her Elijah had been a crewman on Huey helicopters at Kirtland Air Force Base, not too far away, just south of Gibson Boulevard. And she had set up home for them here. Their whole neighborhood long before Toni was born had been Air Force. Nice lawns. Barbecues on the weekends. Dogs barking, children playing, mothers gossipping. Then, out of the blue after the war the officers had moved north, followed a few years later by the non-coms, followed finally by the crewmen. Mama had stayed. Even when the owner had sold the building to the city and the row apartments became public housing and a magnet for the slime of the gutter. This was the only home she and her Elijah had ever had together.

One day in high school at Mama's request, Toni had bussed over to UNM's library, scared as the dickens, looked up the Tet Offensive in the spring of '68 and then returned home to explain to her slowly, and very carefully, as Mama – her eyes tightly closed, chain-smoking her Luckys – listened skeptically to how a simple crewman, too terrified to leave the safety of his airbase in Saigon, could die over there. It had been hard. There was so little real information. So few real details. Fewer than the Pentagon flimsy that Mama had waved around announcing her Elijah wasn't coming home in anything other than a body bag. Even the microfilm footage that Toni had found, burned on to fancy new CDs that her high school would never afford, focused almost entirely on the attack on the American embassy in the city. Nothing about air bases or frightened Huey crewmen getting killed by stray bullets or stray bombs from Viet Cong hell bent on conquest, even at the expense of their own lives.

Eventually, as she kept trying to explain that she had tried as hard as she could, Mama had snapped and reached for the curtain.

"Child! Do you want to end up like her?"

Startled at the question, Toni had looked out to see her friend Lupe, then realized it was a girl a year ahead of her at Highland High School – proud both of its lowest graduation rate and highest crime rate in all of ABQ – standing in a slut skirt on the corner of Dallas Street. As she watched, a large Crown Vic drove up and slowed in front of the girl as she, emphasizing her knockers, bent over and talked through the passenger window to the driver. Then she got in.

"Do you?" Mama was lighting another Lucky.

Toni shook her head.

"Then try harder. Otherwise that is where you'll wind up. I won't be around forever, child."

Toni nodded.

"Now," Mama sat back with a smile. "Tell me all about that big ol' university."

And she had. Everything that she could remember. The clean sidewalks and the beautiful grass, the lovely trees. The large library. The huge construction site for some building named after Dane somebody. The students everywhere. Carrying backpacks with their books. Tossing a football or a frisbee around on the lawn that she would have been afraid to walk on. Silver and cherry sweatshirts everywhere with UNM and the Lobo, the wolf mascot, that she knew from football games on tv.

"And the girls?"

Toni had paused, not certain what Mama meant.

"Child, were they any different from you?"

Not really.

At first, she had thought, of course they were. But in the weeks following her UNM adventure and after a few more trips to the library to look up things that Mama "needed" to know about, she began to feel sheepish at how scared she had been that first time. It wasn't even that far away from home, was even shorter from the high school, though the bus did skirt Nob Hill which was supposed to be full of rich people. She had seen White girls, of course. But she had also seen a lot of Natives. And Latinas. Not any more than one or two Black girls, though.

But then, as Mama cheerfully pointed out, she was both.

***

She was both.

A Blatina strolling along the south side of the White House looking out at the Rose Garden. Who knew such a day could come?

The night was still. Overhead a hunter's moon lit the sky up almost as brightly as the windows along the Colonnade. One of the most famous scenes from the White House, Malcolm had surprised her with its mundane history. They both, the West and East Colonnades, had been built by Thomas Jefferson, stretching out from the main building on each side to help hide the rustic stables and sheds behind the much grander President's House.

Which is what it had been called until it had been repainted white after the British burned it in the War of 1812. Even she knew that.

Except she was wrong. In Malcolm's quiet smile while pouring her a scotch one evening, she detected that he frequently corrected this urban legend. The original sandstone – from which state, Malcolm had told her she was sure, but she couldn't remember – had been whitewashed years before the war and the building had been offhandedly referred to as the White House in those days as a result.

In any case, the building had largely existed all by itself on the grounds for much of the country's history. It was T-Rex who, flexing his new presidential biceps, decided there just wasn't enough room in the building for his grandiose schemes, so he had the stables and some greenhouses just to the west flattened to make room for another office building for himself and his burgeoning staff. Over time, his Executive Office Building became known as the West Wing. (Toni always remembered her confusion when, as a freshman Congresswoman, she had been surprised to find the Oval Office in the West Wing and *not* in the White House. Her face burned at the memory, even today.) He also had had a small East Wing with its large cloak room constructed to receive guests in that carriage and top hat era.

Not content to mark his territory in that fashion alone, it was T-Rex, too, who, by Executive Order, had officially named the President's home the White House.

Not to be outdone, it was his wife Edith – apparently the only one at that time who could handle America's Peter Pan President – who installed the first garden. Wilson's wife Ellen enlarged it into a garden that emphasized roses a decade later and Jackie

Kennedy had it all redesigned during her years into the most
famous Rose Garden in the world.

Toni was stepping into it now. It was large, being about a
third of the Lobos' football field. It was quiet, which made it
easy for her to pretend that she could hide in it. On reflex, she
darted a glance over her shoulder at the colonnade. Sure enough,
there was Rod's straight silhouette aligned against the wall. She
knew without thinking about it that there was no way in the
world he was leaning against that wall. Not him. No matter how
late the hour, and it *was* late, he was standing on his own two
feet. He might be wearing a parka, as was she. Nevertheless,
that man was ready to spring into action at a moment's notice.

Being January, there was not much in bloom, just a lot of
snow on the ground. She didn't mind. It crunched quietly,
soothingly underfoot. All too soon, the first daffodils would be
poking up. Right around the time of the South Carolina primary,
if she was lucky.

South Carolina.

She knew that she should be thinking about the Iowa
Caucuses. But South Carolina was a problem. There was a
firebrand down there, a state senator by the name of Nat Forrest
– who proudly claimed kinship with the Confederate general
and, incidentally, founder of the Ku Klux Klan – who kept
threatening to write new articles of secession to break away.
Whose influence kept growing despite all rational belief. The
recent, hyperbolic flaps over the transgender bathroom laws had

only played into his hands, strengthening his cause "to fight against those Big Government Liberals out to destroy our way of life."

Beatie couldn't say his name without spitting.

Toni loved the Rose Garden at night because she often crafted her best thoughts here. In the early days, she had spent so many hours among its blooms, that it had been jokingly termed her second Oval Office. (Which had played into critiques over whether a woman could handle the stress of the job.) Yet, many was the time that an exasperated Janice had entered the room to announce a next guest only to find the door to the colonnade wide open and the President's backside seen departing behind a clump of pink azaleas.

Later, at Warren's strangled hint, Toni had restricted her sojourns to the night when no one could see.

What to do about Fast Eddie?

She couldn't really blame him. If anything she blamed herself. She had almost made the mistake of saying so in front of Beatie but couldn't handle a bursting volcano just then.

It was better to wait.

She had gone through the day. It had been a typical one. The PDB – Presidential Daily Briefing – of all the hotspots of the world, of all the threats to the People. That had come first.

Malcolm had told her of Presidents who had demanded oral presentations, also those who had preferred everything in writing instead, and those who had favored a mixture. Even a few who were rumored to have such short attention spans that graphs and charts were the rule, no written information presented longer than a few sentences. A lawyer, she had adopted the mixture approach. After her early meeting with Beatie, she would return to the bedroom, sit in one of the chairs or lounge on the couch if she had had a bad night of sleep – more often, that, lately – and grind right through the pages they had sent up. Then, she would shower, dress and ask herself which parts she didn't fully understand so that she would be able to question the DNI, or Director of National Intelligence, and his team of briefers in the Oval first thing.

After the PDB, Warren and Janice had sprinkled in the typical mix of a few softball visits from celebrities in town interspersed with harder customers such as the Midwestern Quilting Gals – who had presented her with her very own Bible, then insisted she open it to John 3:16 and read it aloud together with them. She had gone along goodnaturedly for a few additional verses with these tough old birds, knowing the MQG endorsement was tough to get – for anyone – and would be crucial in Iowa. Eventually, Warren rescued her when she finally tapped her left thigh with her thumb. The signal they had worked out years earlier.

Her outrageous notion – MAG, or Mothers Against Guns – had been on the tip of her tongue, but she hadn't dare push it.

She wondered at that. They can make her read a verse about the truth setting her free, yet she was afraid to challenge them to do something about school shootings?

In exasperation with the American public's constant weather-
vaning about guns and mass shootings, she had come up with the
idea. The public had a morbid fascination when some jacked up
seventeen year old grabbed his uncle's AR-15 assault rifle (or
"modern sporting rifle" as listed in the catalogue) with its high
capacity magazine to spray his local high school and his
classmates with .223 Remington caliber bullets. The people
remained glued to their tv sets and tablet screens for days as the
whole drama unfolded like a movie. But, secure in the belief
that such massacres only happened to *other* folks, the public all
too easily moved on to the next diversion when this one lost its
clickability. Thus, any move to limit such weapons of mass
destruction in any way whatsoever – such as closing the gun
show loophole, or universal background checks, or outright
banning of, at least, the high capacity magazines – never went
anywhere. As soon as the gunsmoke faded, the old arguments
began and the American public tuned out.

She had been debating this problem with herself for years,
even way back in the day as a prosecutor for the ABQ DA's
office. She had come with up all kinds of ideas, even wacky
ones such as a national tax on bullets that grew so high that guns
would go out of fashion, much like legislators had done myriad
times to cigarettes and smoking.

Sometimes she had veered away from a national solution and
consoled herself with the notion that it would prove to be a state
by state fix. Let the liberal Coasts pass the most stringent gun

27

control measures possible. Let the Heartland states keep their guns – which were, as she well knew, inexpensive entertainment, not to mention inexpensive pest control, in rural areas that knew few other options – until they finally went out of fashion. Lincoln had adopted just that same wait-for-it-to-die attitude toward slavery until the Civil War had forced his hand to the much more radical – not to mention quite possibly illegal – Emancipation Proclamation.

But then, a new study would come out showing that guns traveled quite easily across state lines, such as ⅔ of the gun violence in strict gun control Chicago was committed by guns brought over from Indiana – a state which had no gun control to speak of and lay just a moment's drive away. Literally. Or that the Iron Pipeline – a conduit of guns from the Old South working their way north to Manhattan – had doubled in size every time a new gun control measure was passed in Albany.

No.

She had a lot of friends who blamed the National Rifle Association for the recent mass proliferation of guns these last decades. But she knew that they were only selling what the people were buying. The NRA certainly were not helping matters. However, the true culprit was the culture of guns itself. What to do when owning a gun was considered a sign of manhood in the local town? When men who refused to join the gun club or go hunting were rejected by the local girls as weak and effeminate and couldn't find a date?

After a particularly tragic school shooting, she finally had come around to her Outrageous Notion, as she called it. The notion of Mothers Against Drunk Driving from her childhood years and how those brave women had taken on the Tavern League – who, like the NRA, were not making things any better in those days – to make the idea of holding one's liquor while controlling a car at high speeds *not* a sign of manhood. They had revealed it to be what it was. Asinine. One conversation at a time, through hundreds of heart-to-hearts, thousands of discussions, millions of shaken heads or grimaced expressions displayed at just the right moment, they had gotten their message across.

It was stupid. Stop it.

And they had changed the culture.

In the end, it had proven to be not the men who had fixed the problem. It had proven to be the women. And the men had followed.

It was their very own version of Aristophanes' *Lysistrata* – his classic comedy of wives denying their husbands sex until the men stop making war on the Spartans and peace is declared.

Oh, she had asked around and learned there were a sprinkling of groups on the ground thinking along the same lines. None, however, had made a serious dent at all in the gun culture of America. A couple, she suspected, were silently funded by the NRA to act as safety valves, designed to give anger a vent to harmlessly dissipate when indignation boiled over after a mass shooting.

Why not take it to the top? Why not take that bully pulpit that T-Rex had bragged about and let Mothers Against Guns, or any organization heading that direction, use it? It would be ironic. T-Rex had been about as gun crazy as any President could be. Well, she smiled as she abruptly remembered one of Malcolm's stories about Andrew Jackson fighting a duel. Okay, maybe not as gun crazy as Andrew Jackson.

Still, she had fought her own duel today. With herself. And she had lost.

With the MQG today, with the Gals, her Outrageous Notion had been right there. All she had had to do was say it. Out loud.

For all her bitching about T-Rex, she knew in her heart that he wouldn't have hesitated to bring up an idea of his.

Why had she?

***

Waking in the middle of the night, she couldn't figure out why. Just this sort of hazy impression in her frowzy brain that she had been dreaming of Cesar. She hadn't seriously thought of her childhood crush in years. That trim high and tight that he had sported, years before anyone called them that. Those spectacular biceps that he wore in homemade wife-beaters that she had made for him, making Lupe jealous, as she cut the

sleeves off t-shirts he had gotten from Goodwill. That tall
Spanish nose that had made her wonder – after she had seen a
documentary on tv about the Roman emperors and had put the
meaning to his name for the first time – whether he had some
Italian throwback genes in there somewhere.

If it hadn't been for Mama, Toni's hymen would not have
survived for long around Cesar. Lupe's definitely hadn't. The
day she hit fifteen, with her mammoth tits really starting to draw
attention from gang boys, she was all over him. Like a tigress,
she had confessed to Toni at lunch at school one day. "It hurt so
bad, chica!" she had crooned with pride, making Toni so jealous.

But Cesar had always had a roving eye. Even she knew that.
All too soon, he had moved on from Lupe, leaving her friend
tear-stained in her arms. "Por que? Por que me dejo?" she
repeated over and over. All Toni could think was how grateful
she was Cesar *did* leave her friend. *Before* she could get
pregnant since over time it became obvious that that had been
Lupe's plan all along. The thought that Cesar would simply
move on, leaving her friend to clean up the mess, simply didn't
penetrate Lupe's mind. Mama had an awful lot to say on the
subject, of course. For a while there, Cesar even stopped coming
by with bags of date expired whole chickens that he got cheap
for her at Lowry's Cash & Carry. Which also meant he couldn't
feed his street soldiers for free anymore. The whole situation
started getting downright serious until Mama relented, and only
when Toni could see the bottom of the large freezer out back one

day when she was fetching out another chicken. Life returned to normal after that. However, Mama made doubly sure that Cesar didn't get much time alone with Toni from that point forward. Her mother's funeral became the one exception, and Mama had gone through almost an entire pack of Luckys in the short half hour that Toni had been gone.

Nevertheless, the tumult of her high school years had soon passed into the steadier rhythms of the University of New Mexico. After repeated phone calls hectoring Highland High School's guidance counselor to come out and visit her, since Mama wasn't leaving her kitchen for anyone, through sheer force of will and several trays of fried chicken both eaten there and taken away as leftovers, the two intrepid souls managed to cobble together a doable action plan. It was heavy on affirmative action admission policies, heavy on affirmative action scholarships, heavy on Catholic scholarships, which made Toni suddenly start going to Mass on Sunday mornings, heavy on work-study jobs, a little less heavy on student loans, and a hostessing job at a local greasy spoon restaurant through the graveyard shift.

What to study?

"Hell, child, I don't know. Do I look like university material to you? Ask the padre." Father Manuel had quickly become a sort of joke with Mama. After all, she had been raised Southern Baptist so priests, with their cute little black outfits and white thing-a-ma-jigs at the Adam's apple, she thought hilarious. Still, as she would sigh, often, at that time, "Money was money. The Good Lord Jesus made damn sure of that."

Father Manuel at Sacred Heart Catholic Church was certainly different. White-haired, soft-spoken, gentle, Hispanic. Wise. Wise in a different way than Mama, but Toni sensed it right off. She listened.

"Study everything, mija," he had counseled. "That is the point of a college education. Basket-weaving, ballet, biology, ballistic physics. Sample everything. Eventually, your heart with the help of several Ave Marias will choose for you."

And then he would start, almost as if it were rote. And, almost as if it were rote, she would join him.

Dios te salve, Maria

Llena eres de gracia

El Señor es contigo...

She would think long about those words years later. Would recite them repeatedly throughout bad nights after Artie's unit, the 58th Wing, got sent to Afghanistan. Almost as if it were a talisman. Because she knew how seriously he took the prayer: Hail Mary, full of grace, the Lord is with you...

And her favorite line, which was destined to take on new meaning in the decades ahead...

Bendita tú eres entre todas las mujeres

Because she hoped that she, too, could become blessed among women.

In any case, her years at UNM would prove Father Manuel
correct. It was best to sample as much as she could, though
Mama kept clucking out loud at the Film Appreciation class she
took until Toni bought her off by agreeing to take an African-
American studies class. English lit, European history, chemistry,
geometry, pottery, economics, statistics, acting... The list was as
endless as it was varied.

A whole new world was opening to her. One class at a time.
One book at a time. One paper at a time.

And yet her old world was still there. Kind of. Somewhat.
As her university years passed, she saw Lupe less and less. Her
friend was too busy trying to attract the attention of airmen at the
air force base. Besides a little voice at that time began to
whisper the unhappy thought that they were growing apart, had
less and less in common. Toni barely even saw Cesar in those
days.

Feeling restless now, she stretched her back, her legs kicking
around in her presidential sheets. Wondering why she was
dreaming of a handsome gang member from her childhood, she
got up and sloughed across the room in her slippers and
bathrobe, out the door, barely nodding at the agent sitting outside
her room, and crossed to the little kitchen that was just off the
Prince's Room. This was the kitchen that Malcolm and the chef
prepared her breakfast in. She knew that Malcolm would be
upset finding her tea cup in the morning, and that she would hear
his cautious reminder that staff may be called at any time of day

or night, but she went ahead filling up the kettle herself and putting it on the boil anyway. In the cabinet, she found some chamomile tea, put a bag in a mug and waited for the water to steam.

Leaning back on the counter, fluffing out her messy tangle of hopeless hair, she looked at the island that ran through the center of the kitchen. The same island counter on which Gerald Ford – determined to prove to the nation that the Imperial Presidency of Richard Nixon (and the nightmare of the Watergate Scandal) was over – had toasted his own English muffins to the delight of the press at that time. It had created quite the stir.

Staring at the island now, it suddenly dawned on her how much it resembled Mama's kitchen table. And that's when she realized why she had been dreaming about Cesar.

Of course.

Unlike this afternoon with the MQG gals, she hadn't flinched at that moment. Awful though it had been.

One night, when she was just getting home from the greasy spoon after the bar rush had ended, she had found Cesar lying in front of Mama's door, blood pooling all around him.

He had passed out.

She woke him and helped him inside. Calling Mama from her bed, and helping her up, Mama cried, "Boy, what you done got yoself into!?"

His features beaded with sweat, he kept clutching his middle, and managed a "Sorry, Mama."

To Toni's picking up the phone to call an ambulance, Mama shushed her with the admonition, "Child, what on earth is you doing?"

Toni hung up, confused.

Mama was shaking her head, lighting a Lucky. "Ambulances mean hospitals, child, hospitals mean police, police mean this fool of a boy here gets into the System."

Ah. The System. Mama had a lot to say about the System. None of it much good.

Instead, Mama began rapping out orders: bowl, cotton swabs, rubbing alcohol, sewing needle, thread, paring knife, towels. Toni jumped to respond.

Then, as Mama directed her, Toni got Cesar up on to the kitchen table lying back on some towels to soak up the blood. She got his shirt off of him, taking a furtive glance or two at those delicious abs of his. And rolled up a towel for him to chew on.

Next, she washed her hands, poured out some rubbing alcohol into the bowl, put a bunch of cotton swabs in to start soaking, and threaded the needle and dropped it in the bowl, too, along with the paring knife.

She washed her hands with the alcohol and, at Mama's direction, took out a swab and wiped his belly clean around the bullet wound that was puckering up the skin. The blood was slowing, making Mama hum in appreciation, "Mmm-hmmmmm-mmmmm. You'll be fine, boy."

Gritting her teeth, Toni picked up the paring knife and, ignoring his cries and moans muted by the towel in his mouth, following Mama's instructions she cut two lines, each one snaking out from the wound. Then, she dug carefully in the wound for the bullet, as Mama yelled at him for he began thrashing, "Grab the table, fool! You the full-blown idiot that got yoself into this mess. Grab the edges of the table!" Which he did.

After far too long of his crying out and writhing around, Mama shouting over him, and her own sweat falling into her eyes, stinging them, Toni felt something. She kept prying up with the tip of the knife, terrified at the thought of cutting something inside there that was vital, finally catching on to an edge of the bullet. Slowly, painfully, it came up, then out.

Followed by a fresh trail of blood streaming up and out.

Mama grabbed the bullet from her and brusquely told her to jam some swabs in the wound. After a fair number, the bleeding stopped.

Cesar had stopped too. Writhing. Looking at him, Toni realized that he must have passed out, for his chest was still, thankfully, moving up and down.

Mama said it was a blessing and directed her to quickly sew up the wound.

Only then did Toni realize from the ache in her back that she had been standing the entire time. She sat down.

Mama lit another Lucky.

And they sat there. Not a word passing between them. Mama's hand shaking as she took puff after puff after puff.

Eventually, the horror of the moment had passed, Toni remembered now.

The tea water was boiling. She poured out a cupful.

She didn't want it.

She hadn't frozen back then. Why not?

***

Spotting Warren and Beatie squaring off against one another in the Roosevelt Room a couple of weeks later, she did what Janice hated and walked right in.

Her scheduler, following her at the time, stood there for a moment, flummoxed. "Madam President, Mr. Koval is waiting just outside the…"

"Oh, we'll get to Levi's Corn Growers soon enough," Toni purred over her shoulder.

Beatie had her set look. Warren, his defiant one. Warren – a DNC apparatchik from way back, his early 20s, in fact – was a holdover from Hap's administration, serving as chief of staff when Hap was governor. He wasn't as blueblood patrician as Hap, but he was definitely a courtier to the monarch. Why he had stayed, she had never really understood – particularly given the flood of others when they realized that she was little more than a caretaker – other than to remain where he had hoped to be, right at the center of the whirlwind, no matter who was the reigning sovereign. In any case, after the obligatory push-me-pull-yous of the early days when he was figuring out her boundaries, he had eventually settled down.

It wasn't like Hap had wanted him for his expert policy analysis, anyway. He truly was excellent at keeping the machine lubricated and running smoothly. How he did it, Toni didn't know and, to be honest, didn't really care.

As usual, he was wearing his gray hair clipped short over his de rigueur bespoke tailored dark blue suit with bowtie. Wags claimed that Hap had insisted Warren drop his Savile Row tailors for American ones as soon as Hap had declared his candidacy for President. After chewing it over for months, Warren had, reluctantly, settled for some Manhattan tailors whose suits regularly went for $3K or more. Shoes were $1K.

Beatie sat opposite him in her regulation rasta locks, white t-shirt that emphasized the balloon nature of her boobs, barely contained within her rattey-assed jean jacket adorned by its large peace symbols stitched all over it. Her lenses were pink today.

Rumor had it that Beatie was the only one in the entire Madison administration that could regularly demand Warren meet her outside the Chief of Staff's office. Toni hoped it wasn't true, for she thought it juvenile. But, as she had learned in the very first days of her first run for Congress, you either take Beatie as she was entirely, or you didn't take her at all.

"Hi," she smiled at them, hoping to break the tension that had swooshed her in the face as she entered.

Warren quickly stood, as was the custom whenever the President, whomever he or she was, entered a room. He hailed her, "Madam President!"

Beatie did neither.

Oh, dear.

Warren glowered at Beatie who, reluctantly, shuffled to her feet.

"Ma'am."

Smiling more brightly than ever, Toni sat so that they could.

"I've been thinking."

Warren had given her his full attention. His cheeks were flushed red, she could see. His smile was strained.

Beatie was still glowering at him.

What on earth? Well, whatever, Toni thought, and went on.

"I've been considering the possibility that we might treat this spring a bit differently."

That got Beatie's attention.

"After all, this is our fourth one together, and we certainly don't want it to be our last."

She paused, wondering how to resume. It wasn't like she had planned this.

They were silent, watching her. Warren's face was frozen, immobile. The corner of Beatie's lip twitched.

Finally, a new thought sprang on Toni, and she followed it.

"We have faithfully given the country three years of Hap's administration, securing his legacy as best we may. Three full years."

Warren frowned, his eyes moving down to the table in thought. Measuring? Contemplating? Challenging? Toni never knew with him. Warren was as fully closed off to her as Rod.

"Three full years," she repeated. "And yet, it strikes me that the Iowa Caucuses are two Mondays from now, and we have yet to explain to the people, who will be faithfully voting, what they can expect to see from us in the next four years."

Beatie leaned way back in her chair. Her hands – festooned with so many rings today that Toni had wondered upon seeing them at their morning meeting whether her strategist would be able to hold a Beatie Cake – came to rest on her ample belly. A very slow smile was beginning to form.

Warren was still looking down. Then, as if struck by a thought, he suddenly looked up out a window at the Oval Office's foyer.

"So, take forty-eight hours. I want to see a whole new range of ideas presented to me on…" Glancing at Janice, whose eyes were about to pop out of her head, Toni tried to remember what day it was. "Warren, set it up."

He briskly nodded.

As she rose to her feet, she used a trick she had learned handing out assignments to her first Congressional staff. "And

I'm going to hope that creating jobs while solving the Artificial Intelligence and Climate Change crises will be on that list."

Walking away, she smiled at the thought of what makeup sex must be like between those two.

***

It was Warren.

It was the Joint Chiefs.

Calling her down to the Situation Room in the basement.

She sighed.

When she had first arrived, she had this dream. It would repeat itself endlessly, driving her mad. Over time it had faded. But each time, still, that it arrived, amidst her sweaty, strangling night sheets tangling her legs, her ankles, her feet, her hands, it was no less poignant.

She was Sol.

She was the sun.

Part of it was founded, she knew, even as she didn't really understand it, on the expectation that the 21st century would prove the moment when the people would make their home on other places than the pale blue dot. Whatever the plan, and there were many – heavy helium factories on the moon, for example – it would happen just as surely as the first colonies in Virginia, then Massachusetts Bay, then Rhode Island and the others. Hap used to talk about it during their (his) campaign.

He would deliver his fiery rhetoric about the little guy getting ahead again at last, then, when the audience had tired – since he could, truly, go on for hours just like Fidel did in the Plaza Mayor of Havana, his listeners standing there, spellbound, for hours – Hap would wax lyrical about what he called "the dreams of the people."

We would have hotels on Luna, the moon, he said. He could see them. Where instead of the sunrise you could see the Earthrise. People talked about a long weekend in Vegas, he said. Soon, they would talk about a long weekend on Luna. Forget about the seven days it took for the Apollo missions of the 70s, he would say. This would be a fast rocket out to Luna in a day, two days on the moon, and a single day return. "Don't talk to me about proposing at the top of the Eiffel Tower!" he would clamor. "Guys, you want to impress her? Drop to one knee up there!"

And then, as he pointed dramatically up to the sky, "All because you dreamed large enough to put me in the White House!"

Our children would walk on Mars, he would say. "Our tenth President from now," he would shout, "will have lived there! A few months riding the rocket out, then a half year living there, actually walking, working the surface of the Red Planet, followed by a few months return. My daughter wanted a gap year in Europe before going to college. Well, guess what! That's nothing!"

(Space experts would, from time to time, question his numbers, but only half-heartedly because they were so delighted he was actually thinking about the subject.)

"We will mine," he used to roar, "the precious metals of the Asteroid Belt, just as surely as we have plumbed the precious oils of this Earth. Remember the 49ers? Well, guess what? We're going to have a second set of 'em!" He foresaw large corporations such as Exxon or British Petroleum funding it all, and he had wanted to help them. "If Congress won't let me create your children's and grandchildren's jobs out in the Belt," he would bellow, "I'll do it by executive order, so help me God!"

His Hapsters would scream with excitement.

Even as Toni wondered whether they truly understood what he was saying.

That was the source.

In some ways.

Of her dream.

She knew that, but she didn't have to like it.

A second wellspring was the power she held now.

In her hands.

She was the Leader of the Free World.

Experts from the State Department and Department of Homeland Security debated whether her power was more absolute than, say, Eisenhower's in the 50s. She didn't care. It was too much, as it was.

Others, mostly from the Pentagon, which had surprised her, spoke more quietly and respectfully of the lessons learned from the brush fires of the last empire. The British one. When they were responsible for keeping the bad boys at bay. Worldwide.

Learning about Khartoum, for example, had given her nightmares for weeks. You send out a general with what you are pretty certain are pretty clear instructions. Just to have him find Jesus out there in the hinterland and – rather than bring the boys home like he was supposed to – fortify the town, instead, in the face of astronomically superior numbers. Of the Mahdi. The whirling dervishes.

Oh, it gets better. Your handpicked general uses the newfangled telegraph to send back cherry-picked Biblical messages about God's Grace saving the savage from their own Hell, and now your homegrown evangelicals are beating the drums to send more boys out there to be wasted, reinforcing failure, because... Well, because, God ordained it, right?

Right?!

Sol.

She was Sol.

She was the sun.

She was having it now, she realized. The nightmare.

Dammit!

She tossed and turned in her sheets, struggling to get free, only to have them wrap her more tightly. Fighting. Suffocating. Grappling. Screaming.

She was the sun.

Of all humanity.

Of all the solar system.

There were two forces.

That could sway events.

Sol used gravity. It was inescapable. Ineluctable.
Inexorable.

No matter who you thought you were. No matter how
powerful you imagined yourself to be. No matter how large a
petty duchy you had created – like John D. Rockefeller with
Stanford Oil, or Andrew Carnegie with Carnegie Steel, or Henry
Ford with Ford Motor Company, or Bill Gates with Microsoft,
or Mark Zuckerberg with Facebook, or Jeff Bezos with Amazon
– no matter how large your edifice, your monument to yourself,
you could never escape the sun.

Or the President of the United States.

What to do with such power?

The power to compel. To investigate. To arrest. To question.
To seize. To impound. To occupy. To requisition. To
expropriate. To declare. To conquer.

Elizabeth's Star Chamber could only dream of the power that
Toni had at her fingertips.

Why did they give it to her?

The people.

Why?!

She hated them for that.

***

She woke with a snap to Rod's quiet knock.

Thank god. She couldn't deal with the Witch this morning.

She mumbled. Something.

Malcolm was there. How did he know?

Rod was opening the door for him. Her steward was bringing in the tray, just like the old days. Coffee and a croissant.

Then she realized the time. It was 3.

Shit.

She looked at Rod.

He stared right back at her. "Your chief of staff will be here in a moment, Madam President."

Never President Madison. Never Ms. President. Never Ma'am. Or anything else. Certainly, never Toni. Oh, no. It was always "Madam President."

Warren appeared in the doorway, breathless, in a sweater and jeans. ? She saw the head of that...new guy? Sticking just around the corner of the doorway. Borgenson? Burgenson? Her new National Security Advisor. They never lasted more than a few months these days. (Why bother? Everybody knew she was a doormat for the Kim Jong Uns of this world.)

Toni smiled.

What else to do?

"Come in, Warren. Have some coffee with me." She looked down, then realized Malcolm was already at a nearby cabinet – when had that appeared? – and was drawing out a second porcelain cup.

Warren was still standing in the doorway. With the NSC guy now.

"Madam President, you are needed in the Situation Room. It's Boko Haram."

She sighed.

Wahhabist Islam – which she had actually learned about at UNM taking one of those sampler classes that Father Manuel had suggested – was a political creature of thugs. Ibn WhatsHisName – she couldn't remember it right now as she was blinking the sleep out of her eyes – had made a deal with one of the Saud guys. You scratch my back (religiously), I scratch yours (politically).

It was no different than Ronald Reagan and Jerry Falwell in the Moral Majority days.

Or Julius Caesar and the Optimus Maximus priests in Roman Empire days.

Or Hap and Family Worship in their time.

Who cared?

She grumbled. Another sleepless night. Just somebody wrapping his need to conquer the next couple of counties over in some kind of religious mumbo-jumbo.

She took a sip of coffee and, seeing Malcolm's eyebrow arching upward – when the hell did he arrive? – took a bite of the croissant which was, as usual, splendid.

She slipped toward the edge of the bed, watching Malcolm gently take up her bathrobe. Didn't he have a home to go to?

She turned as he was settling it on her shoulders. For the first time it struck her that he was gay.

She didn't know what she thought about that. A gay steward? Anyway.

Oh, right.

Ibn Abd al Wahhab. Son of the Slave of Allah.

Nice. Not a bad moniker for a priest.

No, wait. She paused, staring down, then looking out, trying to remember. Son of the Slave of the *Giver* of Allah to the World. Or something like that.

Anyway, his buddy bad boy Sowww-uuud – right around the time that George Washington was telling the other George to go fly a kite – which was weird when you thought about it – decided that he would like to take over the Sock (her private name for the Arabian Peninsula) and needed someone to give him a veneer to whitewash his, ummm, conquests?

Bad boy Saud had made a nice deal. Get the local pope to recognize you as Top Dog – like Leo crowning Charlemagne – and both boats rise together. Anybody who didn't meet the newly crowned high priest's definition of holy got put to the sword.

It worked. If Saud didn't conquer the Sock entirely, his kids did, eventually, creating Saudi Arabia. And the Wahhab priests were right there, every step of the way, blessing their blood-soaked battles, every hack and stab. Wrapping each in the holy green flag of The Faith.

Even celebrating the downing of the Twin Towers.

Which Toni would never forget.

Ever.

Ever.

Ever.

Shaking her frowzy head one last time, she abruptly realized that the people needed a President, not a sleepy girl.

Ceremony.

Christ!

She swallowed. She stood tall, paused to take another long, slow sip of Malcolm's coffee, then nodded to the NSC guy, to Warren, to Rod (who, as usual, appeared not to notice). Then, summoning up as much majesty as she could, she swept out of the room. A trick she had learned as a Congresswoman. Everyone else followed or, like Malcolm, she assumed, cleaned up the mess. Just as she used to.

In the Situation – or John F. Kennedy Conference – Room, essentially a long corporate board room with video screens at one end, she entered, told everyone to sit.

They did.

Boko Haram had six Green Berets that they were holding hostage. In Chad. That was, essentially, the problem.

Far cry from the Tet Offensive days of '68 when Mama's Elijah had died. One of forty-seven who died every day that year in Vietnam. On average.

No matter.

These were her six.

She was responsible.

Why they were in Chad (Loufa, a small town, barely), to begin with, assisting the British – whose Royal Navy used to rule the world but was now reduced to six destroyers – and the French was not really relevant. To her.

She was bringing them home. To *their* Mamas.

She had demanded a rescue plan. The Joint Chiefs had offered her a choice of three.

She had chosen one. That was, essentially, the heart of the matter.

Essentially.

But it wasn't supposed to happen until around noon. It was 3 am.

What had gone wrong?

She listened, numbed, to the droning of the four star generals and admirals who sounded much like plumbers telling her why her toilet was stopped up, back in her ambulance-chaser cheap-ass apartment ABQ days. When Artie had held her at night.

What would he think?

About this.

There were six guys out there. That's what Artie would say.
He – given the chance – would plow his PAVE Hawk helo – no
matter what the hell they were firing right back up at him – into
whatever shitstorm existed – to extract them. That was his job.
It had always been his job. To insert. To extract.

His quick, nervous smile flashed in her mind. His chubby
cheeks and sweet moustache that had always made her melt.

...Something about a possible intelligence leak from a CIA
asset on the ground, but they weren't sure...

Now the fur started to fly.

Accusations thrown back and forth. JCS, DNI, NSA, CIA,
DHS, and all the rest of the alphabet soup going at each other.

She didn't care.

Artie would go get them, leak or not.

She stood.

Warren stood. They shut up, stood.

"Get them. Get them out of there. Now. Bring them home."

Yes, Madam President.

***

She awoke to the sharp rap of the Witch.

Malcolm was there again.

With his tray. With his coffee. With a blueberry muffin this
time and, of course, Beatie's cakes. In the bedroom, though.
Which was odd.

Twelve SEALS had died getting out the captured six Green
Berets.

She had sent them to their deaths.

A wren was singing outside the window. Ridiculously
cheerful.

It made her want to weep. It made her want to throw up.

At the hands of Boko Haram.

How was she going to explain that? Boko Haram. Who was
Boko Haram?

The latest mushroom, right? The African version of the
Afghan Taliban. Or Saudi Al Qaeda. Or Syrian ISIS. Or Thai
BRN – her personal favorite – because they loved to cut off the
heads of gentle Buddhist monks. Why not?! They were such
easy targets.

Killing the thugs made no difference. They came back,
anyway. Like a bad rash. It was whack-a-mole. No matter what
the world did, some thug on horseback would rear up, wrap
himself in some religious flag near at hand, claim to be a true
believer while he went about the grisly business of putting a gun
to his neighbors' heads while he was robbing them. No different
than Jesse James.

Why was she here? For what reason?

Feeling as if someone else entirely, she asked to see the service records of those that had just...

Beatie frowned. Her lenses were cherry this morning.

"Bitch, they coming after you on this one. I have no idea what you was thinking last night, but you just handed Fast Eddie the nomination."

A cup was flying through the air.

Coffee was splashing, milling all around it, right up to the moment that it shattered against the Imperial Golds and Tan wallpaper that Hap's wife had...

"Madam President, would you like a moment?"

Malcolm's soothing voice crept in.

She nodded.

And, somehow, miracle of miracles, the Witch was gone.

***

Beatie, as usual, proved to be right. The House Oversight Committee announced hearings that day into "the SEALS Last Stand at Loufa." The Senate Armed Services Committee, more circumspect, announced that hearings on "Operation Redeem in Chad" would begin in two weeks.

Neither looked good.

Surprisingly, she heard about it not from Beatie, or Warren, but from Malcolm.

She was walking in the Rose Garden that afternoon, scrunching around in the snow, when he suddenly appeared, sans parka or hat, scarf or mittens, with a thermal mug of coffee for her and a large slice of carrot cake.

He asked her to sit on a bench and served her, barely repressing his shivering (she knew better than to protest) holding the mug while she balanced the cake plate on her knees and took a bite.

Without preamble, he abruptly – if a bit self-consciously, she could see – launched into a story about how Eisenhower had handled the Joe McCarthy Red Scare hearings of the 50s. Congressional investigations that claimed to be unearthing hidden Communists in the State Department. When some wanted Ike to speak out against McCarthy, the President had refused – so the legend went, Malcolm said – for fear it would only give the Wisconsin Senator the stature he needed to challenge Eisenhower in 1956. When his friends later wanted him to shut down the hearings, the President had thundered, "No, he needs just a little more rope!" And McCarthy had hung himself. Or so the tales said, Malcolm sighed.

She listened with welling tears in her eyes, for she realized what he was telling her. Without telling her. Without ever meeting her glance. When he was done with his two anecdotes, he merely waited for her to finish the carrot cake, and without further ado, took the plate and fork back into the White House.

She took his advice.

In the days following, she shut her mind to the hearings and focused on her Climate Change and Artificial Intelligence bills. The Iowa Caucuses would be what they were. Her campaign manager Levi had said as much at their meeting right after she had first popped out the two new ideas.

She needed to take a legislative win to New Hampshire. Maybe even two. She needed to look stronger. He had said that as well.

She liked Levi. Maybe it was because he was a Jew and she was a Blatina. Perhaps it was because someone had told her that his surname, Koval, was Slavic for blacksmith. He certainly hammered away at his opposition.

He already had the whole year sketched out…

- Take her CC & AI legislative wins to New Hampshire a week after the Iowa Caucuses
- Survive the South Carolina primary a week later in early February
- Rebuild momentum a few days after that at the Nevada Caucuses (sure to support a Southwesterner)
- Come out of California's primary on Super Tuesday strong enough to nail the nomination
- Kick the ass of Connor Raines (or whomever) in the General Election in November

She would use Iowa's rallies to introduce her new ideas to the nation. It was time. She would use the intervening days to get the bills out there in the relevant committees of Congress. If not both CC and AI, then just one. Which, she could hardly care less, at this point. There was always time to pick up the second one later.

She needed a win.

After Chad, she needed a win.

***

Iowa.

Caucuses.

Noise. Crowds. Happy ones. Excited ones. Balloons. Trailers. Smiles. Hot dogs with dripping mustard. Tinsel trailing from the rafters. Brats heaped high with sauerkraut. Posters shouting proclamations. Glitter. In the air. On teen girls' eyelids. High school bands wailing out old favorites. Adorable applecheeks smeared with cotton candy. Placards being waved in each other's faces. People.

The people. Even the kids in their endearing tiny Sorel boots with the cute little felt liners.

It was cold. Not too cold for them to eat roasted corn, and certainly not too cold for warm kettle corn!

It was fun. She was having fun. She never got to do the Iowa and Nevada Caucuses the first time around. Hap hadn't even asked her onto the ticket until mid-July, just before the Convention. After she had reluctantly, almost belatedly, accepted, the *McDougal & Madison* ticket had finally been born.

(Along with the predictable candy reference. Some enterprising soul had designed and private-labeled some dark-blue, coated chocolate candies for the Convention. M&M styled on one side, the Democrats donkey on the other. Within weeks, they were everywhere. Beatie loved them, swallowed them by the handful. Toni had quickly sickened at the sight of them.)

Nevertheless, first time or not, walking around this drafty barn, ignoring the Uncommitted space taped off in the corner, scooping sweet caramel popcorn into her mouth, in this, the Fourth District of northwest Ames, she was enjoying herself. (A secondary location, this barn, for the boiler had burst that morning in the first location, a local Baptist church. *Des Moines Register* wags were already tagging it as an omen for her presidency.)

Still, Iowans took their job as first vetters of serious candidates seriously, no matter where the caucus wound up. They studied the issues. They didn't have a lot of time for snake oil. They were earnest. Maybe even a little too earnest for her taste.

Even so, she liked them.

Even if they didn't like her so much. Or, she reminded herself, crunching another handful while she reached down to smooth out the hair of a sweet blonde-headed toddler, or...

More precisely – as she watched a farmer wearing a cruddy and crumpled John Deere cap over an old Ethanol Burns 4Ever jersey on his potbelly stare at Beatie's rasta locks and lilac lenses with undisguised disgust – she reminded herself that they didn't understand her.

Yet.

Levi had quietly asked her that morning if they could put Beatie in a hotel room somewhere.

Yeah. Uh-huh. She could see that.

He was everywhere. Des Moines, Cedar Rapids, Davenport, Dubuque, everywhere. And she with him. Pancake houses, churches, factories, corn fields, slaughtering houses, delis, big-box stores, high school auditoriums. Parking lots. Movie theatres. Baseball fields white with snow. On the bed of a pickup, she shivering beside him as he bellowed away in his megaphone. She was seeing Levi ascendant. Large gatherings almost one thousand strong at University Baptist Church of Iowa City or small ones at a local dusty hardware store in Council Bluffs boasting no more than thirty attendees. It didn't matter. He worked his magic. He connected. Levi might swear up and down on the Madison for President bus that the "corn-fed Flat Earth Society" was "the end of everything." It didn't matter. Somehow, in ways she would never understand, these Old Time Religion believers would always accept her fast-talking Brooklyn Jew far sooner than they would her.

Maybe it was his off-the-rack-suit. In DC, he was as every inch the bespoke tailored aficionado as Warren. Out here? He was as strip mall racked as you could get – on the days when he wasn't sporting a parka with blue jeans and hiking boots.

These Iowans ate him up.

She had seen him, maple syrup proudly staining his tie, standing on a chair at the Des Moines Radisson, hammering out instructions to a large roomful of caucus captains. "Our President has stayed the course and now it's time to move forward! Toni's Tomorrow. She has been true to Hap's legacy, and now it's time to plant her own. Toni's Tomorrow! Let's bring Toni to Iowa! Maddies!!! Let's bring Iowa to Toni! It's time for Toni's Tomorrow!"

(For all his "Toni's Tomorrow" rhetoric – which Beatie sneered at – it worried Toni that his field volunteers didn't warm to Levi's characterization of them as "Toni's Maddies." Hap had had his Hapsters. What did she have?)

Well, she had Levi. He was a rock star. Even if she knew that, standing next to him, she was a pipsqueak. He talked the future. She talked climate change.

Yeah.

Climate change was – except for the precious few enviro hardliners – like eating spinach before having some chocolate cake. She knew that.

For example, for every gallon of gasoline saved as a result of higher fuel efficiency standards, twenty-four or so pounds of global warming emissions were eradicated.

Woohoo! That was a panty-dropper!

Her own path – as a climate change skeptic – had changed the day that the Antarctic Shelf had dropped into the ocean. Before that, she had simply tuned it out. Global Warming? Shit, it was always hot in the Southwest. Try Lake Havasu City at Christmas.

Somehow, after the glacial shelf had dropped, suddenly everything else that everybody had to say about the issue became noise. The shelf drop itself was clarifying. Crystal.

Houston, we have a problem. That kind of crystal.

It had become a clear dividing line.

Sort of like that bizarre notion she still dreamt of, of putting the AR-15 on the same list as, say, the Gatling Gun or a home-baked dirty bomb. Either you believed that all three were a menace to society and should be outlawed... Honestly, who would claim Second Amendment Rights for your neighbor to cook up his own dirty bomb in his garden shed?... or you didn't.

In any case, when it came to climate change over the years, as a Congresswoman, through her studies, she had taught herself "the Three Cs." The Three Cs were the cause of global warming – in order of importance: cars, coal and cattle. The numbers weren't right. But they gave her a handle on the issue whenever she attended a briefing on the subject by, say, the National Oceanic and Atmospheric Administration, since those briefings typically made her, and those around her she noticed, drowsy.

The Three Cs. Cars, Coal, Cattle.

Cars. Almost ⅓ of the country's global warming fuels came from transportation. Simple enough. Double the fuel efficiency standard since, for all their bitching, the Big Three had proved quite successful over the last hundred years at adaptation. Shoot! Just take a look at their retooling from making sedans to making tanks in World War II. And back again when the shooting had stopped. Oh! How they had groaned! Had demanded public financial assistance. From the taxpayers. Yet, somehow, they had made it happen. Ahead of schedule. As usual. As they were now with the latest EPA demands for more efficient mile per gallon vehicles.

That was the first C.

Coal. The second ⅓ of the country's sin against the planet was the production of electricity to keep Mama's tv on at night. ⅔ of *that* came from burning coal, natural gas, and oil. Add to that another ⅕ of the sin coming from industry burning that same evil mixture of fossil fuels just to keep everybody in a job. That's bad.

Simple enough, though. Switch over to renewables. Oh, wait. The country wasn't ready for that, yet. Okay, switch over to nuclear energy. Except the country wasn't ready for another Hanford catastrophe. Hell, look at how long the country had fought over whether Yucca Mountain would become our long-term nuclear rod storage site. Not happening. Back to renewables. Oh, yeah. The country wasn't ready. *The Petros* on Capitol Hill weren't ready. Sigh.

The SEALS who had died rescuing the six Green Berets at Loufa, Chad, interceded here. Interrupting her thoughts.

Staff Sergeant Ryan Atkins, of Shreveport, Louisiana, one of the Green Berets, had died of his wounds an hour ago. Rescued at the end, only to die anyway, at Ramstein Air Base in Germany. He had two very beautiful children. She had asked to see their pictures. A boy of five with a gap between his two front teeth, and a girl of three, clutching her bunny. Who would never know their father. Because of her. Right?

On the plane to Des Moines, Foster – her Rhodes Scholar legislative aide for Capitol Hill – had glowered at the news. Knowing what he was thinking – that it made her look incompetent, weak – she avoided his glance and tried not to think about how that would affect negotiations over her climate change and AI bills.

Cattle. She shook her head. Tried to focus.

Her last C was a bit whimsical, because the number was even looser than the others. Still, in a topic overwhelmed with overheated rhetoric, her third C helped her find her bearings. Whatever went up a chimney stack every day lighting homes and factories, 10% of those same fumes could be wiped out if old growth forests being cut down in places like Brazil and Uruguay were left in peace. Because of all the carbon dioxide they ate up. Why were the locals cutting down the old rainforests? To make pasture room for massive cattle herds of millions of tons of fast

63

food hamburgers each year. Many of those tons devoured right
here in Iowa. Today.

Funny. Or not.

Right.

Besides, it wasn't like she was even asking for the treaty with
China yet. All she wanted was for the country to start a pilot-
project national cap and trade market, modeled on the one
California was already using to great effect.

Didn't matter. People tuned out as soon as you mentioned the
words cap and trade.

Like being forced to eat your spinach before having your
dessert each meal. That was climate change. If you were a hard-
core enviro, spinach was a gift from God. If you were the other
98% of the world, spinach was a chore.

Nevertheless, Toni believed in the American people. If only
because she knew their history. When slavery stopped being
considered a benevolent institution and, instead, a cultural – even
economic – evil, the people had responded. It had taken half a
Civil War for Lincoln to work up the political capital needed to
free the slaves. Even then, his successor had tried to put them
right back into chains. Yet, the American people did make up
their minds. At last.

The same with Civil Service Reform, probably the hottest
political topic (therefore, the most boring mint julep topic) of the
Gilded Age following the Civil War. The Pendleton Act had
wiped out all that corruption that so many banana republics

around the world struggled with, even today. Not the USA. When the occasional Oval Office holder tried to bring back the old spoils system, which did happen every thirty years or so as Malcolm had quietly pointed out to her one morning, the court system stopped the guy dead in his tracks.

And the Native Rights question. Wounded Knee happened – like so many of those battles – in that brief twenty-five year period between the end of the Civil War and the dawning of the new century. Whether the "conquered peoples" would come along or continue the fight against the United States was a question that would occupy the nation for the next century and beyond. However, compared to other cultures, other nations, Toni knew, at least the Americans discussed it.

Then, the first harbinger of income inequality: the Great Depression. Hoover, the President who denied its existence for three solid years – until being defeated for re-election opened his eyes – only opened the door for later political leaders who would savage this topic all through the 20th and 21st centuries.

The Civil Rights Struggle of the 60s. The Feminist Movement. The Gay Rights Brawl. All in their time, after enough Americans, just like Mama, had had enough space to wrap their minds around the change being requested – had gotten on board.

Toni believed in the American people. Given time, they could change.

She just honestly wondered as she went on and on in her speeches – at Iowa University in Iowa City, at Second Baptist Church in Cedar Rapids, at Christ the King Cathedral in Council Bluffs, at Trinity Church in Des Moines – about an international cap and trade system for toxic emissions – since China, for all their noisy posturing from time to time, was the top polluter by far. Twice the amount of the US. Well more than that of the European Union – the other great offender. (Of course, India alone, and Russia alone, and Japan alone, were all doing their level best to darken the globe's skies.)

Toni wondered. She stood there, speaking, watching their eyes dim.

Levi had worked them up just before her, making their eyes sparkle with his brave talk of Toni's Tomorrow. Had gotten them charged. Had gotten them screaming.

Then, she had put them to sleep.

AI was worse.

Artificial Intelligence – the single greatest threat to jobs, no matter the color of the collar.

Did anyone care?

What she wanted was simple. Since careful study over the last two years had proven to her that *nobody* knew what was coming – but *everybody* feared it in some way or another – she wanted a national job training program. If you lost your job because of automation – whether by robots or code – then you were automatically entitled to free training, plus lost pay, to learn how to maintain the robots or code that were now doing your job.

She had asked for a much larger, more generous jobs training program, of course, but that had only sparked one of the most vociferous squabbles she had ever seen. Between Beatie, of course, championing her idea, and Foster claiming that it was a "Boondoggle of Big Guvment Giveaways" that the Freedom Caucus in the House "would nev-ah saddle, nev-ah."

Foster was descended from the Brown and Root construction firm of LBJ Texas times. How he was a Democrat was a mystery to her since everybody else in the "all hat and no cattle" state these days seemed to be Republican. Nevertheless, when Foster spoke, whether Toni liked what he had to say or not, she had learned to listen. So, she had downgraded her expectations, over Beatie's objections, to the quid pro quo bill: lose your job cuz of AI, you get free training to learn how to run that robot.

(She had, from time to time, flirted with the whole Universal Basic Income idea, even if it was as low as $500 a month, but given what Foster had to say these days, she had shelved it. For now.)

**

A week before the Caucuses, she had sent Foster and his team of "shit-kicking Ivy Leaguers" up to the Hill to quietly unveil her two freshly hammered-out ideas to the leadership of both House and Senate and to friends on the relevant committees.

She had warned him to take it slow, given that these were her first initiatives after three years of minding Hap's store. Go slow. Be ready for honest surprise.

To which he had drawled with that beaming smile of his that could charm the cookies out of any Southern belle, "Go slow, but go whole-hog, Ma'am?"

And, by all accounts, they had. Beginning early, at 5 am, talking up the leadership staffers, giving them plenty of time to text their bosses on the way in to work that something new was afoot. Each member of Foster's team had had a list to work their way through. He had shown it to her. It was designed based on common interests or past history shared with the target staff member. If her Texan had the reputation of cutting wide night-time swathes through the hosts of Congressional aides and pages, it was surely because he was thorough. And because he could – as he liked to claim – "sell fridges to the Inuit."

The reception had been cautious, welcoming. As it typically was. Not that that said anything.

As Congresswoman, she had used the same smiling reception for a myriad of bills she hated on sight. It had given her time to figure out how to say "No" without burning bridges.

For her climate change bill, the only Nos they had received – and they had been immediate – had come from the Petros. Nicknamed for their adamant defense of petrochemicals in an age when the entire globe was investing – one way or another – in renewables. While sprinkled throughout both houses of Congress, there were two hard-core hubs…

Her studies had revealed that the Longhorn State was the largest producer of wind-power in the nation. Yet, Big Oil was still very much at home there: in the Texas 7th (Houston – ConocoPhillips, Halliburton), Texas 8th (Woodland Hills – Anakardo Petroleum), Texas 24th (Irving – ExxonMobil), and other places.

Up north in the Mitten State, the Big Three might be cautiously embracing hybrids, nevertheless, their primary products still burned fuel and would for decades, thus Congressmen from the Michigan 5th (Flint – General Motors), Michigan 11th (Auburn Hills – Chrysler) and Michigan 12th (Dearborn – Ford) all counted among the devout.

And, it went without saying, the Senators of both states also worshipped regularly at the altar of Big Oil.

How an international cap and trade agreement would adversely affect the Petros was beyond her. But, as she well knew from her years on Capitol Hill, Representatives and Senators almost always voted the way that their districts leaned. And if their districts regarded climate change as a liberal hoax then, well, it was a liberal hoax and that was that.

Still, she thought there would be some wiggle room. Should be. Could be. What it might be would reveal itself in a day or two. She knew that from experience.

About her AI bill, however, Foster had reported that there were only absent-minded smiles or gapes of outright bemusement. That was disappointing. The House Speaker's domestic policy advisor had even quipped, "Her Accidency going all Isaac Asimov on us, now?" The Senate Majority Leader's chief of staff had remarked, "Now why would she want to worry her pretty little head over that?" A House Appropriations Chair's advisor had shaken out a sour grimace, "And she plans to raise the cash for this just how?"

And that was that. At least at first.

Two days before the Caucuses weekend, while there was still no interest on AI, Foster had finally brought her some wiggle room on the climate change bill.

Jenkins of the Pennsylvania 3rd (Cranberry Township – Westinghouse) had promised to back her climate change idea if a consortium of Nukes, led by guess who, could build nuclear power plants in China. The Middle Kingdom's President Xiang would not agree to American nuclear plants without her approval. Another wrinkle. They, she and Xiang, already had their hands full with Space Age squabbles. As in, who gets to put what up, out there, over our heads? He didn't want any more spats.

Chinese nuke plants. Built by...who cares? After construction, the power plants' safety protocols would be inspected by Chinese officials, no matter what the original contract had promised. She knew that from experience.

Toni could just see the enviro reaction to that notion. After the Japanese fuckup at Fukushima? But, she reminded herself for the umpteenth time, it wasn't like enviros could be bothered to get out of their armchairs to vote on Election Day, anyway, right? Nevertheless, it was a place that she couldn't go, just yet. Trusting Americans with their spent fuel rods was one thing – even after Hanford – but, trusting the Chinese? The country that had sold their own people poisoned baby food, then poisoned pet food, then triggered the global SARS epidemic by pretending it wasn't originating there.

Sigh.

One step forward. Two steps…

***

The Uncommitted space had a few more souls in it now.

In this drafty barn in the northwest quadrant of Ames, Iowa, there were, as always, traffic cones set up with ribbons tying them together into rectangles, grouping off sections of the floor.

Rod was standing next to one. Her primary Practorian was there with his team, of course. Rod was always there. Looking extraordinarily fit in his gray suit that carried God knew how many weapons. His eyes always watching. Everything. Everyone. Resting on her, just for an instant, because she had looked at him, then moving on when he saw there was no threat.

71

She felt that warm moistness tickling her pussy. He didn't need a bespoke tailored suit from Savile Row to make him look like a honey.

She growled at herself. What was up with her?

Foster strode past, fiercely arguing with someone on his cell.

He had brought her the welcome news late last night that Jenkins had come through. The Pennsylvania Congressman had worked the Petros hard over her climate change idea. They were coming along with him, he had said, so long as the fuel efficiency targets currently agreed to remained as fixed. She had looked at Foster with confusion over that one. Was the Sierra Club kneecapping her, their best friend, by trying to mount some effort to get those targets raised? Some friend... Foster had shrugged that he was hearing nothing, but if so, it was probably only a fundraising gambit on the enviros part. Besides, it strengthened their hand because it was an easy giveaway.

Also, the Petros demanded that the funding for the cap and trade pilot program could *not* come from a gasoline tax. Another easy give.

Best of all, Foster's count said that with the Petros and the Nukes on board, they had just enough to pass the House. The Senate would be another battle. But that was for another day.

Now, all she had to do was pay the piper. Give the green light on nuclear power plants in China. A simple statement supporting the development would suffice, the Congressman had suggested. She groaned. A simple statement?

Whatever.

She refocused on the traffic cones, scooping up another mouthful of caramel corn. This was the way that Iowa Caucuses worked. The Republicans filled out a simple secret ballot, like any other election. The Democrats – given the chance – had decided to make the process more complicated. There were two rounds. In the first round, all participants gathered in marked-off spaces representing the candidates they were supporting. There was even a space for the "Uncommitted Voters." The judges walked around and counted up heads. Any group that didn't measure at least 15% of the total was ruled invalid for the second round and that's when the fun began. The other groups then descended on the woeful voters and begged, pleaded, cajoled, even threatened them to join *their* group to support *their* candidate. After thirty minutes or so of this, the judges blew a whistle and recounted. Winners were declared, sometimes, depending on the tradition of the county. But, everywhere, all caucus sites called in their results to the state headquarters, who tallied them all and released their final numbers to the media.

In years such as now, when the incumbent was a Democrat, there were usually only two spaces marked off – the President's supporters and the Uncommitted – even if the latter was a mere formality.

All evening, here in Ames, Toni had tried to avoid looking at the Uncommitted space. She had spotted it, of course, as soon as entering the barn. It had sported a surprising number of people.

Maybe it was people just visiting, not voting yet, she had told herself.

Right up to that moment, she had not missed Levi. He had been upset with her decision to go to Ames. Des Moines was the largest city of the state, where the state leadership was. Where anybody who was anybody was. She, the candidate, belonged there. She should be there. She knew it.

But she was tired.

Tired of getting off the plane, hoping that it would be different this time. After all, she was the President. She had *not* been expecting the loud shouts that had greeted Hap everywhere, the jovial hand-clasps, the wide hugs, the gathering of balding white heads protruding over large pot bellies, all bending over to hear the latest "So this pretty little blonde in this huge black SUV drives up…" joke, followed by the explosion of guffaws, and hearty back slaps. The first time around had taught her not to. Everywhere she had gone those last months of the campaign after joining the ticket, at rallies, speeches, parades, demonstrations, factory tours, church services, university symposia, the reaction had been the same. A sort of genteel discourtesy. The welcoming handshake, a bit distant, a bit cool, but respect for the candidacy, respect for Hap's choice. At first. Then, the white balding heads bent over paunches closed ranks, shutting her out.

Determined to enjoy herself no matter what the circumstances, she had tuned it out as best she could. She had learned, had taught herself, to focus on the things that made her happier. She focused on blue skies and green lights, on the marching bands with their eyes screwed up in concentration, focusing on every note, on the children running here and there with excitement because everything was so new.

As a last resort – what she suddenly realized with a jolt here in the barn she was doing right now – she turned to the women. They weren't as openly rude. They would smile, blushing as they lied about their excitement over her candidacy. It was a white lie. A fib. But it had gotten them past the moment. It was doing so, now.

She was tired.

When she asked, then had demanded, the freedom to spend Caucuses Night at third rate Ames, Iowa, Levi's eyes had bulged almost to point of bursting. Of course, she was expected to spend the night with the Grand Poobahs of the Iowa State Democratic Party in the capitol, Des Moines.

But she was fed up with being disrespected to her face.

Instead of saying so, she had merely taken his hand and smiled, "Levi, you will have things well in hand here, I am sure."

He had agreed, reluctantly, but only if she promised to take Foster and leave behind Beatie. (Beatie had ignored the directive with a snort. Making Levi yank Foster over into a corner for a frenzied conversation, Brooklyn to Texas.)

In Ames, she had reasoned, things would be humbler. The people not so grand. Simpler. Not so full of themselves. More willing to open their arms to a stranger.

So much for that idea, she thought, watching a fat farmer with a face brightened by whiskey abruptly close shut and turn away as soon as he realized who she was.

She sighed, and sought out the eyes of an elderly woman, quite possibly his wife, who looked down and away out of embarrassment. Toni moved to her, watching the woman muster up a grin that flickered on, then off, then remained turned on, fixed for the duration of their conversation until Toni's hand reached casually, instinctively out to caress the tow-headed locks of a darling little boy. He looked up and smiled. Toni smiled back and knelt down.

"What's your name?"

He frowned in concentration as he considered, then looked up at her partner.

"Gamma?"

"Yes, sweetie." The matron bent with difficulty then, with an assist from Toni, lifted him into her arms and settled him on one hip.

The matron gave Toni a speculative glance, then shrugged and smiled, a real smile this time, even if a bit tentative, still. "This is my June's Georgie."

"Oh, how delightful," Toni cooed. "He's so handsome! And how old is Georgie now?"

And they had gone on, making rather stilted conversation in a rather desultory fashion.

All the time, the back of Toni's mind continued glancing from moment to moment out of the corner of her eye at the Uncommitted space. It was filling.

That morning, as their cavalcade motored over to a Des Moines supporters' breakfast, CNN breathlessly broke the news of the identities of the twelve SEALS who had heroically died in Chad trying to rescue their fellow Green Berets. Foster looked at her, his eyes reddening, his mouth opening.

Beatie had grunted. "You'll get screwed."

Foster had then turned his ire on her, instead. "She'll look weak as a possum in daytime if she doesn't. Lahk she can't sell it."

Beatie chuffed.

Foster gaped at her with amazement, all Rhodes now, no Texas. "After this!? After Loufa!? On the night of the Caucuses!"

Beatie smirked at him, repeating to her, "You'll get screwed."

Toni took a deep breath.

Foster darted another glance at her, then started texting someone. Furiously.

After another quiet moment or two, he took his own deep breath. Looking at the floor, he asked, "Madam President. You've met the farmers. You've met Iowa. Who would you support if you had just gotten this news?"

Beatie growled, "Oh, Jesus fucking Christ! Levi don't know shit!"

Toni raised a hand cutting her off.

"Release the statement."

Yes, Madam President.

***

The Enviros screamed aloud. To the heavens. All afternoon. As if they had been raped. Sierra Club, Greenpeace, Friends of the Earth, Critical Mass, Alliance for Nuclear Responsibility, Coalition Against Nukes, and a whole range of others. Even the International Atomic Energy Commission reached out, then released a statement of concern after Toni let the call go to message.

Oddly enough, or just as she had expected, she didn't hear a peep about it in Iowa. Not all late morning, early afternoon, early evening or this night. She visited about twenty-five caucus sites that day, she lost count. Shook hands beyond number, ignored the men turning away, went to their wives, and listened. Not a word. Not a sound. Not to her staff traveling with her. And certainly not to her.

Not from the media that had been crowding the barn this last hour, either. Not a one. Just the usual run-of-the-mill Qs that she had been answering for the last three days. Over and over again. The stress was on making her answers sound fresh, not scripted, not repeated hundreds of times already. Then, gratifyingly, some new ones. About her climate change bill successfully reporting out of committee and moving to the House floor. Tonight! Well, that was nice.

Not a whisper about nukes in China.

Foster was ebullient. "It was the right move, Ma'am!" Texas forever. All over the barn, she was watching him right now, sidling up to these corn-fed beauties of the Heartland. As their wide eyes ran over his Brioni suit, it dawned on Toni that her legislative aide was going to get lucky tonight. Several times from the appearance of it.

Someone was tapping a microphone over a harsh squelch, announcing that the first round of voting would commence. Explaining that all groups contending must number more than 15% of the total in order to be judged valid to participate in the second round.

Rod was staring at her. Hard.

She sensed it, then turned completely around and found his eyes across the barn. It wasn't a threat, at least not a physical one. She could see that because his team were all in their usual places. He was just staring at her. His chest was heaving.

For what?

She searched for Foster. Then noticed a teen girl checking her phone for a message and showing it to her daddy. And another. And another. And another.

Foster's face fell just as she found him in the crowd. Barking at his phone, he removed his arm from around the shoulders of a heavily-busted girl in flannel buttoned low enough to make her mother faint. He was looking for Toni, his boss. He started for her.

"Madam President! The House just voted down your cap and trade market bill by a margin of two to one. Do you have any comment?" A microphone was being shoved in her face.

"Madam President, what does this say about your level of support in the House?"

"Are you worried about what this means for your re-elect––, sorry, your election this fall?"

"Madam President—?"

And then she saw it. The judges commanded everyone to take their places before the head count.

As she watched, her group shredded right in front of her eyes. First one, then another, then a couple, then a few more, then more and more and more. All moving over to Uncommitted. All resolutely not looking in her direction.

Someone blew a whistle.

The barn was so quiet, you could have heard a mouse in the rafters.

The judges began counting. They didn't really need to, but scrupulous to the last, they went through the entire procedure. The small, lonely group of Madison supporters left by themselves, expressions of defiance on a few faces, a couple with tears streaming down their cheeks.

It was clear.

Numb. She had watched it happen with her own eyes.

Even the media was stunned into silence. Before they quickly got on the phone to other places, muttering fiercely, then turning to look at her, some openly gulping.

Her supporters had failed to qualify in Ames. The President's supporters had failed to qualify.

And from the expressions directed at her – from embarrassed discomfort giving way to eager, predatory framing of the question as they raised their microphones – from their eyes, she could see that Ames wasn't the only place that that had happened.

She smiled.

What else could she do?

II

She looked up into the dark sky above her.

She was seeing her own fear.

Her fear of becoming the President.

For real.

It was a nebula. A great, gaseous cloud of extraordinary beauty. It spread all across the great black sky. Festooned with a myriad of tinsel-colored stars playing back up vocals, it occupied center stage, much like Levi did. It was a great wonder. A great bright, cotton candied, fuzzily thick oval, tilted above her, stretching the very limits of her vision – from horizon to horizon. She craned her neck to take it all in. So many colors, so many shades, so many hues punctuated by so many bright stars within the mix, she couldn't possibly count them all, much less name them. Some hues standing out, so bright. Others lurking behind, so dark. An entire universe all in itself. So many worlds contained within that whole. So many souls.

Her fear.

So many dreams, so many unfulfilled.

So much unwritten poetry.

So few adventures embarked upon.

Really?

Or was she simply chastising herself for being a wuss, once again?

She refocused on the celestial wonder unfolding above her. So prodigious in all its rainbow colors. As if Crayola had taken it all in stride and – giving it over to the hands of the toddlers she would never have in her womb – let them decorate it, as they chose.

All belonging in, all contributing to, this great big donut in the sky tilted above her. Its wafting, woolly arms spiraling clockwise out from its bright – too bright – like staring directly into the sun too bright – center. Like she had on the day after her mother's funeral, trying to hurt herself, to punish herself, staring straight into the sun, because she was still alive and Rosa Isabella Madison was not. A girl who, at sixteen, had – like Lupe wanted to right up until the day of her rape – wanted

83

to fuck any boy who crossed her path in hopes of getting
pregnant so that she could get married.

Rosa was no different.

Toni suddenly realized.

She was on Hap's Mars.

She was dreaming.

Her mother had died at the age of 33.

Was she up there in Messier 106? Was that Heaven? The
famous nebula?

For that was what Toni recognized it as now. M106. From
her astronomy class at UNM. One that Father Manuel had
suggested. M106. Perhaps the most famous nebula. Because,
other than the Andromeda Galaxy, it was one of the brightest.

After humans had successfully populated the solar system and
figured out – Star Trek like – the mystery of faster than light
travel – as steam had succeeded wind blown clipper ships – so
that the people could move on to its neighbor, the Andromeda
worlds. To dream of moving beyond them, some day, some year,
some lifetime, to visit M106.

A joke Beatie had told her a year ago interrupted her
wonder...

Conservatives enjoyed an entire lifetime smug in the belief
that only bad people got AIDS right up to the moment when,
furiously indignant, they died of it.

Liberals knew the disease could hit anyone and wasted an entire lifetime terrified of it right up to the moment they died, feeling somewhat guilty that it hadn't.

Yes, the world, the humanity that she believed in was one that gathered together to solve whatever new, horrifically wasting disease Mother Nature threw up every decade or so.

It didn't seize on some random sickness, such as polio, and use it as an excuse to prove why one random group of people was superior to others. And they certainly didn't say God had deemed it so.

That was the humanity she believed in

So what?

It was not like she was doing anything about it. Not like she was leading them.

She was just sitting there, staring in wonder at M106.

What was she so afraid of?

Her own voice?

Beatie would smirk at that.

Well, sometimes she honestly hated her best friend.

Rod reached out to her, the wild winds swirling around them. His frame — or was it Artie's? She couldn't tell behind the mask. It couldn't be Artie because he was dead. In Kandahar. Wiping dust off her faceplate, she focused on the body encased, like hers, in the thick atmosphere suit. It was taller, trimmer, more muscular than Artie. It was Rod.

She took his hand. They walked, their white suits encompassing everything but their fingertip touch, their booted feet stirring up small swirls of the Martian regolith – strange name, but soil for Earth had already been taken – with each step. The home planet itself a pale blue dot just above the horizon.

They were walking toward a small dome.

It was cone shaped, to handle the ever-present wind storms, much like living on the Great Plains in the early days must have been, such as sod-busting in Nebraska or the Dakotas. Their home was white, with the red sands of Mars staining it daily. One of many cones in the colony village. All strung along like stained pearls on a necklace with plenty of space between.

Above all the beads, the necklace, that celestial donut in the sky continued to slowly gravitate. Swallowing her, making her feel utterly insignificant, as his grasp did, whenever she allowed it to.

Not too far away, she could see the oxygen and water factories, generating their wares on a daily basis. Without human hands to help, just human minds to maintain. Beyond that were the beginnings of the gardens, much like Jericho so long ago, as Dr. Whathisname had talked about, explaining the end of the Paleo – wandering – gathering – one guy fucking five women – protecting them and their children until the guy in the next meadow beat his head in – lasting for a few million years or so – age. Because there had been some sort of global drought that had forced the wandering bands to stop picking berries and take up gardening instead. Like at Jericho.

It was Port Hap. All of it.

Someday, someday *it would have return to Earth capability.*

Port Hap. She had named it so.

Whatever others might think of his attempts at fidelity, she had truly admired the man. His visions. Besides, even if he used to stare at her tits when in his cups on the campaign trail, all the other times he had truly been kind to her, had respected her. Or so she told herself on a good day.

But Rod was gesturing her up the three steps that functioned as their front porch on Mars. They were walking up them. Together. Their home. They might as well have a picket fence. With a dog. Okay, maybe not a dog.

Rod was opening the hatch. A puff of inner air blew the clinging strands of regolith away from the edges of the portal.

He was opening the door for her. Just as he did for her on the bulletproof limousine back on Earth. Where she was President.

But didn't know why.

And felt guilty as a result.

What? Was she President merely because she felt entitled to it? Like George Bush had. And his son, after him?

She thought people became President because they wanted to make the world a better place. Like Hap did.

What was her problem?

Did she just simply suck?

Rod was ushering her in. Time to stop thinking big thoughts, and instead, focus on that large cock of his filling her.

Completely.

Making her feel all woman.

Just once.

Again.

He was behind her, wiping his feet on the inner doormat. How odd to have doormats on Mars. He was closing the hatch. She felt, rather than heard, the shooosh of pressure changing. Rod was bending to take off his helmet, the dichroic glass that obscured his features sparkling in his hands.

She reached up to her own collar to take off her own. Already feeling, in her mind, the muscular hardness of his lips, his jaw, pressing into her own. Just as she could already feel the hardness of his hips pressing into hers. Making her ache for him. Melt. Into him. To become one. Forever. No secrets between them. Ever. No shields between them. Ever. Just them. His growing manhood already felt through the atmosphere suit.

Making her moist.

His helmet coming off with a final twist, and he beginning to straighten.

He was turning to smile at her. But his hair was all wrong. It was shorter, buzz cut. It was dark.

It was Artie.

***

She woke, feeling the tendrils of disaster clinging to her like those smoky ones of regolith on Mars.

What was that poet's line?

The night shelters me

From her worst

She sighed, trying to recall whether it was Rod's soft tap or the Witch's hard ——

Rod?!

Jesus!

What was she thinking?! The man was married. She sat straight up in bed feeling so… Feeling...what, she did not know. Rod. She took a gulp. Then realized that she was choking. So took another gulp of air while she smothered her gasps from Malcolm under a pillow knowing that he would smack right through the door if he heard them.

Like Rod.

She might know absolutely nothing about the man, other than the curve of his ass, but at least she knew that he was married. At least she knew that much. Beatie had gossiped – in her roustabout way – once upon a time that the man had managed to create two perfect replicas of his wife. All white powdered sugar.

Toni had snarled.

Not that Beatie had noticed that morning. She was too busy taking a bite.

As she was this morning.

Before long, they were sitting in the West Sitting Hall, as usual. Their first early morning meeting since the return from the Caucuses. The Tiffany lunette was spilling its stunningly bright sunshine on them both. Not that Beatie noticed. Either.

"Fucker's coming for you, bitch. You know that."

Team Madison had returned to DC looking battle-weary and bedraggled. Foster had been atypically silent, staring out the window, meeting no one's eyes. On the South Portico lawn, filing out of the Marine One helicopter, she spotted Warren standing granite-faced to greet them. His eyes blazed as he looked at her Texan, who actually seemed to flinch a bit.

Warren, a hard-ass? When had that happened?

Toni had touched him gently on the shoulder with the murmur "Rake him over the coals if you must, but..." as she passed him. Warren had nodded. Tightly.

Later, Beatie had brought the grimly cheerful gossip that Warren had demanded Foster's resignation – for getting played by the Petros or being so distracted by Iowan boobs that his candidate had had to learn about the fuckup from the media – Toni was never quite sure. Foster had immediately agreed, then stood ashen-faced, as Warren had ranted for a good ten minutes – the staff could hear him through the door, another Madison White House first. Beatie had quoted him with a smile. "Never before in the annals of Presidential electoral contests has such asinine incompetence ever been witnessed. Such fatuous, brainless, absurd stupidity! This?! This?!! This is what the London School of Economics brings to bear?! Give me any, I swear to God, any hapless twit from any public university who spent one tenth the amount you wasted on your dross of an education and they would have done better!" He ended by thundering, "The only thing – *only* thing – standing before you falling on your sword is the President herself!"

Apparently Foster had protested at that point because Warren's voice had risen into an entirely uncharacteristic shriek.

"No!! You won't go near her! You won't bother her! You won't come within one hundred feet of her. You have done enough! God — God help me! How in the world could — ?" His voice had failed at that point. Yet their conversation had continued on for another painful twenty minutes or so until Foster had left, white-faced, drained. Later he had been seen crouched on a bench bordering the Rose Garden, weeping. Wags had grinned that the "whipped cur" (one of her Texan's favorite epithets) was afraid to enter the garden for fear of running into her.

As well he hadn't. She had spent many an hour there herself pondering Warren's question. How in the world could — ? Second Oval Office jokes or not. She was out there night and day. Iowa was a bust. They were still recounting but only because she had managed to scrape enough votes from smaller towns and rural areas. Many of the major cities, and particularly Des Moines, had meted out the excruciating humiliation of voting Uncommitted.

Levi announced that the major donors had suddenly snapped shut the purse. No money now to reserve major media market buys for the fall when prices now were at their cheapest. The President's campaign was suddenly broke. Embarrassingly so.

That the Petros and the Nukes had played her was obvious. Why they thought they could get away with it was another question altogether. Because of their ploy, she was now committed publically to supporting American nuke plants in China. And it wasn't like she could reverse herself. Not after Iowa. She had endangered her reputation as an enviro of sterling credentials as a result. Had potentially jeopardized and definitely weakened one of the most crucial bases of support she would need in the fall. If evangelicals enthusiastically carried yard signs for Republicans, enviros and unions carried them with gusto for Democrats. So long as they believed in the candidate.

After the boys on The Hill had gotten her official green light, Jenkins and his fellow Nukes had dumped their support for the Climate Change bill. The Petros had followed shortly thereafter. If they had ever supported it to begin with. That much was clear. Any more, however, was as certain as reading tea leaves, for no one would say. Capitol Hill was sealed up as tight as a drum. Even the old reliable sources for leaks about inner-workings and smoke-filled conversations had dried up.

The entire city seemed to be in on the joke.

She had been played.

Tepid requests about the AI bill weren't even given the dignity of a response. So much for standing by our workers in a future growing steadily less certain in the face of increasing automation. The unions were abandoning her, too?

Lose the enviros *and* the unions? She couldn't win. No one could. No Democrat.

How?

Why?

She shook her head this morning, clearing her mind of self-pity in her lunette sunshine. She hadn't taken a sip of coffee, not even a nibble of the heaping bran muffin sitting idly on a small plate. Malcolm was standing by. Rod down the hall. Beatie was staring at her. Her lenses were emerald.

Her strategist heaved a sigh, shook out her rasta locks irritatedly, then took a bite.

Yes, yes, to all of that, Toni's inner argument continued. Maybe she should have seen it coming. Maybe not. Who wanted to go around in life assuming people were lying to you when pledging to stand by your side? When they *went out of their way* to promise to have your back?

What bothered her was why they thought it would be okay to pull off such a betrayal. Such treachery made for entertaining fiction in a movie. In real life, you always needed your fellow legislators for the next bill. And the one after that. And all the ones following. She knew that from her own years in Congress. So, yes, recklessly burn as many bridges as you please, but only when you were retiring.

The answer had come just last night. Even now, it was difficult to admit it.

It had been a moonless sky. Very dark. Rod's silhouette was reassuringly there, as ever. It made her bitterness a little more palliative. A little. She was absentmindedly crunching through the snow, lighter now that the first hints of spring had hit. Bringing with them some soft rains that were washing away the vestiges of winter. Her fingers trailing along the first buds of some bloom, she couldn't remember which. But she remembered she liked it. It was a large bush. Comforting. Real. The passage of time. That healed all wounds.

Why? And then the answer had come...

They did it because they thought she no longer mattered. She was about to be retired as surely as if she had pulled the plug herself.

She had lost her party.

She was no longer the standard-bearer. Had she ever been? Truly?

She would always be the first Blatina President, but never an elected one. Her Accidency.

Suddenly, she felt relieved.

It was over.

The last President to lose his party during the election cycle had been LBJ, right after the Tet Offensive that had cost Mama her Elijah. And that had been because of the war. Toni had shaken her head at that gruesome thought. Bad enough as it was. She didn't need to whip herself as well.

Then, what? The following thoughts came rapidly. Don't bother with a New Hampshire humiliation in these next few days. Announce tomorrow. LBJ's words sprang to mind, oddly. She didn't know that she knew them.

I shall not seek, and I will not accept, the nomination of my party for another term as your President.

She had always preferred the fire, even if a bit apocryphal, of William Tecumseh Sherman's refusal, when Grant's supporters were looking to draft him to run as his former commanding general was about to retire.

If drafted, I will not run. If nominated, I will not accept. If elected, I will not serve.

She never thought she would ever be in a position to be considering which, if either, her own refusal to run would more closely resemble.

At any rate, announce, then sit out the campaign. Watch the next standard-bearer come forth to receive the accolades and laurels of his party. And she had no doubt it would prove a he. A White he. That would be certain. Still, she sighed, she promised herself that she would campaign for him, or at least go graciously silent if asked not to.

She refocused her attention on her strategist just now selecting one of the best from the heaping tray of Beatie Cakes. How would she explain the decision to her?

"Loufa made you look weak," Beatie was saying. "A woman playing with a gun she had no bizness messing with." That was ironic, given that her friend had crafted her Billy the Kid brand when Toni first ran for Congress.

"Then your Rhodes Scholar got played by the Petros and the Nukes so the Tree-huggers could scream victim and abandon you. The Wrench-turners..." (Beatie's nickname for the AFL-CIO, or unions in general, depending on the day) "... saw both and got spooked about the AI bill. They holding back for a better sales...man."

Toni closed her eyes.

Beatie was continuing, her voice grating now. "Soros, Sussman and the other barons agree. Why throw good money after bad?"

Yes, yes, she knew all that. Or had at least guessed it. How was she going to explain to her oldest friend that she wasn't going to run?

"Fast Eddie arranged it."

That got her attention. But then she chuffed. This was Beatie's shadow-side. Gifted, preternaturally talented at spotting crises before they even formed, she sometimes became paranoid. More often lately, it seemed.

"Ed didn't even know about the negotiations."

"Warren told him."

Pause.

Unbidden tears sprang to her eyes. No. Not now! She blinked them away, avoiding Beatie's hard stare. She looked down the hall to Rod. Who was watching her. Intently. She could almost see his muscles tensing to spring.

She looked down.

Malcolm was clearing his throat. "Madam President…"

"He told me last night," Beatie was continuing. Beating her with each word. Slapping her. Smacking her.

So, what now, Toni thought, abruptly dazed. We return to ABQ together? Open a coffee shop? Two Black chicks who never should have dared to leave?

Another breather.

Then Beatie's voice softened. "He offered to resign."

Toni looked up, her voice caught.

Her friend was…chuckling? "Said he got played, too. By his old friend Fast Eddie. Even used the nickname." Her eyes glinted. "He offered to fall on his own sword."

She brushed some crumbs off her mammoth boobs.

Then grunted. "Told him not to."

Toni paused.

Then, thought, why not? "What do you want me to do?"

***

As Beatie began talking, Toni found her mind caught up in an abstraction. It was like watching someone get raped.

Her patrician chief of staff. Her bespoke tailored, blue-blood chief of staff.

Who could believe it? Betrayed by someone he was supposed to be able to trust. And there was nothing he could do about it. Not a damn thing. So much for the silver spoon.

It was Lupe's rape that had made her a lawyer, she abruptly remembered.

Not just the rape itself, but everything that swirled around the tragedy, including one of the few disagreements that she'd ever had with Mama in all the years that she had known her second mother.

She had gotten a message to come home from her Anthro class. It was a family emergency, the student carrying the message had earnestly blurted out.

Getting out of class, Toni ran to the first pay phone she could find and called home.

Mama was curt. Get home now. It's Lupe.

She had caught the first bus she could and, a breathless thirty minutes later, found herself walking up the steps of home with a tight knot in her belly. Even if she already suspected what the problem was.

Mama had lectured Lupe on her "whore's wear" often enough. "Child!" she would say, blowing out a plume in exasperation at

Lupe's newest, shortest mini-skirt. "You gonna wind yoself up in a world of hurt!"

But her high school friend had always turned the carping aside with her trademark smile. Her smile and her boobs. That was Lupe.

Until it wasn't.

Now her vivacious, dare-devil, damn-the-torpedoes best friend was a shattered, tear-stained wreck, lying on the couch, holding her middle.

Not unlike Cesar, Toni couldn't help but think at the time.

Bizarrely, the healing triggered the argument. All afire with her years of higher education, eager to take wing, Toni wanted to use it by taking her friend through the process. By calling the police, getting a rape kit done. Lupe could identify her assaulter —

Mama had hissed, "No, no, no! We are not getting that silly girl in the System! We are going to handle this the Trumbull way."

But here was the thing, Toni countered, "Lupe's legal. We can do this the right way."

"And get screwed by the System!" Mama had bellowed. She lit another Lucky before realizing the last one was half-smoked. She angrily stubbed it out, her eyes growing wide as she beheld her daughter. What has happened to my child? Where did she go? Her eyes pleaded.

Toni saw the fear. Stroked that beefy arm. Caressed that plump cheek.

"Please," she asked. "Let me try it the real way."

"Real way!" Mama snorted and lit another Lucky. Then realized in exasperation her mistake again and stubbed it out with a loud hmph. "You are just going to hurt her all over again."

Lupe had stood, somehow, in the midst of all this. "Chica, you are smart now, with your university ideas. If you want to try, I trust you." And then she started crying all over again. Toni hugged her, then just held her.

And that had settled it. Almost.

"I'll make my own plans," Mama had grumbled. "Just in case."

In some odd way, the whole, awful experience had brought the two high school friends closer together, Toni realized years later, even if it also further highlighted their growing differences. For, after it was all concluded, she never really saw Lupe again. Oh, years later when Lupe was happily married to a vacuum repairman and working on child number four. But Lupe wouldn't approach her – it was at a campaign rally during her first run for Congress – Lupe had merely smiled, with tears in her eyes, and babies in her arms, waving.

At the time of healing, though, they had come together. Right down to the nights sleeping in her bed together again. Her arms around her friend, listening as Lupe described what it was like.

The harsh thrusting that terrified, even as it hurt, bruising her within. Followed by the slow realization that his eyes were too focused on his own pleasure to hurt her more than that. If she played her cards right, and got away, she would be okay. He might be a monster, but he was no killer. And the odd relief that hit her as he was coming inside her. Just get away and she'd be fine. After all, it hadn't lasted for more than a few minutes.

As for the way he had smacked her around in the back seat when she had changed her mind and tried to leave, well...what boy in their neighborhood didn't slap a girl around from time to time?

And then, surreally – except she watched it become all too real – the growing feeling her friend had of something gone spoiled deep within her as the months passed. As if she were ruined forever. Lupe's tears on her shoulder again and again, as Toni held her each night. The fear of being ruined.

It was that feeling, more than any other, that made Toni want to shoot the bastard.

That and her own growing feeling of impotence as the entire process went forward. Eventually, she had to agree, Mama had made the right call. She *had* been too idealistic.

On that night, though, Toni called the police and helped Lupe fill out the statement, including the airman's name, the club where she had met him near the airbase. Had gone through the entire process. Gone to the hospital, had the rape kit done, including the scary blood tests over the following months.

Taken her home. Cared for her. Met with a prosecutor.

And that was where the troubles began. He was clearly bothered by other things. His mind kept wandering. He had taken in Lupe and her at a glance. Not worth his trouble. She saw it, recognized the same look from the more arrogant professors at UNM. It made her angry. It made her rage. So, Toni forced him to go over the details again and again. Sparking his own irritation. Freaking Lupe out, and herself, with her daring. Finally, his agreement to see that the airman was arraigned as quickly as possible and, should he plead not guilty, brought to trial. In some civil rights history class that Mama had made her take, Toni had picked up the phrase "justice delayed is justice denied" and – in some kind of furious trance over his evidently cavalier attitude – she kept hammering away at it until he finally just kicked them out of his office.

On the bus ride home, Lupe had sheltered in her arms, crying again. Clearly frightened. She, herself, was confused. Why the indifference? What good were prosecutors if they weren't going to do the job of charging criminals for their crimes?

Mama had merely smoked her Luckys. Moodily. One after another. Toni made a hamburger and noodles dish which nobody really ate.

A few weeks later, at the arraignment, the mystery was revealed.

Sitting in the chairs behind the table on the prosecutor's side as far from the rapist as they could get, they watched him smirk at the sight of them. Until his very well dressed attorney made a comment to him, forcing the asshole to turn around and sit up straight.

The judge had come in, the bailiff had bellowed out that everybody should stand. The judge told them all to sit. Then, he focused on the defense attorney. His Honor clearly didn't like him, which made Toni's heart lift a little. Even as, she noticed, the judge refused to look at Lupe. Not even once. Then followed a lot of gobbledygook that Toni barely understood. Darting a glance at Lupe, she saw, as expected, that her friend caught even less.

Then the defense attorney was explaining that the airman was urgently needed in the Mediterranean to support an operation in that theatre. A rescue operation. The attorney could say no more, of course.

The judge wanted to know why this particular airman was so crucial to the mission.

The attorney replied that he could not divulge those details, was not privy to them himself, but that his client's commanding officer had insisted on the need. He requested a stay of proceedings for ninety days.

The judge had sighed. He turned to the prosecutor who made no objection.

The gavel came down and that was that. The airman smirked at Lupe again as he left with a saunter, a free man.

All walked out, leaving the courtroom deserted. All avoided their eyes.

Money? The leverage a military airbase has on the surrounding neighborhoods, the surrounding political structure? Power? Over two Latinas with no other resources. Toni had pondered that miscarriage of justice many times over the years.

Mama, however, sprang into action that night.

Cesar came over, flanked by a couple of his Trumbull Soldados. Soldiers. They ate as much of Mama's fried chicken as they could manage. She smoked one Lucky after another with a grim smile on her face. It was Toni, now, who was avoiding their eyes.

The next morning the airman's body was found hanging from a lamppost on Wyoming Blvd SE, just outside the club parking lot. Lynched. Every bone possible in his body was apparently broken. His eyes gouged out. His cock cut off and shoved down his throat. He was wearing his uniform.

Now, suddenly, the airbase boiled over with a rage that lasted for weeks. Fiery speeches from all corners denouncing the violence of the neighborhoods surrounding the airbase. Sermons in pulpits. City council members and other civic leaders speaking out each night on tv. The mayor holding a special forum. Politicians seemed to line up, including the district attorney – Toni noticed with disgust – to decry this horror, this preying on "our boys in blue" who "defended this great nation with their honor."

After a week straight of such disgusting hyperbole, Toni pounded the kitchen table one night in frustration, swearing she would call an investigative reporter she liked on KOAT7, a local tv station.

Mama had uttered one word. "No."

The way she voiced it ended Toni's thoughts on the subject.

Yet, it hadn't.

Not really.

Months later, when Lupe was finally coming around to a semblance of her former self, and getting back out and around to visit the wider world. When Toni was finishing up her classes and getting ready for graduation, wondering just what the hell to do with herself now. One day, she found herself walking by the UNM School of Law. On impulse, she asked to speak with someone.

He was a nice man. He reminded her of Father Manuel with his professorial manner. Surrounded by his photos of a much younger, and much slimmer, version of himself back in the 60s with Bobby Kennedy and a very different Cesar – the grape picker Cesar Chavez. Signs shouting United Farm Workers and *¡Si, Se Puede!* in the background.

He listened to every word she had to say. Gravely.

When she had finally run down and felt herself, maddeningly, tearing up, he had only looked out the window saying, "Senorita Madison, I cannot promise you justice for this tragedy that you have just suffered. That is beyond the power of this law school."

Then, returning his eyes to hers, he had smiled, gently. "I can, however, promise you justice – or at least the chance to achieve justice – for the next one."

Thus, even though it was typically far too late to be accepted, her grades, her fire, and of course, her ethnicity opened that door for her.

Which made her grow only taller in Mama's eyes – who had immediately set everything else aside to figure out how they would pay for it. Much more expensive than her undergrad years, law school turned out to be, rather prosaically, a variation on the same mix of funding. With the hearty addition of what Mama only called "help from the community." What that help was, Toni decided not to ask. She did notice that Cesar began coming around again more often. Also, that there was a new, heavily locked trunk, bolted to the pavement next to the freezer out back.

She decided that she didn't want to know.

Just as they never really discussed Mama's Trumbull solution to the rape. She couldn't. She loved Mama with all her heart, even as she disagreed with her, vehemently, about the choice. She was also furious with herself for being so clueless, so idealistic.

If there was anything that she learned, overall, from the tragedy, in all its aspects, it was this…

Power responded only to power.

In whatever form.

***

First In The Nation.

A string of house meetings – such as with old Hapsters the Johansens and their six guests in their living room in Nashua – where she arrived, stomped the snow off her boots, gave over her parka and settled into a chair all ready to talk CC and AI and where those two bills were going, how they would improve the future of America.

Peggy, the hostess, asked instead, "Is it true that your vice president is running against you?"

Or that church basement with eight people and their minister, Reverend Wickham, himself another old Hapster from the early days, in Concord. Same question.

Or at the Larsens, their living room with four friends – also all old Hapsters – in Chesterfield. Same one.

The gang at the Colchesters in Walpole with its beautifully sculpted hills let her get a few minutes into her pitch about AI and securing the future for our workers, blue collar and white, before someone popped the question.

And so on.

Through it all – in living room after dining room, restaurant after deli, church after VFW Hall – the same question. Whether Woodstock, Littleton, Lancaster, Conway or a dozen other places that she rode the old travel circuit on those three days before ending, finally, at Dixville Notch (notch, in local speak, meaning mountain pass) not too far from the peak of Sanguinary Mountain. If New Hampshire was an L turned backwards, the township – population of seven (or eight, depending on who was counting) – snoozed quietly at the top of the letter, just across the border from Montreal.

Dixville Notch was an American past-time. Its voters gathered at midnight the night before – or the morning of, locals would argue – primary day in New Hampshire so that they could vote. The process took about sixty seconds. Then, they counted up the results and released it to a hungry media – who often outnumbered the actual voters in the fusty Ballot Room of the Balsams Country Club – becoming the first in the state to announce their picks. Which made them first in the nation since everyone in New Hampshire knew that their state held an official primary and Iowa only held – harumph! – lowly caucuses.

There was even a large white decoration on the wall, styled like an old-fashioned signpost, proclaiming the "First In The Nation" tradition.

Levi thought it cute and, therefore, not really worth their time.

After three days of fielding the same damn question about Fast Eddie, though, Toni had had enough and insisted they go to the Notch. She couldn't give a damn what the rest of primary day held for her. She was going to be there to stare the voters in the eye.

Entering the surprisingly small room, seeing the litter of annotated photographs, from Warren G Harding onward, decorating the walls, the legendary ballot box, taken out of its pristine case built into the wall where it sat locked away all year, now standing proudly in pride of place in the room on a table, she spotted her vice president.

What a surprise! His schedule had been strangely vague of late, so Warren informed her.

Edward Langton was chatting up an elderly couple. As he was posing for a photographer and, apparently, answering a reporter's question. All at the same time.

As was Connor Raines across the room. Incorrigible playboy turned software impresario of the Silicon Valley, founder of the holographic social media site That Moment that had made him a billionaire by thirty, Raines was standing by the ballot box talking with an old farmer who was carrying a gavel. Well, well, well. Connor Raines was the GOP favorite, if only because, as he argued quite convincingly, it was time for the GOP to stop being the enemy of Big Tech. She didn't see any other Republican candidates.

Fast Eddie or Connor? Levi was breathing, heavily. His flannel shirt not at all hiding his paunch sticking out over his jeans.

A reporter was approaching her with that predatory gleam in her eye, microphone extended like a lance in front of her. Levi snapped to action, almost impaling himself on the microphone, allowing Toni the chance to skip away.

Slipping past Rod and one of his team, she spotted another couple just arriving. The farmer was pulling off his knit cap, his wife was taking off her wool scarf. Both looked rather sour at the hour, if a bit expectant.

Perfect.

She strode right over, hand outreached, and engaged them, noting Fast Eddie's right eye had begun fluttering. He was protesting to a reporter, a little too loudly, "Of course not! I am here to support our President, that is all!"

Ah, well. She hoped Beatie's plan worked.

For now, it was interesting to know that Fast Eddie had a tell when fibbing. She didn't know that.

The couple, Clarence and Evelyn Baxter, had a farm just a couple miles away. Their children – Clarence's gnarled fingers could barely handle the photos on his newfangled cellphone their granddaughter had given him – lived in Boston, mostly. Toni helped him with the phone as Evelyn gave her the rundown: one son a lawyer, another a doctor, the lone daughter in commercial real estate. The granddaughter who gave him the cellphone turned out to be an activist with Greenpeace, as evidenced by a shot he showed her of two divers – one of whom was her, Clarence grunted, still a little unnerved by it – wearing scuba gear as they plugged a large sewage pipe that was apparently dumping sludge in the Charles River in west Massachusetts.

Toni took her cue and launched into a full-throated pitch of her cap and trade market idea. Hap always used to say that Iowa and New Hampshire voters "might look as dumb as stumps in flannel, but they know the issues." Clearly, they took their vetting of early candidates gravely.

Evelyn waited until she was about three sentences in, then lay a hand on her arm to stop her.

Toni took a breath and forced a smile, waiting for the Fast Eddie question.

"But, Ma'am, what chance does that bill even have after such a clear defeat in the House? Two to one, wasn't it, dear?"

Clarence nodded, grunting, "Near 'tenough."

Finally! Toni felt her smile brighten. "Yes, and that was just the first step. A reading of the lay of the land to show us..."

Where the hell did that lie come from? She wondered. Then, shrugged and went on with their "plans" to come back in another month with a second go of it, incorporating every single concern that was voiced during the dry run.

There were seven voters in all. Two more had shown up in the form of another elderly couple. They could easily be mistaken for cousins of Clarence and Evelyn. Connor scooped them up with a neat turn of the foot and a wide swinging handshake that she had seen Hap do a hundred times or more. Raines was the favorite of the evening. Everyone understood that. Dixville Notch historically voted Republican on that night.

The Democratic candidates had to be content with scraps from the table.

Nevertheless, she used the opportunity to step around a photographer clicking away at the room to meet the farmer holding the gavel just as he was taking the time to slap the backs of the late arrivals. His name was Billy. The others' she really didn't quite catch, but they were obviously Raines voters. The wife even blushed as Connor took her hand in both of his. She blurted out, "Let it Rain!" To which Connor leaned back that already famous leonine head of white hair of his and let out a hearty guffaw.

Toni smiled and turned back to Billy asking if he could introduce her to the couple that Fast Eddie had been engaged with. Surprised, Billy nervously swept his few wisps of gray hair back and openly wondered if that were showing preference.

Not at all, Toni protested with a smile. And – struck by inspiration – gushed, "Just think, I've come all the way across this great nation from the Southwest to stand in this room tonight. And, let me tell you, Albuquerque might dip below freezing at night in the wintertime, but we cannot boast any of the charming drifts of snow that you have here every day."

That thawed him outright. He walked her right over to that couple. Eddie, mysteriously, took this opportunity to move over to Clarence and Evelyn. Musical chairs.

Right after the introductions, Toni took the moment to ask Billy about the ballot box. That she understood it to be a gift from a local woodsman. Which wound him up like a top. He, assisted by the couple, began lobbing out different stories associated with the ballot box, highlighting how Neil Tillotson was the first to start the tradition and "who created rubber balloons, ma'am" – "now, Billy, they were latex, just like the gloves he invented that every hospital uses" – "whatever!" – and on and on.

Nimbly, Toni managed to slip in her AI worker's training bill, riding on Tillotson's coattails for being such a creative entrepreneur and changing our world for the better. They listened to her pitch about rewarding rather than penalizing our workers because of the creativity of our entrepreneurs. Of standing by our workers, whatever the color of their collar. And so on.

Until the wife nudged Billy, who looked down at his watch in shock. "Grand consternation! We'd best get started."

He actually did a double-take right then, as if he had lost track of time...listening to her...and couldn't really quite believe it.

In any case, Billy gathered them all to the front of the room, asking the media to make way at the back. He made a pretty little speech, obviously honed over the years, welcoming everyone, beginning with her and her veep, and including Raines. Then, he held up a ballot, pointed out the spot for write-in candidates at the bottom, and the three slender voting booths that had been set up along one wall, curtained by plastic flags that covered the entrance for each.

All of this, as everyone seemed to keep one eye on the large clock on the wall behind him, over his head. It might be rural America, but the stage-management was pure Hollywood. He turned to count down the last five seconds and, at the stroke of midnight, he crowed, "Ladies and Gentlemen, the Dixville Notch polls are open!" and smacked the gavel down on the ballot box.

The three ladies went first. They disappeared behind the flags, one to a booth, and emerged a moment later. Each carrying their ballots, neatly folded over. Billy stood over the ballot box with great gravity, nodding solemnly to each as they slipped their votes through the slit at the top. Their husbands had taken their places in the booths and voted, then Billy surrendered the gavel to Clarence and went to vote. A moment later, he emerged, slipped in his vote and, retrieving his gavel, watched Clarence rejoin Evelyn in the semicircle that had formed around the box and, with a glance at the clock, smacked the box with the gavel, roundly declaring, "The polls are closed. Please wait while the ballots are counted."

At this point, he cleared his throat of some noisy phlegm while reaching out for a grand skeleton key to open the reverse side of the box and, with a nod to Evelyn, he took a step back. Evelyn and another woman stepped forward to take charge, whispering, with an austere decorum as they totaled up the votes and wrote them down for Billy to read aloud.

Somehow Levi had managed to slip in next to her shoulder. "Remember," he whispered while jerking his head at the photographers who were sneaking around the edge of the wall, "those cameras will be on you. Not Raines and certainly not the Schmuck." Levi's Yiddish contribution to the host of nicknames for Vice President Langton circulating the West Wing these days.

Evelyn thanked her assistant, then set the stack of ballots down on the box and primly resumed her place at her husband's side. Following her walk, Toni saw the way her eyes flickered at Raines. Oh, well. He was reputed to be a ladies man.

Billy was noisily fumbling around in his overalls, checking his pockets for his reading glasses. Clearing his throat of some less agreeable, stickier phlegm. Finding his specs at last, taking them out after an even longer theatrical pause, he put them on his nose, adjusted them just so and peered at the crowd. Then, he looked down at the totals and, blinked a moment, darting a flick at her, then resuming in tones of majesty.

"Ladies and Gentlemen, distinguished candidates, guests, members of the media, and citizens of this Great Nation. We here at Dixville Notch proudly announce our results in the New Hampshire primary election, first to be reported to this state, this nation, this world."

He paused, looked around the room, then continued.

"For the Grand Old Party, Connor Raines, four votes."

No surprises there. Guess she and Fast Eddie would have to squabble over the remaining three. Billy's glance darted at her again.

She sighed. Oh, well. It wasn't like Beatie hadn't prepared her for this moment.

"For the Democratic Party, Vice President Langton, two votes."

The cameras began flashing. The reporters were stirring. Levi was growling something in Yiddish. Or maybe it was Polish. The cameras kept flashing. The photographers moving around in front of them now, no longer bothering to hold back. One reporter was already firing a question at Raines.

As Billy read out his last result with a blush, Toni abruptly smiled. She couldn't help it.

She knew where her single vote had come from.

***

It was going to be a struggle, Beatie had warned. The man who was supposed to be carrying you had stolen a march instead. Think back to a time in your life that had been a long struggle.

That was easy. Reyes Latino.

After graduating from law school, thinking of Lupe, she had become an ambulance chaser. She worked quite hard at it for a few years. Mama had helped her find her first clients who were, inevitably, from the neighborhood and had to pay with barter. Paying clients came slowly. Just soon enough, though, it seemed, for her student loan payments.

Whether she was making a difference, however, she honestly couldn't say. She simply worked one case at a time. Trying not to answer the question. Let the world be what it was. She was going at it just one case at a time. One day, at a law school alum gathering, a classmate wearing a vintage Chanel dress suit asked her why she hadn't gone corporate.

"You've got the brains for it, Toni. You know you do."

She did not know that.

"Do you want me to talk to one of our partners in LA? I think you'd be happy at our firm."

Corporate law. She had never even considered the possibility. Litigation – the courtroom – had seemed the only choice.

As for everything else, such as a boyfriend, well, who had time for that?

Besides, she was starting to feel self-conscious that she was still living at home. It was cheap, but… She wanted her freedom, some independence. Mama's sermons didn't pack the same savor as they had a few years earlier. Particularly when Toni was meeting her clients around that smoke-filled kitchen table.

And that trunk out back weighed on her mind.

So, she had focused on the little things. One case at a time. The treadmill. Getting to know the judges. Getting to know each of the prosecutors – which played fair, which screwed you as soon as you got distracted. Getting to know the law. Juvenile law. Robbery law. Armed robbery law. Vandalism law. Grand theft auto law. Arson law. Drug possession and/or sale law. Prostitution law. Repeat offender law. Assault law. Armed assault law. Even Murder law (once, which she had lost). Domestic violence law. Rape law, the hardest for her of all, defending accused rapists.

One case at a time. Bartering changing slowly into actual checks. Figuring out how invoicing worked. Using a secondhand PC that she set up in the corner of Mama's living room. Actually being paid. Slowly working up a surplus, even with student loans. Then, working that surplus into a sustainable stash of cash that would, someday, make a small apartment realizable.

Mama had cried.

It was a teeny one bedroom in Silver Hill, a few blocks away from the university and, yet, still south of Central Ave, so she felt like she was not going too far from her clientele. She borrowed one of those new digital cameras hitting the market, printed the photos at a copy store and brought them to Mama.

Who had cried harder. Then, insisted that Cesar and his Soldados check out the neighborhood before they moved her in.

It was painful moving out.

Yet, life was life.

Besides, Artie was coming into hers just then. Her short, shy, chubby, helo pilot. Arturo Pedro Gonzalez. An undocumented.

She had met him at a club one night, practically the only time that she ever went out. He had asked her to dance. His bashful grin, flickering on and off like an uncertain neon sign. Gulping, swallowing, as she stared at him, not certain that she had heard him right with the noise of the music.

His very careful handling of her. Gingerly taking her arm after she had complained about the head-throbbing beat of the DJ's choices and leading her out onto the street. His anxious scan of the avenue and careful choosing of the best lit side as he walked her to the campus to look at a fountain that he said was supposed to be pretty cool.

As the evening was. A typical, breezy ABQ cool evening of summer. He had taken off his pilot's jacket and put it around her shoulders. And had listened to her concerns about how she didn't know what the hell she was doing as a lawyer. So much pain, so much violence, so little hope, so little change. She had wondered if it was the vodka talking or something about the sweetness of his warm eyes that made her unlock feelings that she didn't even know were under key and give words to. Aloud. To a stranger.

And he had wound up taking her straight to her favorite place on campus. The Mother Earth fountain. Which always reminded her of Mama. She pretended not to know it that well, making light of it. Because she was suddenly afraid that she had blabbed out her entire life too much to him and must sound like a nutcase. Instead, as they sat there, she wondered if Artie knew that the artist was Vietnamese and wondered what he thought about that.

At the time, though, she had simply kissed him.

Only to have him stand up in horror, exclaiming, "Senorita!" His eyes gone wide, staring around them, checking to see if any had seen.

It had proven difficult luring him into bed. But what a sweet, warm and wonderful, gentle ecstasy had awaited her there. It was worth it. Even with his constant agonizing over what the Santo Padre would say about them using condoms (the Pill was out of the question) those first two times. Struck by inspiration one day soon after, she gave him a truly amateurish blowjob. Her first. It didn't matter. Boy, was he happy! After a few more months of this, she taught him how to go down on her. Then, on those nights she wanted to cuddle more, how to give her some fingertip love while holding her.

It was worth it.

Even better once she had figured out the pattern of starting on him, then getting him to satisfy her, then finishing him. They lay in her tiny bed in her cheap-ass apartment several hours at a time, making each other giggle, on one of his few days off.

It had proven even more difficult to get him to admit that he was a Special. His unit, 58th Special Air Wing, trained for the most dangerous of jobs. Insertion and extraction of special forces teams operating in the bush. RPGs being fired at his helo was accepted as a daily nuisance. Like gnats. Getting "the guys" in and out safely was his quiet pride. He would only talk about it after she had blown him. Lying flat on his back, breathing out, "Madre de dios, Toni, madre de dios!"

(Which had always made her smile. They couldn't use condoms, but he could take the Madonna's name in vain after receiving a blowjob. Oh, well, she had reasoned. Maybe God was smiling down at her vastly improved technique.)

Only then would he talk – would share with her – in hushed tones about his work. How he went about the daily business of launching a piece of machinery eight tons heavy and then some with all the men and gear. It was precision. It was care. It was humility. Approaching a PAVE Hawk helo with anything less was the act of a fool. One saw them. The Rambos. The silly bravado. That was downright dangerous. They never lasted long before being washed out.

(She had asked him three times what PAVE stood for, but could never remember anything except "vectoring." Besides, once he had laughed, saying, "Vida mia!" – which made her melt – "it means the eyes and ears of the bird!")

That was enough. He was safe, she was sure of it.

Until he wasn't.

In the spring of 2003, as his unit was being called up to Kandahar – in answer, she was sure, to her feverish prayers that he not be sent to Iraq – he had proposed.

She had cried. Accepted.

And, in her eagerness, accidentally tore their one condom trying to get it out of the package on their last night together. It wasn't like she had had a lot of practice with them. Artie had freaked, but eventually relented. She was a lawyer. She could be persuasive. Very persuasive.

Still, he left looking a little green about the gills, yet one more *Dios te salve, Maria* on his lips, she had smiled.

Until she stopped.

Her flimsy didn't come in the mail like Mama's telling her about her Elijah. Toni's flimsy came in the form of a phone call from his sister. Artie wasn't coming home. They were even having trouble securing the remains.

What followed was a long grinding down of her life. Energy. Happiness. Will. To. Breathe.

She moved back in with Mama. Who, thankfully, welcomed her with open arms. No complaints of being forgotten, of how wrapped up in Artie and her career her child had been these last years. Not one word.

Just the loud cry, "Child, you come here! You have some of my fried chicken, now. Best in the world, honey. You looking like a scarecrow."

Too exhausted to argue, she had merely sat at the table and bit into a greasy leg while she watched Mama grow blurry while lighting a Lucky.

She spent about a year trying to get it back together. Some suffering she struggled to give voice to. Some sorrows she knew she never would. Mama was patient. She understood. She had lost her own airman. Had never loved another.

Her law career flagged. She just couldn't work up the energy to meet with anyone, let alone go to court. Her loans were just about paid off, anway. It was easier to simply lie in bed all day, trying to catch the birdsong of a lonely adventurer. And cry. About her man. About whether she had killed him, by distracting him during battle, by freaking him out so much fucking him, that one last time, without a condom. Was he saying a Hail Mary about her, about him, about them, when an RPG had gotten him at last?

The days turned into weeks, turned into months, effortlessly. Would they turn into years?

Maybe she and Mama would wind up like this forever, Toni began to think. Two women with a kitchen full of fried chicken and a suspicious trunk out back.

However, as she learned to recognize years later, the world has a way of continuing to rotate. The sun had a habit of rising in the morning and setting in the evening, no matter what we had to say about it.

Reyes Latino. The Latino Kings.

They showed up slowly, quietly. On a corner. Selling drugs. Buying hookers. Beating them. Raping them. Killing their pimps. Turning them into their own product. Selling drugs. Charging protection fees to local merchants. Taking the local gambling joints for their own. Selling drugs. Buying cops. Buying judges. Buying political leaders. Selling drugs.

Challenging any who felt threatened by them. With fire. With ruthlessness. With savagery.

Cesar's Soldados were among the first to die. She and Mama never got the chance to save them. Not a one. Just the memory of a boy's raucous laughter, a happy face streaked with fat from Mama's fried chicken. Here no more. There another empty chair. Then another absence. And another.

Cesar grew old, even gray-haired, almost overnight.

She tried to ask what it was, but he waved her away.

It was meth. She was sure of it.

One heard on the streets what a goldmine it was. Easy to manufacture. Easier to hide. Easiest of all to transport.

And then the day came when Cesar was no more. Gunned down in a pool hall that was shredded by AR-15 gunfire. The whole place destroyed. Several Soldados dead with him.

On that night, she prayed. She prayed to Artie. She asked him. Where were the police? Where were the prosecutors? What should she do?

She thought of the way he spoke with quiet pride of what he did. You never give them the initiative, he used to say. Never give them the momentum. Let them take the momentum away from you and you are lost.

So, she decided.

To do what he would do.

To take the fight to them.

If there were no prosecutors willing to fight the Reyes Latino. She would.

***

From Dixville Notch to Garnet Gap in just a few days.

Team Madison had returned from New Hampshire to a capitol buzzing about the stand-off between LEOs – the Marshals Service and the FBI – and some separatists at some little known hamlet in a mountain pass named Garnet Gap. The media were already gleefully pronouncing the name with relish, pointing out the cherry color of the gemstone, found in plentiful numbers in the Idaho panhandle, helping the audience imagine the blood about to flow up there after a marshal had been killed.

The Deputy US Marshal had been crouched behind a towering Douglas Fir, soaring into the sky above him. His name was Hank. He was about to make history. What were his last thoughts? Anything? Get home to his picturesque sweetheart? Get a pizza along the way? Stop at a bar to bang some other broad because his former cheerleader girlfriend had lately turned into a shrew about the low pay of federal law enforcement officers? The world would never know.

For her part, Toni was pissed that she didn't even get to enjoy the New Hampshire victory. Dixville Notch was an embarrassment, sure. But they had fought it out across the remaining election sites anyway. Iowa was one thing – the noisy, exciting, disorienting caucus environment, where herd mentality reigned, making sudden shifts in a voter's support possible, not really thinking so much as following his friends across the floor from one space to another. New Hampshire, with its formal primary – where voters marked a ballot, on their own, in a booth – was a different ball game entirely. It was slower, more thoughtful. They had managed to eke out a victory over Fast Eddie and get the Granite State's stamp of approval as Democratic nominee to be President for four more years.

Can't win for losing, she grumbled.

Beatie – who had remained behind to work on her plan – had greeted her on the South Lawn outside Marine One with three words. "Remember Loufa, bitch."

The United States Marshals Service – America's first cops – was founded soon after the Revolution as part of the first judicial legislation that Congress had, empowered by Article III of the Constitution, passed to set up a legal system of courts. Unlike the Texas Rangers – and certainly their most famous one, The Lone Ranger – the marshals were quiet. Always had been. Toni had seen a poster once of the first marshals. She couldn't identify a single one.

That Judiciary Act of 1789 created thirteen judicial districts, each having its own attorney and marshal. The US Attorneys did their lawyer work. The US Marshals chased fugitives. Often ones who had skipped bail or had refused a summons.

Well over two hundred years and a host of duties added later, marshals were still chasing fugitives. Well, that is to say, their deputies were. Like Hank had been. Chasing Jedediah Templeton Meyers who had skipped bail out of Coeur d'Alene after beating a local Sikh grocery store owner into unconsciousness. Meyers had been heard to shout by several bystanders, repeatedly, "Take your stinking hat, your dirty skin, you shit bag and go back to whatever hellhole you came from!"

Not surprisingly, the local DA had decided to try the assault as a hate crime. Toni would have done the same.

But Meyers skipped town not ten minutes after bail was settled upon.

Hank and his fellow marshals had tracked him over the following weeks to a series of huts that looked, from their placement and the walls between, suspiciously like a fortified compound with interlocking fields of fire. It was hard to tell with all the old growth forest covering it. The compound belonged to The People, a white supremacist group, long judged by the Southern Poverty Law Center as "quiet, yet worth keeping an eye on." TP was led by Gideon Israel Browne. An engineer turned preacher in the old, simple Baptist mold, he had rejected the world as beyond redemption, carted his wife, his sons and his flock away from Sodom-like Spokane, Washington, to create their utopia in fine American-style, off the grid in the panhandle of Idaho. Other than his predilection for collecting assault rifles and powering his compound with solar panels, Browne had led a very quiet couple of decades. Thus, her morning's Presidential Daily Briefing.

But the pot boiled over with the shooting death of Hank.

Where had the shot come from? Why? Who knew?

What had started out a simple snatch job – five buddies wearing vests and carrying Glocks, as per reg, but also sporting hiking boots and water bottles in their determination to enjoy a day in the woods – appeared to have mushroomed overnight into a major operation – led by the FBI and staffed by hundreds of special agents and marshals wearing combat uniforms patterned to match northwest flora, complete with body armor and helmets, carrying M16s. Ringing the site, high in the trees, perched snipers with rules of engagement that, a friend at the DOJ leaked, seemed to be changing by the hour.

Beatie had groused, "Nat Forrest – hell, all of South Carolina – is drooling over those changing ROEs." Warren kept his eyes on the floor. Odd.

Beatie kept staring at her until she ordered Warren to call in the attorney general, an old friend of her chief of staff, for an update.

US Attorney General Max Evans, former governor of Pennsylvania, came over in due course. A Hapster, more eager to burnish his credentials on his way to the Supreme Court than rock the boat, Toni had been content to let him proceed with Hap's original orders.

Evans had turned in a few racketeering convictions, using the updated RICO laws to kneecap a wiseguy or two foolish enough to long for the old Castellammarese War days of yore. Also, a handful of quiet investigations into sexual harassment by Congressmen of their staff, forcing resignations. A couple of labor disputes. Some corporate polluting. A couple large mergers sniffed and scratched. But, no dramatic policy shifts. No precedent-breaking cases. Nothing major, really. The garden variety of work that had marked the quieter Department of Justice of administrations past. Evans had done just as Hap had ordered: "Keep things quiet at home so I can get to work on colonizing Mars."

Evans leisurely strolled into the Oval, not even carrying a folder, which irritated her. Still, his old-town courtly ways were charming. He smiled warmly, commented on her win in New Hampshire, inquired after a friend or two in the state legislature in Concord.

She invited him to sit. And waited.

Max's grin wavered a bit.

Growling within, Toni smiled, "The update on Garnet Gap?"

His toothy beam widened. "I'm sorry, Madam President, is Ed running late?"

Jesus.

She didn't know what he saw in her face, but he clearly didn't like it. He glanced over at Warren for help. Her chief of staff, she could see, had his eyes on the floor.

What the…?

Max went blank for a moment, then as if wetting a finger to test the wind and liking what he sensed, he relaxed back into the couch.

"Madam President, I can assure you that matters are well in hand." Don't worry, little missy. Don't worry your pretty little head.

"Good," she chirped. "The update?"

That threw him. He cleared his throat and began reciting in monotone all the relevant facts and recent history that she had just read this morning in her PDB. She waited until she saw him winding down.

"Yes, thank you for summarizing my morning briefing," she heard her voice grow curt. "An update?"

He looked like she had slapped him. His genial, avuncular cheeriness reformed in an instant to a sudden mean, toughness that would have taken her breath, except. Except she was angry.

She made to speak.

He held out a hand. "Now, hold on Madam President!" Then he turned to his old college roommate. "Warren, what in Sam Hill?"

Her chief of staff cleared his throat, raised his eyes to the couch opposite. "Perhaps the President is entitled to an update without having to ask a second time?"

Max's mouth dropped open. He swallowed. Swallowed again. His warm, dimply beam worked its way back, almost.

Still, it was something. Toni had to marvel at his speed of adaptation.

She also had to wonder at Warren, filing that away to consider another time.

"It's...well...Madam President..."

And then she watched him throw it all in. As if handing her the gavel. Not my problem, anymore.

"It's not good."

Since early morning, FBI negotiators, including a couple of Coeur d'Alene Police Department negotiators to assist, had been trying to establish contact. To no avail. The compound refused to respond.

Moreover, drone flights overhead revealed that the innocent looking canopy of dense old-growth forest sheltering the compound was actually a sophisticated lattice of cloaked netting that minimized heat signatures. Even their very best thermal imaging cameras were only picking up blurs.

On the ground, with the even denser growth outside the compound and its placing of concrete walls reinforced – it was recognized now – with several alternating layers of brick and some other masking material, it was worse. The LEOs could see tell-tale signs of movement from time to time. Nothing more. Nothing definite. Except a sign.

She waited.

"That says?"

He glanced over at Warren, then shook his head in disgust.

"That says," she repeated, hearing her voice harden, just slightly.

"Take that Black Jezebel"

The corner of his lips twitched. But he managed to suppress his smile. An eyebrow arched, waiting to see her response.

"Options?" She kept her voice cool.

Evans had dropped his facade entirely by now. He didn't like taking orders from a woman. Especially, she guessed, a woman of color.

His answer was as detailed as it was helpful. "The usual. Wait it out. Or go in."

She had in her mind an image. It was from one of the standoffs that had come back to haunt the country in the latter decades. Prior to that, so far as she knew, they hadn't had problems like this since...well...Harper's Ferry just before the Civil War, and before that reaching all the way back to the Whiskey Rebellion and, a few years earlier, Shays Rebellion, both of the Colonial era.

That was pretty much it. Until lately.

She was troubled by that image. From one of the standoffs. Of a mother, walking alone, on a trail, through old growth woods much like what was masking the compound in Garnet Gap. Her head bent down. Her arms crossed over her breasts. What was she thinking? Of her children? Was she afraid for their safety? Terrified? Was she angry? At her husband for letting things get

out of hand with his juvenile fantasies of making war on the US
government?

Toni was all for libertarian impulses. This country was
founded on them, for God's sake. But this?

"Is there a plan laid to assault the compound?"

Evans snorted.

"Any information on how many women and children are in
the compound?"

He shook his head.

"But they are there? Families?"

He shrugged. And beamed a smile that did not reach his eyes.

Right before she sent him on his way, Warren stepped out of
the room, then returned to whisper in her ear.

Another agent had just been killed. They couldn't place the
location of the shooter.

Christ, she thought, remembering the Reyes Latino.

They were taunting her.

***

Becoming a prosecutor with the Bernalillo County District
Attorney's Office was harder than she expected. But, then,
having relied on her ethnicity to open the last two doors – even if
she truly didn't know what she was doing – she was damned if
she was going to use it to open a third.

She bided her time. Taking on clients again, she quietly approached prosecutors she was matching wits with after their cases closed. But, she found the door firmly shut. If they had beaten her in court, they just smirked when she asked if they could put in a word. If she had beaten them, they were usually not in the mood to entertain the slightest suggestion. Even her favorite prosecutors were cool to the idea. One simply said, "Toni, you're a defender. Why not just stay on your side of the courtroom?"

Finally, after several months of waiting, in exasperation she tailed the DA himself, all three hundred lumbering Latino pounds of him, to his favorite watering hole one night. Emboldened – if not a little drunk with her audacity – she approached his table just as his guest, a simpering blonde the thickness of a runway model, was being seated.

She stuck out her hand. "I'm Toni Madison. Lawyer."

He looked at her, his small eyes in that large round face staring right back at her. Coldly.

"I know who you are."

This had surprised her. And made her stuck. But, seeing the blonde gawk at her as if she had mold on her forehead, she found her game and plunged on.

"I grew up in Trumbull Village."

He began rolling his eyes.

"I want to put the Reyes Latino behind bars."

He chuffed.

"You don't have to pay me." Where had that one come from, she wondered? "Just give me a chance."

He looked at his guest a moment, who was already clearly bored. He began, "Look, Ms. Madison—"

"One month."

He was getting annoyed.

She jumped. "One week! If I don't get a conviction in one week, I will never bother you again."

He was distracted by his blonde's locks now. Was even reaching up to smooth one away from her cheek. She smiled beatifically back at him.

"One week. I'll never bother you again," Toni repeated.

He waved a hand at her. "Sure, whatever."

Not certain what she had just agreed to, she beat a retreat.

And then charged forward to the precinct headquarters not too far from her apartment. She walked in, asking to speak with any officer, any detective working street gangs. Having started, she was too scared to stop.

Thus began an odyssey. She collared the first cop that would listen to her. Became the gum under the shoe of the first detective that gave her a chance, even if he stared at her tits the entire time he was talking with her. And if they didn't have what she was looking for, she filed away the relationship for a future case and moved on.

Not getting too far ahead of herself, she kept her eye on the ball. She had one week to secure a conviction. Best go for a simple one.

Jaywalking.

Why not? A conviction was a conviction, right? It didn't have to mean jail time. Or so she told herself.

She was talking to a couple of cops a few mornings later sitting in their unit on San Pedro Drive when an RL – as she had started to term the gang members – began crossing the street in the middle of the block not twenty yards from them.

"There," she cried. "Arrest him!"

The two uniforms looked at her, then laughed. Yeah, laugh, she thought. They all knew Toni now. Word had spread about the Blatina, her tits and her obsession.

So, she ran right over to the RL by herself. He was typical. Big, large, heavily muscled, with lots of bling hanging around his shoulders, his ornate Reyes Latino tat standing out on his neck, over his heavy t-shirts and the flannel thrown over them, his jeans hanging down his ass, over his high tops. She grabbed him by the arm.

"Yo, chica, que pasa?"

She all but shouted, "I'm arresting you – a citizen's arrest – for jaywalking!"

He laughed. "Not now, bitch. I've got biz."

"No!" Then, she repeated herself, even louder.

Until she found herself on the ground, staring up at a bright light in her eyes and a pounding pain on the side of her head.

"Freeze!"

"Loca! Fuck me!"

She turned her head and, fuzzily, saw one of the uniforms in crouched position, his service weapon out. His partner was just squealing their unit around to a stop in front of them.

"On the ground! Now, meathead! You hear me! Hands on your head, meathead! Hands on your head! Now!!"

Getting down, the boy-who-would-be-a-man swore. Shaking his head while eating pavement. "Pendeja! You enjoy your life. While you have it, puta."

"Gun!" The uniform pulled a Glock from the waistband of the RL.

"Cabrona!" The ganger muttered at her.

Fascinated, she wondered how he could store a handgun in his pants if they were falling down his ass.

The other uniform was picking her up, dusting her off, taking her aside.

"Toni, this is some serious shit, you know that?"

She smiled. "Yeah, well, I want him arraigned this afternoon."

(A chorale had started up in her head. Was this that "happy warrior" feeling Artie had once told her about? When he was steering his bird into battle?)

In any case, she strode off down to the courthouse to find a judge who would help her. She hoped the RL had given her a whopper of a black eye, wondering how she could highlight it with makeup.

The jaywalking violation rapidly transformed – with her spunky fire, moral high ground, and winning smile – into a felony weapons charge. Of course he could provide no license for the handgun and certainly had no permit for a concealed weapon. Besides, he was a felon anyway, out on probation. More potential jail time was added to the list. That afternoon, knowing the drill, when his public defender advised him to plead guilty in hopes of a lighter sentence, the RL followed suit.

He didn't get a lighter sentence. In fact, he got a harsher one, for striking an officer of the court. The judge was really quite angry about it. The ganger's threats to her after sentencing only made it worse with the judge adding one more year. Which was questionable, legally.

(She wasn't going to say anything.)

Overnight, Toni became a celebrity. The lawyer who nabbed an RL for jaywalking just to see him put away, mere hours later, for years on felony charges.

She granted one interview, on the steps of the courthouse, just after he was hauled off. Having learned a little political tact since her teen years, she lavished extravagant praise on the DA for believing in her, for believing in both the large Hispanic and teeny Black communities, for believing in a safer ABQ.

Mama was ecstatic. She also calmly arranged for a new generation of Soldados, led by a boy who was way too handsome for his age, named Diego, to mount around the clock protection for Toni.

Who squawked.

To give in when Mama slyly explained that she herself would have the same 24/7 guard here at home. So long as Toni agreed.

She did.

But only if her escort wore ties. Anything else she could explain away. She knew the judges well now. Ties were non-negotiable.

And that set the tone. Her list of convictions grew. She found simple ways to have gangers arrested – having Diego plow into an RL car with a wreck, for example, just to see them drive away from the accident since they thought it not worth their time while she wrote down their license number to have them picked up later. Soon, a digital camera Diego had given her – carefully not telling her how he could have afforded it – expanded her range of possibilities. She tooled around at night taking shots of, for example, gangers tagging a future target to be robbed, to have them picked up later – shots of them smoking dope were also good – shots of them selling guns even better. Even parking violations were handy and quickly proved a favorite – any minor violation was fair game. The list grew with her creativity. Including her ability to wear disguises.

Not to mention going without sleep.

She also learned to husband her resources. She may have rushed that first conviction into jail. Later it made her smack her head at the thought she could have turned him. To get insider information on how the RLs operated.

After thinking it over, she decided to try it anyway. She asked the judge if he would reduce the sentence in exchange for information about RL operations.

It was in his chambers. He sat way back in his chair, looking her over.

"Are you certain you know what you're doing, counselor?"

She gulped. But nodded anyway.

"It better be real." And then he had waved her away.

Flirting with Diego to get a ride out to Central Correctional became a routine occurrence. How long she could keep it up without giving in to his entreaties was another question. She became a favorite with the guards there. And, from the increasing number of fox whistles coming from the exercise yard each time she visited, with the inmates as well. Sitting in a dingy, dusty barred room at a crummy stainless steel table opposite a convict with several black teardrops tatted down his cheeks – symbols of kills – became routine as well. Even if their answers were cagey, evasive, often designed to compel her return more than give her anything useful.

Nevertheless, a wall in her room at home was soon given over to photos taped to it, yarn strung between them as she struggled to figure out the RL's hierarchy, its operations, its expansion plans. Even when she finally got a desk in the DA's suite of offices in the Schiff Building, she did her best work at home. She liked her fellow prosecutors. She also knew, from one of her convictions, that at least one prosecutor was on the RL payroll. She just didn't know which.

Not the DA. Of that she was certain. He didn't like her. That was also certain.

She didn't care. She was winning.

She knew because one night the RLs exploded a Molotov cocktail on their front steps. And shot the guard that had lept to protect her when she came out in a righteous fury to smother the flames. She held him as he died. Too young. Sixteen. Rodrigo. He had had a crush on her.

They shot him. Not her. They could have. Could they have missed?

The police were angered, as were several new friends that she didn't even know she had among the city leadership. Mama complained about the number of flower bouquets that kept getting sent all that week. But not too loudly.

After a few days, when the police escort had been withdrawn, the RLs did it again.

Again they shot her guard, but not her, as she ran outside to confront them.

She didn't run outside after that.

She couldn't. She understood now.

She, a heroine of the day, an officer of the court, might well be untouchable now. Certainly not worth the price of retribution they would surely pay should they try a hit on her.

No. Instead, they had decided on another strategy.

For all the tv, radio and newspaper coverage lauding her courage, her strength, the Reyes Latino understood her better. They knew her weakness.

And they had decided to reveal that weakness through...

Taunting her.

***

Get me General Woodruff.

Yes, Madam President.

Perky was a boffin, as he liked to say. An analyst. He had worked for decades at NORAD – North American Aerospace Defense Command – in Colorado Springs. Retired now, giving over almost entirely to fishing and reading classical Greek, he had worked in the alternate, worst-case scenario, site under Cheyenne Mountain. What he liked to call Erebus, the ancient Greek name for the Underworld.

She had met him on a routine visit while a Congresswoman. She had noticed a photo of Athena Parthenos – the Nashville recreation, of course, since the original Parthenon statue had been looted by God knew which invading army centuries ago – above his desk. She had shyly asked the general if she was correct. Of the few Greek gods she could actually remember, Athena – the warrior priestess who took no shit – was a favorite. They had struck up a fun, if a bit odd, friendship ever since.

She had learned to call him whenever she felt that she was being fed crap on any subject close to the military.

She quickly gave Perky the rundown at Garnet Gap. She told him everything they knew. And through her inability to answer his most basic questions to her in return, she learned what she didn't know.

How many? How many combatants? How many non-combatants? What weapons stockpiled? What supplies for a siege?

But the image that was haunting her, she broke in. Of the mother.

Yes, he said. He remembered the image of the mother on the trail. It was haunting. If not clear. We assume that she feared for her children, forgetting that she was the one who had put them there in the first place. Do we know that, in fact, as historical fact, that she was the victim, the hostage, all those years, and not the inspiration for that standoff to begin with? Why do we assume – Toni could almost see the twinkle in his eye – that to be a woman is by definition to be the weaker sex?

And that was a relatively simple standoff. Not anything remotely on par with what she faced now.

Cloaking devices that could repel thermal imaging was high tech. Or, more precisely, given their location in the world – an affordable low tech response to a high tech threat. There were advanced engineers in that compound. There were weapons specialists. These were no hillbillies. This took years of planning.

Most troubling of all, he said, they were aggressive. They knew their target. And it wasn't the LEOs that they had, quite possibly, lured there. They knew their target and they were speaking directly to her all the way across the country with a sign designed to be seen through cloaked concrete walls. Everything else hidden by those masked walls. The *one* thing that could be seen. Clearly. By design. This wasn't just intentional. This was symbolic. This was pageantry.

Jesus, she thought. How could she have missed that? Browne, their charismatic leader, wanted this showdown. With her. For what?

"But I don't even know them," she protested.

"Do you have to?"

She didn't know how to answer that.

"Are you in the Oval Office?"

She mm-hmmmed, her voice catching, afraid of what she was about to hear.

"Well then, Madam President, I suggest you look in a mirror to see what they see. The threat to their existence that you represent. Just by sitting at the Resolute Desk in the Oval Office. You, ma'am."

Beatie was frowning. Her face, an expression of study. Perplexed.

Warren was waiting.

When she looked at him, he stood straight. He stood tall.

"How many more LEOs have to die while I wait?"

No one said a word.

She heard her voice grow hard. "Take them."

Yes, Madam President.

***

The butcher's bill was bad. But it was over.

Oddly, the country stood by her. They were proud of her, their Blatina President, for standing up to a bunch of Armageddon-crazy White Supremacists.

Seventeen dead, among them Browne and Meyers, the fugitive who had played the bait, the lure. For that was becoming the theme. Beatie had huddled with the White House Communications Team and, likely breaking a few intelligence laws in the process, hammered out a meme to be spread round the world in the minutes after the shooting began. They were likely finished even before the combat.

Five women, mothers all, among the dead. Three armed and shooting. The other two, victims of crossfire. By their own, by the LEOs, only ballistics could tell.

Beatie highlighted the Black Jezebel sign. That was the lead off. Then, the cloaking technology. Finally, the pièce de résistance, the hunting of LEOs. Beatie was a firm believer in threes. Especially when it came to the voting public.

In any case, all the Hapsters on the Comms Team had long departed. They were all Maddies now, and had been since last fall. Their enthusiasm for their task was evident.

Maybe a little too evident, Toni grumbled to herself. Torturing herself with pictures of the dead.

Two boys, one fifteen, the other sixteen. Both carrying shotguns. Both in the thick of the fight and had paid for it.

But it was over.

Let the editorials decry her decision. Let them applaud it (and most were, whether Dem or GOP). She cried alone in her bedroom. She didn't know what else to do.

Malcolm had mysteriously appeared later with a very large scotch, an ale, a cheeseburger, fries and a deck of cards. After she managed a few bites, he shuffled the deck and played a simple game of Go Fish with her while Rod stood, reassuringly, near her bed. Until she finally fell asleep.

***

And dreamed.

Beatie was out back. On the South Lawn. At the foot of Marine One.

Digging. Her rasta locks dripping sweat on her overalls, smearing her amber-colored lenses, her mammoth boobs getting in the way of each thrust of the shovel into the deep, heavy loam.

Digging her way to China? It was on the other side of the world, everybody knew that.

No, someplace closer.

Where?

South Carolina. She had found the key.

The key?

Yes, to the treasure map. It had taken her a couple weeks of hard thinking. After all, it wasn't like she could call up any friends anymore. They had all turned on us. Look at Warren. They were all following Fast Eddie. Which—

And she had stopped to wipe some sweat off her brow with a large garnet-colored handkerchief that left drops of blood on her cheeks.

And spoke.

Which is your fault, bitch. For being such a doormat for three years. What was you thinking?

Toni swallowed, began to cry. She thought she could trust Warren now.

Yes, cry, bitch. Go on being their doormat.

Her friend watched her, without pity.

It don't matter, bitch. I done found the treasure map. It leads from Ames, to Dixville Notch, to Garnet Gap, to Charleston.

I've got Fast Eddie by the balls.

She cackled.

And went back to digging.

***

Nat Forrest didn't sleep.

All through the night, Toni realized upon waking, Forrest had been beating his States Rights drum. But, then, States Rights was a South Carolina tradition.

Maybe it was because it was one of the few colonies to be named after a king, Charles II. Virginia – named after the (in)famously virgin Queen Elizabeth – too, had its pretensions to greatness. Even though the Johnny-come-lately to the Civil War, once it had finally joined the Confederacy, Virginia decided it simply must lead it.

South Carolina was no shrinking violet. Even its capital was named after the feminine personification of the country – Columbia – though its leaders seemed to forget that from time to time.

In any case, the state's political leaders in Andrew Jackson's day decided that they simply could not, would not go along with some newly passed tariffs on trade at that time. So, they simply passed a resolution in their majestic State House in Columbia, nullifying the national tariffs. As far as they were concerned, the tariffs no longer existed.

President Jackson, in true tender-hearted, let's hug-it-out fashion responded…

I will hang the first man of them I can get my hands on to the first tree I can find.

Fortunately, cooler heads prevailed and a gentler, more politic solution was found.

Nevertheless, just a few decades later, right after Lincoln had been elected, firing up visions of Yankee bluebellies coming down south to free the slaves (not that Lincoln intended anything of the sort at the time, truly), the South Carolina leaders of that day gathered in Institute Hall of scenic Charleston and passed their Ordinance of Secession. Given that the declaration would spark the Civil War that engulfed the country in a years long, fiery conflict of tears and suffering – killing more soldier boys than all the other nation's wars combined, including World Wars I and II, until Vietnam tilted the scales, just – given all this, one would expect a mighty document. It was not. It numbered just over a hundred words.

We, the People of the State of South Carolina, in Convention assembled do declare and ordain, and it is hereby declared and ordained, That the Ordinance adopted by us in Convention, on the twenty-third day of May in the year of our Lord One Thousand Seven Hundred and Eighty Eight, whereby the Constitution of the United States of America was ratified, and also all Acts and parts of Acts of the General Assembly of this

State, ratifying amendment of the said Constitution, are hereby repealed; and that the union now subsisting between South Carolina and other States, under the name of "The United States of America," is hereby dissolved.

And just in case cooler heads might try to talk them out of this particular piece of tomfoolery, they fired on the local federal fort, Sumter, out in lovely Charleston Harbor. There was no going back now. A year later, most of the city along with Institute Hall had been burned to the ground – by whom, no one could say. Picturesque Charleston lay in ruins, not to be rebuilt until well after the war.

Not to be outdone, after conquering the state capital in the final months of the war, General William Tecumseh Sherman burned the State House to the ground.

To listen to modern day Nat Forrest's drum-thumping about the need for secession "before those big government liberals led by that feminista autocrat" and "the carnage at Garnet Gap would come to Charleston over my dead body!" one might have thought it was the 1860s all over again.

A few months ago, Nat Forrest – descendant of Confederate hero Nathan Bedford Forrest, or so he claimed – was a crank. After Garnet Gap and "the slaughter of The People" as he termed it, he was listened to. All over the Deep South. He had found a new career in the carnage of Garnet Gap.

That South Carolina's primary was a week away did not help matters.

The People.

One of the few ideas that had ever caught fire with her in college had been termed something like the Migration of the Peoples. There was the usual haggling of historians over the most appropriate name and the centuries in which it occurred. Nevertheless, it was a powerful idea that had hit her – maybe because she was Blatina and, by definition, on the margins of the centers of power? In any case, the notion was that for a period of a few centuries, a very small group of people went on the move, creating wholly unforeseen consequences. Empires died. Wars raged. New countries formed. The estimates triggered the usual barstool debates, but if the population of Europe at about 500 AD was around fifty million, the adventurers on the move numbered only 1% of that total. If that.

Yet look at what that minuscule group of malcontents achieved. The Goths, in all their flavors, assisted by the Franks and the Vandals, brought down the western half of the Roman Empire. If they ever got tired of their exploits, they had the Huns from their eastern sally ports pushing at their backs, egging them on. The Huns also managed several smash and grabs in their local environs, sundering Constantinople from the rest of the Empire, forcing it to go its own way. All this splintering of the behemoth made room for new dynasties, such as the Merovingians who would rule Francia, giving rise to the later, grander Carolingians. Also on the move, the Saxons of the Germanies invaded the British Isles, followed by the Jutes, and then the Vikings. Transforming that cockpit of the English speaking peoples into a veritable melting pot of cultures. One of the first.

There would be others.

This great migration of malcontents, no matter how few people were actually involved, had moved the beating heart of civilization from the sunny, placid eastern shores of the Mediterranean to the frigid, stormy northern coasts of the Channel, never to really quite retreat, even to this day. (Particularly if you asked a European what they thought of the Yanks.)

The idea – of so few changing so much – had so caught her fancy that she was seriously considering going for a master's in anthropology – if she could believe in herself enough to attempt it – right up to the moment of Lupe's rape.

She doubted that the powers that be in 6th century Europe were any happier during the migration of the malcontents than Old White Guy patriarchs in 21st century America. This century that opened new doors to people of color, particularly women of color, all over the world. That forced the OWGs to share the microphone, if not the gavel. Isn't that what she represented, whether she liked it or not? Look in the mirror, Perky had said. See what they see. The threat that your dark skin and boobs represent to their power structures.

The People.

Garnet Gap.

Nat Forrest. What was she supposed to do? Hang him from the nearest tree? Throw him in jail for treason? That would go down well, on the eve of...

The South Carolina Primary.

***

Unfinished business.

Or, as Beatie had termed it, "Armoring our Black asses."

Toni had to admit, securing their rear flank *was* wise.

The day before flying to the Palmetto State, she asked Warren to meet her outside. It was early March in DC, so she donned her usual parka, knit cap, mittens and, followed out by Rod in his own parka, wondered how Warren would look. She might have guessed. A lovely cashmere tailored coat costing surely in the thousands adorned his frame as a warm cashmere scarf wrapped around his neck, with stylish dark gloves covering his hands.

He slowly walked up to her. Stone-faced. Not unlike a man approaching the gallows.

"Madam President."

She abruptly realized that he was thinner than she remembered. Older. Gaunter. She gestured him to sit.

"I want to apologize to you, Warren."

He began to protest. She lifted a hand. He went silent.

She waited a very long few moments, then resumed.

"I was...too...cautious. I truly never expected to be anything more than the first Blatina vice president. Was grateful for that place in history. But only back of the stage. What I was used to. Never, in my mind, did I think I would ever take center stage. This was supposed to be Hap's show."

He nodded. A bit raggedly.

Still waiting for the blade to fall, she could see.

"I'm sorry," she said to him. Softly.

A sob wrenched out that he quickly suppressed.

"Madam President...!"

She raised her hand again. Again, he subsided.

She breathed. "I...should have tried harder, I guess. To take the reins in my hands. Sooner."

He swallowed. Then again.

She continued, "If not for my own happiness, then for the sake of the nation's."

He sighed. Then cut it off. Still waiting.

She realized just now that she had never been able to read him so clearly. Not in all these last years.

"You know," she smiled, "it occurred to me the other day that I never officially asked you on as chief of staff."

He went very still.

"That night at the ball when Hap died, we just...seemed to assume it, I guess."

He nodded. "Yes, Madam President." Then, "Ma'am, if you—"

She raised her hand a third time. Again he hushed.

"Now. Beatie tells me that her tea leaves – not to mention several private dick hours in three separate states – reveal that Ed sent advance teams, quietly, out to Iowa, New Hampshire and South Carolina, with three separate messages. In Iowa, it was go Uncommitted. In New Hampshire, it was go Write-in. In South Carolina, she expects he'll be on the ballot. Somehow, some deal, even given the late date. In short, a coup. She expects him to announce tomorrow."

He nodded. He was relaxing now. He no longer looked so anxious. Instead, he looked more thoughtful.

"I remember what you did for me with Max. I know he is your friend."

He snorted, quietly. His eyes had closed, his head giving a little shake. Of disgust? Of self-disgust?

Hap used to always say, "The President rules best, if he rules at all, through persuasion."

This was the moment.

Beatie had been unsure about this next move. She, herself, had been. Until now.

Time to take the plunge.

"I'm certain a mind of your caliber…"

He jerkily swung to her, a haunted look staining his eyes, like a lost little boy. She was right. He truly was looking drawn, far more than she had ever seen him.

She continued, "...understands the high regard in which I hold you after I've opened my mind to you like this."

He blinked. Tears sparkling his eyes. He blinked them away, glancing off, down, somewhere else.

He mumbled, "Yes, Madam President."

"What do you think of Beatie's digging?"

He pursed his lips, appearing a lot better all of a sudden. He looked around the Rose Garden, at a bush for some time. She looked at it with him, noting its early buds, trying to remember which flower it bloomed.

He moved, a bit. "Ma'am, the only way he could have pulled that off...Madam President, they have their own careers to worry about. The only way to get them to go out on a limb with him like that was to show them evidence that a solid win was a lock."

She nodded in agreement. "South Carolina."

He smiled, chuffing in admiration. "An early, solid win."

After a moment, he stirred again. "Ma'am? Did Beatie find evidence of Nat Forrest visiting Iowa or New Hampshire?"

She let her head slowly fall back so that her own tears could fade before forming. A winter wren had begun singing. Cheerful. This time, she didn't mind.

***

He volunteered to take an early flight out. He left practically that minute. Eagerly. Like a school boy about to pull off a prank.

The next morning, an embattled, hot-faced Nat Forrest stunned the nation with the news that he had reliable information President Madison was planning to move on several leaders of South Carolina. To imprison them for insurrection.

In light of this intelligence, and particularly in view of the merciless manner in which she had massacred the good people of Garnet Gap, he had drafted Articles of Secession that he would present to the State House in Columbia this afternoon. He had no choice.

"I am assured," he said staring into the camera with a fierce eye, "that this move ensuring the safety of the good people of South Carolina, protecting them from the depredations of a liberalized woman gone drunk with power in the White House, I am assured that this noble endeavor enjoys the full support of the most powerful corridors in Washington DC."

They boarded Marine One en route to Joint Base Andrews, which never failed to give her a pang of Artie. There, they boarded Air Force One. And settled down in front of the tvs in the airborne Oval, sipping coffee and chatting about the odds.

After another hour or two, CNN announced that State Senator Nat Forrest, in a terse statement, had withdrawn his support for Vice President Edward Langton in the South Carolina Primary.

Beatie mawked, "I didn't know he was supporting Fast Eddie."

As they were touching down in Charleston, MSNBC announced they would shortly be carrying a live statement from the Vice President.

His right eyelid kept fluttering as he spoke of his devotion to the Madison ticket, that he had no idea that various friends had been making a last ditch lobbying effort to include his name on the state primary ballot, that President Madison was the Democratic leader needed to carry this great nation forward four more years.

III

Super Tuesday.

Eight states, including the great enchilada California were deciding today. Toni blinked away last night's dream while standing in the Galleria of the storied Biltmore Hotel in Los Angeles. A long, voluminous, sumptuously decorated hall of golden tans of art deco splendor. Thronging with admirers.

She could hardly have cared less.

It was a power dream. Borne of that awful night after Garnet Gap. Rod standing by her bed until she fell asleep. In her dream, she had awakened, pulled him to her with all her presidential power, the inescapable strength of her gravity well, inexorable. She was Sol. Undeniable. Had then pulled out his Rod of Rods, waving his objections into silence. And edged him – the Queen of all blowjobs – nibbling the edges of his cock, over and over, only rarely taking his head into her mouth, again and again and again, until, her jaw aching, his gasps and moans roaring in her ears, his voluminous splats of opalescent cum, shining in the moonlight, had spattered all over her dark tits with their even darker nipples.

She had bent her head while lifting one celestial orb to her mouth, tasting him.

Like honey. Or mead from some medieval fairy tale.

Grrrrrr! What was with her?!

Things were going well. Even Levi was actually starting to smile again.

Rod was standing near her in the Galleria.

She turned to him, saying, "It's going well, tonight, don't you think?"

As usual, he didn't respond.

She waited.

Those liquid gray eyes of his – that made her weak – looked her over, then resumed his search of the vastly crowded hall. What was he looking for, she grumbled to herself? Guns? Knives? Dirty bombs?

"Not even a 'Yes, Madam President' tonight?" she asked him.

He darted a glance at her eyes, then looked away.

She growled, inwardly.

"You know, after everything we've been through, you could manage a "Hey, Toni!" every now and again, don't you think?"

"Yes, Madam President."

"Fuck you."

And she walked away. After a few steps, she waited – sure enough, he was right behind her. Goddamn him! What, was he a machine?!

She woke up.

***

Super Tuesday and Levi was *not* smiling.

She was in the Biltmore. Rod was right over there, just ten feet away. The California state Dems chair was sweatily grasping her hand and wheezing some joke about what Universal Basic Income meant to Republicans. The Galleria was overdressed. And overfull. Everything was the same.

Except Levi was not smiling. At all.

The votes were going well. All eight states were dutifully pulling for her.

After all the Sturm und Drang of Iowa and New Hampshire and the breathless last minute flap at South Carolina, the Democrats had settled down into what was turning out to be a typical race of an incumbent for an office.

News flash: She was boring everyone to death. As usual.

Levi had already asked to speak with her later. She already knew what he was going to say. After conscientiously pulling the numbers, he would point out that Dems were voting in smaller blocs than Hap had commanded four years earlier.

Well, she growsed to herself, Hap was Hap. How do you compete with a rock star?

There was an enthusiasm gap. Between Dems and Republicans. She had looked up the numbers, quietly, herself. On Republican primary days, they stormed the barricades to make the voting booths. Eager to vote out the Black Jezebel. Dems, on their primary days, grumbled as they hoisted themselves out of their lazy boys to make it down to the polls, grumpy about missing their favorite Tuesday night tv show. Maybe. Or maybe they weren't making it out of their chairs at all.

What did they expect?

Fireworks?

Fast Eddie – as much as she hated to admit it – had provided most of the pyrotechnics so far this cycle. Right now, after all his plotting and planning, he was a wounded cat, hiding in his lair at the Naval Observatory. Which were actually pretty nice digs. Particularly after Nelson Rockefeller had furnished it when he was veep in the 70s. She should know, even if she had never actually lived there. Just toured it during the transition before the Inaugural. She had been looking forward to living in a

Victorian, wondering what Mama would have made of it. But then Hap's appetite had gotten the best of him, and…

Word was that Ed was expecting to get fired. Any day.

Toni certainly wanted to.

Beatie certainly wanted to.

It was Warren who had asked that the Sword of Damocles not fall on the hapless veep just yet. Wait, he had counseled, to Beatie's fury. Let us get through the lion's share of the primaries.

"And then?" Beatie had hissed.

"Let him go," her chief of staff had softly rejoined. "Choose Perky, or an ally from Congress, just before the Convention, as FDR did. As Lincoln did."

That had silenced Beatie.

And, mostly for that reason, Toni had agreed. She certainly liked the idea of Perky as her veep. He would be close at hand for all military matters. Certainly better than the NSC advisors that kept cycling through the West Wing every few months on their way back to K Street and plush lobbying jobs. But then, she reasoned, Perky was too much the artist to ever be a politician. Ordinary people, with all their silly foibles, annoyed him. And it showed. She had seen it. Your average Joe felt stupid standing next to Perky and resented him for it.

Robert Tinder of the Connecticut 3rd, on the other hand, came to mind. He had befriended her when she was a freshman Congresswoman, even as he was a bit patronizing. She liked him because he was one of the few colleagues in Congress who hadn't stared at her breasts when talking down to her. Of course, that could have been his New England Baptist upbringing. He had mentored her, even. Showed her around. Introduced her. Helped her fill out her staff with experienced professionals that gave her a leg up on her fellow freshmen. He got her a seat on Appropriations, arguing that a Blatina voice was needed there. It was good optics, he had said. That he was patently recruiting her to be a member of his Tinder Team ("Light that fire!") for his own run for the Oval someday didn't faze her in the slightest. You had to pay your dues somehow. She had learned that from Mama.

Bobby was also one of the few congratulatory calls after Garnet Gap that she genuinely believed.

It was an intriguing concept, Bobby as veep.

She had forced herself to go through a number of other options, but her heart kept returning to Bobby. She trusted him. Or rather, she trusted his ambition. And she owed him. He would respect that. It was clean between them. Not sticky.

Besides, he looked the part. Sure, he had two (or three, depending) mistresses. But his wife clearly didn't mind. Maybe it got him out of the house. And he had adorable children, one at Harvard, another at Yale. His finances were spotless. She knew this because she had peeked during the transition when he was being vetted for consideration in Hap's cabinet as Labor Secretary.

Labor.

She sighed.

Maybe Bobby was a good idea. Feeling her mind cast off into one of its sojourns – because the California Dems chair was boring her? – she pasted a smile on her face while reflecting for a moment on her troubled relationship with Big Labor.

They had screwed her back in ABQ during her first run for Congress. Just could not support an upstart Blatina. In the first place, many of the building trades were dominated by Whites, and where not, by Hispanic men who weren't happy about a woman in power, no matter the color. So, the Bernalillo County Labor Council had ignored her requests to meet and, instead, voted to instruct their member unions to take their $$ dues and give it to the incumbent.

And she thought that Democrats were supposed to be the good guys. The guys who didn't make smoke-filled-room deals. It was one of her first, and most painful, lessons in how politics really worked. Her relationship with Big Labor had been strained ever since. Oh, she had voted with them. But her heart wasn't in it. And they sensed that.

As far as she could tell, unions were a victim of their own success. The depredations of the Robber Barons on the working class of the Gilded Age were truly horrific. And for that reason, unions – a phenomenon that had not existed in the country before the Civil War – suddenly showed up after the shooting had stopped in the form of the Knights of Labor, asking for an eight-hour workday. And right in time, too. John D. Rockefeller, Nelson's grandfather, had figured out that if he bought up a mom and pop refinery, and put a manager in charge who didn't know the village workers personally, he could squeeze as much juice (or refined kerosene, as it were) out of the stone as possible. If anyone complained, the manager need only fire him. Rinse, repeat.

It was a winning formula. Making the original Robber Baron four or five times – in the dollars of those days – as wealthy as the titans of even today, such as Gates, Zuckerberg or Bezos.

Yeah, like he needed the cash.

So, the birth of the labor unions was a success story of historical proportions. Through the Gilded Age, the Jazz Age, the Great Depression, World War II, their achievements – the eight-hour work day, the forty hour work week, overtime, unemployment compensation, a national minimum wage, child labor restrictions, collective bargaining, OSHA restrictions for workplace safety – the milestones were extraordinary. The lions of the movement – Eugene Debs, Samuel Gompers, George Meany, Walter Reuther, Cesar Chavez to name a few – were truly inspirational.

In their day.

Since then?

Well…

Where were the lions now?

The star began to lose its luster in the 50s when Jimmy Hoffa took the pension fund of the largest union of the country, the Teamsters, and used that money to finance Chicago mob activities. It was no surprise that the Kennedy brothers had used him as a foil to build their own careers in politics.

That turmoil began a slide into obscurity. That continued to this day.

Maybe the unions would come back some year. Or maybe they had achieved everything they were designed to. After all, in a gig economy where almost half the workers in America were self-employed as contractors of one sort or another, manufacturing decreasing year by year, and the service industry not feeling the hunger, a union renaissance was looking increasingly unlikely.

Who could say? Truly?

Nevertheless, despite her own ambivalence, she didn't need Levi to point out to her that unions were not to be ignored. Along with Native casinos, unions were, yet, the top donors to the Democratic Party. Ignore them at your peril.

Maybe Bobby was a good choice.

If Connor Raines became the GOP nominee, as was becoming more and more likely given his performance on this day, Super Tuesday, he would probably recruit an Evangelical as his veep to balance out his wicked Silicon Valley ways. Maybe Bobby could be her version of that.

Beatie suddenly showed up at the far end of the Galleria.
Staring at her.

Toni shook off the Dems state chair, wondering if he had even
noticed that she was moving on. He had a tendency to keep
talking, without missing a beat, about whatever was on his mind,
no matter who entered or exited the group. As if his listeners
were a bunch of cardboard cutouts to him and nothing more.
Even the President.

Shaking hands and beaming "thank you, thank you" again and
again as she worked her way through the congratulations,
through the thickening crowd – getting awfully choked now as
the evening had worn on – Rod at her shoulder, she slowly
approached her strategist.

From the expression on her friend's face, she could see that
she was about to run into the Witch.

She took a deep breath and strode up to Beatie, working up her
brightest smile.

"We need Billy the Kid, bitch."

***

How long since she had heard Beatie call her Toni? Or heard
a "Chica?" And if not those, then maybe a "Madam President?"
But then, asking Beatie to change was like yelling at the rain.

They had originally met in Toni's first campaign office, on
Lomas Blvd in the downtown. It was a shabby affair. She had

gotten a deal from a client whose son she had represented in court, downgrading a felony to a misdemeanor.

She was losing. The latest polling, from the *Albuquerque Journal*, showed her behind by thirty points, with twenty or so undecided. Her opponent was a Democrat in the old boy network. Had represented ABQ in Congress for decades. And this competition between them would be decided on primary day in a few weeks. The general election was a wash. Republicans often skipped putting up a candidate altogether since, barring a miracle or a travesty, ABQ always sent a Dem to Congress in those days.

She was losing, badly, and she knew it.

She was honestly relieved in some ways. She didn't want to be here. She had only agreed to run when the DA had put her name on the ballot, saying, "It's time to take our fight with the RLs to the next level."

Our fight.

Funny. She often felt like she was taking them on all by herself. When she had begun her battle with the street gang, she had imagined that she only needed to get the ball rolling. That others would show up to help. They never had. Fellow prosecutors were out of the question. They had their own crusades. As for city leaders, well, they might make flowery speeches, but after a year or two of rhetoric not backed up by concrete action, she began to understand that because the Reyes Latino were targeting the poor neighborhoods and not those of the middle class, much less of the wealthy, they weren't really a problem worth resolving.

She was going at it alone. In a war that she all too soon recognized that she could not win. With the growing feeling that someday, soon, the RLs would tire of taunting her and, finally, just take her out.

Or that she would come home one day and find Mama sitting at the kitchen table with her throat slashed.

So, run for Congress? Well, hey, yeah. Maybe it would get her off the front lines for a while.

But to lose in such a humiliating fashion?

Well...

And then one day a heavyset Black woman had walked in wearing glasses with blue lenses framed by a wild head of rasta locks and a raggedy jean jacket with old peace symbols embroidered into it.

"You the doormat?" she asked.

Toni wasn't sure that she had heard right. Guessing that she hadn't, she ignored it, put on her best smile and shook hands, saying, "Yes, I'm Toni Madison. I'm running for Congress."

The woman had taken a step back, surveying her from head to toe.

"You getting yo Black ass handed to you on a plate, that's what."

Toni sighed. A heckler. Of all the things she needed right now.

Still, she managed a smile and replied, keeping her voice cool, "I can use all the help I can get."

"Well, least you know that much."

Okay. Toni waited.

"So, what is you, anyway? Black? Latina? Both? Neither? Doormat?"

Feeling her bile rise, Toni forced another smile. "Please don't say that."

"What? You prefer me saying that your Black ass is bent over a desk crying, 'Yes, Massa! Give me one more whack?'"

Toni had been stunned into speechlessness. She stood there, dumb, suddenly noticing that the two volunteers that Mama had managed to guilt into helping out had stopped making phone calls and were now watching her instead. Listening.

"Don't you think you should answer? If you want my vote, that is."

Toni still didn't know what to say. She was caught halfway between rage and frustration.

"You even know how you got into this mess?" the blue lenses were asking.

That spurred her. "I am endorsed by the District Attorney."

"Who wants you out of his office because the chica who's crazy enough to take on the Reyes Latino all by her lonesome just might be crazy to enough to run against him next year."

The woman had sat down. Toni ran a hand irritatedly through her mess of hair. How to get rid of this bitch? Wait, what had she just said?

"You live in a city that is 3% Black, if that. Half Hispanic, who don't, by the way, much like the idea of women running things. The other half is mostly White and they don't like your Nigra ass. So..."

She had crossed her arms.

"Begs the question, don't you think? What are you? Black, Latina, Blatina? Or are you just a doormat?"

Toni felt herself growling, "I'm nobody's doormat."

"Good. Glad we got that settled. Took long enough, though. What are you, then? Cuz the good voters of the New Mexico 1st can't seem to decide. Unless you think I'm just one crazy Black bitch off her meds."

"Are you?"

That made the woman smile.

"Yo beautiful Black ass is thirty one point five points down with nineteen and a half days to go. I see two volunteers who would rather be cleaning out toe jam than sitting here. And not much else. I'm guessing the purse is empty?"

Toni snorted.

"If it was ever full. I'm Beatie, by the way."

Automatically, without thinking, Toni had extended her hand, which was ignored. "Glad to meet you."

"Not yet. But maybe in twenty days you'll be."

Because she thought she was going to scream, Toni walked over to their one grimy window and looked outside. It was a quiet street. Dingy, a few cars moving back and forth. It was a Saturday morning. She should be out doorbelling or something.

"Why you running, anyway?"

Toni ignored her.

"Do you even know?"

That ripped it. She turned, ready to tear into this bitch, and saw...honest concern behind those blue lenses.

"I'm..." she paused. Why not? "I'm tired."

"Of fighting Reyes Latino all by yoself?"

Toni nodded, then teared up. Her volunteers suddenly decided that they needed fresh sodas or coffees or something and beat it for the exit.

Now they were alone. She and Beatie.

"You don't know your father, right?"

Toni stared at her, surprised.

"Yo mother threw it away when you was in high school? Walked into a SunTran?"

Growing mystified, Toni nodded.

"Where was she from?"

"Lincoln."

Beatie had paused, confused.

"Illinois, Lincoln or Lincoln County War, Lincoln?"

Beatie was referring to a small brushfire of New Mexico, back in the days when the state was still a territory and rival gangs had tussled over who would command the lucrative War Department procurement contracts to outfit the federal troops manning the frontier forts as well as chronically abuse, starve and otherwise all around cheat the Indian reservations. Two gangs had come into prominence and their fight had culminated in what became known as the Battle of Lincoln. A five-day running gunfight in a town barely worthy of the name, that had burned out one of the gangs in the process making an obscure teenage tough into the legendary outlaw Billy the Kid.

"My mother was born in Lincoln and followed my father here."

Beatie was still sounding it out. "Battle of Lincoln, Lincoln? The Torreon, Lincoln?" Referring to the aged adobe brick tower in town that had been used as a sniper perch back in the wars with the Apache tribes.

Well, this peacenik certainly knew her local history.

"Murphy-Dolan, Lincoln? The House, Lincoln?" Now referring to one of the rivals and their general store at the time, famous for being two stories tall. The only one of its kind for miles around. Billy the Kid had broken out of it years later when it was the jail, relying on inside help – maybe – a source of local bar arguments, even today. (*Was* there a pistol hidden in the outhouse?)

Her guest was still at it. "The Sante Fe Ring, Lincoln?" The group of shadowy businessmen who had pulled the strings from the Territory capital. "Tunstall-McSween, Lincoln?"

God! "Yes! Yes, to all of that." Toni only knew the history herself because Mama had made her study it in the year after her mother had walked into her bus. Mama said, "Child, you need to know your roots, good and bad."

"Billy the Kid?"

Toni sat, putting her head in her hands.

"Bitch, we gonna turn yo Blatina ass into Billy the Kid."

And she had.

It was a simple two-part plan.

First, they created the icon. They begged some props and camera time from the UNM School of Theatre – who were honestly thrilled to help out – and turned her into a 1880s gunslinger, complete with Colt Peacemakers with her big boobs teasingly on display. With that image, they took whatever money they had left and plastered it everywhere. It was old school. This had been long before the days of YouTube, Twitter, Facebook and other social media platforms. Nevertheless, volunteers loved taping the thousands of 8x11 copies Beatie had made to telephone poles, bus stops, coffee shop and deli bulletin boards and everywhere else they could think of. It was exciting. Made the volunteers feel like they were part of a winning team. For once.

Privately, Toni hated the image. Particularly of her boobs. Especially the guns. Beatie had talked her into it, in part by observing, "Don't forget, chica, we reminding Reyes Latino just how tough yo Blatina ass is."

Second, when the icon generated new media interest in her campaign – the image truly was over the top, downright outrageous in many ways – she went after her opponent, dutifully reciting the talking points Beatie had crafted for her.

She recounted her New Mexico roots, her Battle of Lincoln blood. She was a fighter, she said, by birth. She had taken the fight to the Reyes Latino. Keeping them hemmed into the poorer neighborhoods. Keeping them from expanding into middle class and wealthy neighborhoods.

Toni had quibbled with this, asking what Congressmen could be expected to do about local law enforcement matters. And it wasn't like she had actually prevented them from doing much of anything when it came right down to it. At least not with the nicer neighborhoods.

To which Beatie overrode her. "We gotta scare 'em, bitch! Wake 'em up! Make 'em realize what they be facing without you standing in the way! Fuck 'em and their silver spoons!"

Beatie made her practice her call to action until she could do it without blushing while staring straight into a camera...

"I am standing in their way – Reyes Latino – keeping your kids safe. What has my opponent done but get fat off your taxes? What has he done to make your homes safe? I'm a fighter. Your fighter. Send me to Washington to keep you safe."

Again and again and again, she repeated her call to action. She started getting speaking invitations. Chamber of Commerce.

Municipal League. League of Women Voters. The larger churches. Several other groups.

She repeated that call to action so many times, each time making it sound as fresh and sparkling as if it were the first, that she grew to detest it.

But it turned the campaign around.

In a few days, a pair of Latinas, students at the UNM, came by and asked to volunteer. Beatie wouldn't let them touch a phone or a yard sign. Instead, she bought them a pair of coffees, flavored ones, sat them down and told them wild, hair-raising tales about Toni facing down Reyes Latino gangers in the streets. Saving girls from being raped. Stopping murders on the spot. Personally challenging the leader to a duel. Even jumping over buildings in a single bound.

After the first yarn, Toni decided that she didn't want to hear anymore and had gone doorbelling.

But the next day, those two students had brought back five other girls. And then it was ten. And then twenty. Then fifty.

The day the *Albuquerque Journal* saw her close the gap to twenty points, the Bernalillo County Dems sent over a field director to help out. A real one. With several campaigns under his belt.

Toni had been overwhelmed with gratitude.

Beatie, instead, had merely pulled the field director into a room for a very long Q&A about "Just what the hell yo silver-spooned boney White ass thinks you can do for my Blatina?"

After being reassured that this was real. That he wasn't a mole. She let him get to work. And he did.

"They just hedging their bets, that's all," she had growled, with a grin, to Toni.

Her opponent made it easier on them. He hadn't been opposed in fourteen years. Couldn't remember what it was like. Couldn't find his rhythm. Couldn't re-gear. A development that – stunning as it was miraculous – made Toni vow that she would never let herself get complacent like that.

Asked by the media what he had done to keep ABQ neighborhoods safe, he fumbled his answer. At first, he didn't deign to, loftily reciting his accomplishments in bringing pork back from DC. Which Toni – prompted by Beatie – happily smacked down as being "a wonderful solution to yesteryear's problems. What about today? What about the gangers invading our neighborhoods?"

After she had shaved off another five points, he tried lecturing the media about the proper division of governmental authority – municipal, county, state and federal – demanding they treat his office and his work at the federal level with the respect it deserved. Which Toni, again prompted by her evil genius, shot down by asking, "That's how he's going to keep your babies safe from Reyes Latino, by lecturing the gangers about what Congressmen do?"

Another few days, another few points. The trend was becoming obvious now. Even to her opponent. Who, suddenly,

finally started to grow concerned when the New Mexico State
Dems stopped funding his campaign, declaring the contest a
toss-up. At that point, he just started making things up. Not
needing a prompt now, Toni happily questioned his supposed
accomplishments keeping the people safe, reciting ad nauseum
her own, with a big smile, all her convictions, how many she had
put away, how many she had got to turn state's evidence on their
former partners in crime. The total number of years in
convictions of gangers she had won in court. What had he done?
Why was he lying?

The media loved it. Long before the term existed, she and her
Witch had made the sleepy race for the New Mexico 1st
clickable. They were selling newspapers now. Radio time. Tv
airtime.

Election night was a nail-biter. That morning, she was still
behind by two points in the polls, which put her within the
margin of error.

The contest itself, too close to call that night, went into a
recount that took days. In the end, she won, by a few hundred
votes, only. But, as Beatie had observed, a few hundred was
"close enough for government work."

***

Now, to whip up enthusiasm, her chief strategist wanted to
make her Billy the Kid again. The first spots began running

immediately. Her mother's Lincoln roots, Toni's fight with Reyes Latino, shots from her interviews during that first run, slow pans of the original gunslinger image that somebody must have found somewhere. God, her boobs looked big.

As if in answer, Hamat Allah responded just weeks later. The Bringers of Allah, a new offshoot who, angered that the Taliban were at last joining the peace talks in Kabul, had detonated twenty bombs outside all the major mosques in Kandahar.

It was a massacre. Hundreds died. Hundreds more were wounded.

The Shrine of the Cloak – a reliquary housing a cloak believed to have been worn by the Prophet – and the Masjid of the Hair of the Prophet, an important mosque near the large bazaar – were damaged by the blasts. As were others.

That day easily competed for most violent in Afghanistan in decades.

The peace talks were, of course, immediately suspended.

Her first instinct, after looking at the pictures, the dead children, the body parts, was to have them all hunted down and shot like mad dogs.

Better sense prevailed. She forced herself to focus on the fact that the true casualty of the massacre was the peace talks themselves.

Since the Towers had come down, and the US invasion of Afghanistan weeks later, the war there had ground on and on through the years. Much like the small-scale brush fires of the

British Imperial Raj. They never seemed to go away. Killing thousands of American fighters over the decades and wounding tens of thousands. For what?

Honestly?

And she knew that she wasn't just having trouble focusing because Kandahar had taken her Artie from her almost twenty years ago.

She was honestly disgusted with the whole mess.

Always had been.

Until a particularly illuminating talk with Perky one night – over a bottle of single malt that she had smuggled into his Cheyenne Mountain Erebus – had given her a handle, of sorts, on the whole question.

She had wanted to know – just what the hell was going on?

Her favorite general had taken a large swig, frowned in concentration for several long moments, then begun. She, recognizing the signs of a long oration, had settled in like a cat in an overstuffed chair, even if this one was a hard-edged wooden seat with no pillows.

"*Why* is usually asked," he began. "*How* might be a better method of getting to understanding. Or more precisely, how did we get here?"

She nodded.

"Eisenhower's legacy to all succeeding Presidents – that of gleaning intelligence, via satellites, about our enemies' intentions and capabilities without giving away our own –

changed the game. Groups like Al Qaeda were forced to get creative. So, they developed a new methodology. Choose the most remote, most god awful, butt-ugliest land in the world and move there. Put a gun to the headman of some village, announcing, 'Give us your daughters.' Possessing family ties now, they quickly take over whatever meager means exist in this arid, inhospitable land and use those resources to create suicide bomber schools. Which understandably freaks out all the surrounding countries. Who call for help."

He paused to wet his lips before continuing.

"They don't call London anymore. Or Paris or Berlin. They certainly don't call Beijing for fear the Chinese, once invited in, will never leave. They don't even call Moscow, not after Putin and his cronies bankrupted that country to fill their dachas. No, they call DC."

Of course, she thought silently. It's not that our European allies don't have tanks or gunships. They just don't invest in sensors like we do.

Perky was going on. "Now, what do we do? We can't ignore the phone call. That's unconscionable. Can't build a wall around the baddies shutting them in. This isn't the West Bank – the forbidding terrain makes it well nigh impossible. They can always slip though somewhere. Which was sort of the point. If we send in aid workers to win the hearts and minds of the locals, the baddies simply cut off their heads and upload the whole ghastly affair on YouTube again and again until no more aid workers will come. No. Before drones, the only option the President had was sending in troops. And we won't do that anymore. Not after Iraq. Well, at least not for another generation or two. Maybe not ever again, at all, in the entire history of humanity. No, the days of large-scale land wars are fini. As outmoded as dinosaurs. As are large-scale naval wars. Leyte Gulf, in World War II, was the largest naval battle ever fought and ever will be fought in the long, storied, history of humanity."

Toni lost the thread a moment there, then abruptly recognized the signs of a genius retreating into his own abstractions. Beatie did it to her all the time.

"More scotch?" she had smiled.

He nodded. A little jerkily. Perky was a cheap date.

"What to do, then? Drones? No, drones only get you so far." He was staring off into the distance.

Toni had begun staring off herself. What else was there?

"Buy them off?" she prompted.

"Sure. If you're the King and you can execute any ten-penny-a-nail Congressman who accuses you of aiding the enemy. Presidents can't do that." He blinked. "Well, they could, I suppose. But they'd give up being able to do anything else. And most Presidents, not all, but most are problem fixers. They come to the Oval to make things better." He was starting to slur. "Whatever better means to them, of course. Such as in Herbert

Walker's day, presiding over a country club, he was, except for Panama, which...."

She reached out to touch his arm before he could meander again.

"Keep them talking?"

"How will you get them to the table?" he had smiled at her. A winning smile. A baby's smile.

She had shaken her head.

"Why it's simple," his baby smile still adorning his cheeks. "Kill enough of them. They'll come."

Even the memory of that conversation left her chilled. Sometimes this globe was a pretty nasty place.

At any rate, it was Perky's world view. It didn't necessarily have to be hers.

Thinking it over in the garden that afternoon, she considered her Secretary of State, a Hapster very much in the mold of her Attorney General. She wasn't even sure that the Secretary could claim credit for the Taliban joining the peace talks. Mostly, he just jetted around the planet meeting folks at sumptuous banquets and getting photographed in historic buildings. Harmless.

Hap had never wanted much competition for the limelight when it came to his Cabinet, had always been entirely happy with the B team.

She decided a more direct approach might be in order. Why not? FDR was always bypassing his Secretary of State. Besides, she missed talking with her Texan. He had been left in the woodshed long enough.

Foster came in, looking a bit wary. Warren's face was set in stone. What had they discussed before entering the Oval?

She was seated at the Resolute Desk. Her most – any President's most – auspicious pose.

Foster approached and, with Warren, stood before it.

"Madam President?"

Goodness, he looked like a schoolboy about to get a ruler smacked across his palms. What had Warren caught him doing? Flirting with a secretary, she supposed. Maybe that new one with the big, blonde hair in the bullpen.

"Foster, I'd like to talk to anybody reasonable in the Taliban."

"Ma'am?!"

"Do you know anybody from your days at the London School of Economics who might know somebody else who knows somebody who knows somebody over in Kabul worth talking to?"

He stole a glance at Warren – to see if this was a joke of some sort?

Warren only clipped out, "Well?"

Foster frowned in thought for a moment or two, all Rhodes Scholar. Then his features brightened. Her Texan was back. "He's a got a ramrod up his backside ever since Winslow picked him up for speech writing, but…"

"Winslow," Toni cut in. "The British PM?"

"Yes, Ma'am. Since then Ricketts comes it like his shit don't
— , thinks he can strut sitting down. Course, now that I think on
it, that cowpoke was always a bit too much gurgle and a mite too
little guts. But you can bet the farm on him, sure nuff. I would."

Warren cleared his throat.

"Call him."

Yes, Madam President.

The following morning – since Kabul was eight and a half
hours ahead – she found herself in the Oval with Warren, Foster,
and, a last minute inspired guess, Bobby Tinder. He might not
be able to point out Kandahar on a map, but he could probably
tell you what every city councilman in Peoria was thinking about
the Taliban. Or at least get close.

Warren was speaking. "Madam President, Mr. Herati is
available." She wondered if the man she was about to speak
with had been born in Herat Province, in western Afghanistan.
Since naming children after their birth province was an Afghan
custom. Best not to ask.

"Mr. Herati. Thank you for taking my call."

The connection was clear, on speaker. The voice was soft.
Not strident. Was she expecting that?

"The honor is mine, Madam President."

She doubted that. Nevertheless, she resumed. "With me are
my chief of staff, my legislative aide, and Congressman Tinder
of Connecticut."

"I understand."

"Please accept my condolences for the pain and anguish that the good people of Kandahar have been suffering recently."

There was a silent moment.

This was it. Would he retreat in snark? Would he use this moment to embarrass her? Accuse the United States of war crimes against the peace-loving people of his country? Was he taping this? Probably.

Still, she trusted her Texan. When he wasn't distracted by a woman's scent.

The soft voice was back. "Madam President, may I ask what you want?"

Direct. A glance at Foster showed that her Texan was blushing, but not alarmed. He nodded at her.

Okay. She could go direct.

"I understand that Hamat Allah set off their bombs in Kandahar to punish the Taliban for joining the peace talks in Kabul."

There was another long moment of silence. Was he conferring on the opposite end? Probably.

"That is my understanding, as well."

She heard the English accent better now, slipping through the Arabic. Or, inflection, maybe, was probably a better characterization. Educated in the UK, Foster had said, at Oxford, then the LSE. You can take the jihadist out of the public school, but you can't take the public school out of...

She smiled at that thought.

"The peace talks are very important to me. I want to see them succeed. What can I do, what can my government do, to ensure that this possibility of the Taliban rejoining the peace talks occurs?"

Another break, even longer.

This should be interesting. Foster was starting to look strained. Warren glowered at him. Bobby looked thoughtful, like he was a million miles away.

Finally, Herati returned. "Well, I have an answer for you, Madam President. But you may not like it."

"Give it to me, anyway."

"Hunt them all down, Hamat Allah, and shoot them like the rabid dogs they are."

Later, in the garden, the thought crossed her mind...

It had been her first response as well. Almost word for word.

***

Death.

Could she play the Angel de la Muerte to Hamat Allah?

Or, more appropriately – given their professed belief – their Azrael, sent by Allah to smite them?

She certainly had the means. But she didn't think so. No matter how many they had killed, hurt.

Garnet Gap was bad enough.

Yet, the Taliban had named their price. Boy, had they come quite a ways. The name meant The Students. Because the teacher of the founders, appalled at the violence destroying Kandahar, had dreamt one night that he should lead his students to clean up the mess. Oddly, they had. And instituted Sharia law as a result.

Pick your evil.

Did they wager she was too weak to pay the price they had named? She was a woman, after all. In their world – freakishly similar to the Garnet Gap crowd, by the way – she needed to be guided onto the right path. By someone with a penis and not a vagina.

Were they seeking to embarrass her? Maybe. Did it matter?

She wanted the peace talks to continue. But not like this.

Doing what they asked...aside from the horror of it, death was so...final. Practically speaking, it cut off all other possibilities.

Beatie was approaching her in the garden.

"Chica, the rat's out of the bag!"

Chica?! Well. Wonder of wonders. The Oracle of the Oval had returned. This was nice! Her Oracle was flashing her phone.

It showed a big sign. A Connor Raines sign that said Returning Home.

"We got him!"

Home. Mama. Her strategist's smile was fading in front of her eyes as she thought of...

Death.

In the end, it had not been Reyes Latino that had taken Mama from her, but those damn Luckys.

She nodded at Beatie. "You were right, Beatie. Well done."

"We still going with 'Fighting for...'?"

Toni nodded. Beatie faded again, walking away with a "Got you by the balls, fucker!"

It had been in her third term. One day she had gotten the phone call. She was just walking out of a Government Oversight hearing when one of her staffers – a DC girl – had approached with an odd look on her face. It had been Esteban, a Soldado that she barely knew. Mama had collapsed at the kitchen table. She had burst a vessel and bled all over the floor after a particularly bad coughing spell. They hadn't known what to do. They were sorry. All of them. Very sorry.

It made sense. Even if it had been cruelly ironic. In Mama's kingdom, she did all the thinking out loud and everyone else all the listening. Everyone, and she meant everyone, who had been to that kitchen had been conditioned into passivity. Not to act. Not until Mama had told them what to do. Here, the very people that might have been able to save her had, passively, watched her die, not knowing what else to do.

Toni shook off that absurd, and really quite gruesome thought, preparing to go home. For the last time?

On the flight, she jotted some thoughts down. Of course, she would give the epitaph. Father Manuel was still kicking, if a bit slowly these days, so she had called him to make the arrangements. She knew that Mama would squawk at the idea of a Baptist girl being given a Catholic funeral by the priest she used to mock. But, as Toni had long come to accept – we are all rendered a bit ridiculous in death.

The apartment was smaller than she remembered. Yet it looked precisely the same. The same doilies in the same places on the end tables, on the couch, on the armchair back. The same overflowing ashtrays. The chicken fryer, in the same place on the counter. The same scuff marks from its feet.

Soldados and their girlfriends were everywhere. She sat in her old chair at the table and wept. They let her.

It proved the hardest speech of her life. Standing in the pulpit, looking down over the congregation – probably the only time, outside of marriages and baptisms, most of the Soldados and their chicas would ever come to church – she broke down before uttering a word.

And stood there. Fighting with herself. Gripping the polished mahogany edges of the pulpit. Trying to speak. Taking a breath. Struggling. Getting a grip. Starting again. Staring up at the gothic arches soaring above her. Wondering if her Elijah was holding Mama now.

"Mama…" And hearing her voice falter, crack, she broke again.

And so on.

She felt utterly ridiculous. And helpless. Pathetic. Weak.

Sobbing. Hearing the sobs of others. The chicas in the pews, wiping their cheeks. The clearing of throats from Soldados. One after another.

On and on. It was excruciating.

On the flight home, she had tried to capture the sound of the best speech writers she had heard over the last years. Had tried to use that tone to convey the utmost gratitude, from the bottom of her heart, to Mama for opening her home to a young girl, all on her own. Who had done more than that. Who had proven the most significant guardrails, at the time she needed them, she had ever known. Who had held her in her worst moments of suffering. Who had celebrated with her the happiest moments of joy she had ever known in life. Who had mandated that her Child would go beyond her. Would explore a wider, greater world than she had ever known. Would reach heights that she had only been able to dream about.

All of this, and more, overlooking those times, those moments when her Child had taken her generosity for granted. Ignoring her own pain when her Child had been so taken with the beauty, the danger, the excitement, the opportunity of that wider world that she had truly forgotten her Mama.

For that – the sharpest spear piercing Toni's heart – that evil had begun whispering in the back of her mind, making her a little manic – the awful wisdom of what had truly killed Mama. Not her Luckys. But being set aside. No longer needed by her Child.

All this, coming from the great wellspring of Mama's extraordinarily large heart. Beating proudly, unfailingly for all of them. Always there. Until it wasn't.

And that was when she saw it.

Looking down from the pulpit, yet one more snot-filled, smearing tear dripping from her nose, she saw it in the Soldados and their chicas. They were afraid. They had been left alone. Abandoned.

This day, this morning, this moment was not about Toni at all. Nor would it ever be.

She took a deep breath. Steadied herself. Met their eyes, firmly, proudly. These children of the streets. Just as she was. They needed her to say it. She, above all else. She was the Child. They looked at her like that. She had seen it, this last day. The way they gazed at her. As if she were a goddess. The one who had climbed to the top of the mountain and had looked over the other side. Who had gone farther than all of them. And probably always would. They knew that.

And now she knew it, too. They needed her to say it.

She did.

"Mama is always with us."

She nodded once, tightly, in affirmation. Then had stepped down from the pulpit.

***

Time to grow up.

G7 – the gathering of humanity's seven largest economies.

Her first one, she had been so intimidated that she had come across as a quiet church mouse. She let her Trade Representative Mac do everything. Mac was good, the first to admit that she wasn't fluent. But she certainly seemed to be with her smattering of trade lingo Japanese, Chinese, German, and French. She could hack it out. Or, as she liked to say, she "could drink them all under the table."

She wasn't Ivy League, which Toni was privately pleased by. She was all US Army. Practically stamped in olive. Probably wore that color bra and panties. Immersion school, 24/7, for whatever language she needed for her next assignment. Then, when an IED had taken off her left leg below the knee, just outside Fallujah, she had settled down a bit. Went to school, got her Master's. Or as she liked to say, "whored her way through the syllabus."

Toni wasn't sure if she was joking about that.

All she knew was that Mac had made it easy. Gave her PTBs (the T meaning Trade) on the road. Didn't give her shit for being a woman. And did the job. Mac made it easy for Toni to slip into the background at Tokyo, that first year. Then, Berlin, the second. Shanghai, the third.

And now it was Paris. It was Mac's last one. She was getting married. To an accountant.

The thought of which always made Toni smile.

She was going to miss her trade rep's salty language. Of French President Dubois, for example, she had once opined that "the woman is so crooked, you can't tell from her tracks whether she's coming or going."

One remembered that in all the dizzying round-table topics of GDP, GNP, women's empowerment, interest rates and migration patterns.

She was also going to miss Mac's way of approaching numbers. She didn't throw out a cloud of figures for Toni to memorize. Instead, her trade rep typically gave her a starting point, followed by proportions to communicate the sense of scale. Such as, imagine the USA's GDP – the size of the country's economy – as around $20T. The Chinese GDP was, roughly, half that size. Japan and Germany came next, each being, roughly, half the size of the Chinese economy. Finally, the UK, India and France were next on down, each, roughly, half that of Japan or Germany.

It made things so much easier. She was definitely going to miss Mac.

Odd that during her trade rep's last trip, she was finally going to exhibit some leadership.

She wanted two things. Well, three.

CC: Her international cap and trade market agreement. She expected to defer to the Europeans on that discussion, since they had already been running one in Europe for the last decade.

AI: Her worker training program written internationally. She didn't expect much on this one, to be honest. Only China and the US were making serious investments in Artificial Intelligence. And China didn't dance well with others.

Kabul Peace Talks: She wanted the Taliban back at the table, and she didn't want to have to kill off the Hamat Allah to do that. She expected to turn to British PM Winslow to help with that.

She trusted the Special Relationship, mostly because the more she looked at it, the more she liked what she saw.

Other than the rank manipulation of the CIA by British intelligence back in the 50s about the Iranian populist Mossadegh. MI6 had sworn that he was a Communist, mostly because Mossadegh had run out of other options to inflame his masses so had settled on the radical solution of stealing – that is "nationalizing" – the Anglo-Iranian petro facilities sitting on the beach of the Persian Gulf. The British were understandably quite upset at the theft. But, since FDR had made it clear that the US was not some kind of hired tough to be used to prop up the tottering British Empire, British intelligence, noting the Red Scare McCarthy hearings happening right about the same time, decided to take advantage of that fact and swore up and down that Mossadegh was about to turn over Iranian oil to Uncle Joe in Moscow. Thus, the CIA coup – led by T-Rex's son Kermit and the Dulles brothers, soon to be of United Fruit Company Guatemala coup fame, themselves – deposed Mossadegh and reinstated the Shah. To what eventual verdict of history, who could say? Toni's favorite anecdote about the whole mess was that the Shah had practically fainted at the imbroglio. Just didn't have the stones to see it through. The CIA had had to fly in his sister to stiffen his spine.

Regardless, blind Anglophile Toni was not. Still, she readily accepted the fact that the British had far more practical advice about running a globe than other countries.

For example, just before the extraordinarily complex Versaille Treaty negotiations ending World War I, some senior statesmen in London had formed what came to be known as Chatham House, one of the first think tanks, to help prepare their PM for the talks. Practically the next day, in Manhattan a group of similarly minded American statesmen had formed the Council on Foreign Relations to prepare President Wilson. Indeed, the talks were so complicated, the myriad of issues so thorny, particularly when it came to the protection of the formerly conquered peoples in what used to be known as the Ottoman Empire, no single person could compass it all.

She hoped the British PM of her day would play nice.

After their working dinner devoted to a topic that would have placed Hap in his element – Economic Opportunities in the Solar System – she approached the PM.

A Tory, Freddie Winslow had been elected two years earlier. His polls were steady, if not fantastic. Oddly enough, he didn't seem to care. She had introduced herself at last year's G7 and had been delighted at his wry writ, particularly his droll encapsulation of events or leading personalities of the day. All accompanied by that arching left eyebrow.

"Freddie?" she smiled.

"The Moulin Rouge!"

"What?!"

His eyebrow was arching. "You Yanks are all the same. I warn you, however, the elephant is no longer there. Neither is the garden out back."

She paused a moment, then thought, why not? "How about Jane Avril?"

Both eyebrows shot up at that. "Bless me! A Yank who knows something of the world beyond her shores. Wonders never cease. Splendid. I'm driving."

Which had precipitated a surprising, then increasingly frustrating, and ultimately rather hard conversation with Rod. He absolutely refused, saying that his team needed time to secure the environment.

Which really pissed her off. For some reason. And it wasn't his refusal. Was it?

No, this was the moment. Security be damned. She was sure there was nothing more to this.

At the time, however, she curtly responded, "Because Al Qaeda knew that we would make an impromptu run to see the Can-Can? Honestly." And had walked away taking Freddie's arm.

And just to really piss Rod off, she rode in Freddie's SUV limo. Her security followed close on their heels.

Along the way to the fabled club, Freddie told her of how his grandfather had seen Jane Avril dance the Can-Can back in the days of La Belle Epoque, Paris. He had been a mere boy, there with his own grandfather. Barely six on that day, but he had always remembered it, had recalled the memory many a time for his own grandson.

"'She was so beautiful,' he'd say. 'So shy. So innocent. So sexy. A toxic brew. Unforgettable.'" Freddie sighed with a happy smile, "That little minx took all of Europe by storm."

Which prompted her memories of an obscure World War I history class. She had been taken with the whole lost romance quality of La Belle Epoque. The Eiffel Tower going up, inspiring the creation of haute cuisine sauces and consommes in the major hotels, haute couture fashions appearing among the leading designers, the Impressionists breaking all the old rules by painting the working class in their daily life. All that beauty. All that inspiration. All to expire all too soon in the horrific trenches of Verdun during the War to End All Wars.

Even the name La Belle Epoque – the Beautiful Era – was a term of nostalgia, awarded to that magical period of time only after the Parisians realized what they had lost forever.

"Oui, Madam President. Let us take care we never make that mistake."

"Hear, hear!".

Boulevard de Clichy, however, was densely crowded on this late spring evening. There were gobs of people standing in the street all along the boulevard park, waiting to get into the classic nightclub. She watched a pair of young women wearing 20s flapper dresses stride by. Then looked up to the panes of the club's eponymous red windmill sited on its roof, turning slowly, manifestly, the neon lighting up the sky.

She swallowed a bit in frustration. She didn't care about the club so much as she cared that Freddie had wanted to go. She wanted him in the best mood possible.

"Shall we pull the mighty strings of office, my dear?"

God no. She could just imagine the headlines if it leaked.

Almost grunting, she shook her head.

"Well, you clearly want to talk, and I want to hear what you have to say, Toni. How about O'Sullivans?" He was pointing down the street at a pub.

Stunned, she merely nodded.

What an Irish tavern – complete with Guinness – was doing in the storied Montmartre neighborhood of northern Paris, home to its many moody, dark staircases, with the Sacre-Coeur Basilica presiding overhead, who could say?

The pub was very English, which was good enough for her. Besides, Freddie had suggested it.

He even sprang for the pints, which was good, since she had forgotten with a silent curse that she never carried money anymore.

"Right, then? No more ado. Spill, lass."

She took a deep breath, wondering how to begin. Sell him? No, not after their little nocturnal adventure.

He interrupted her thoughts. "Is that Gunter?"

Her head snapped around to see the German Chancellor enter, look for them and, with a smile, approach to join them.

Rod was giving her a warning look. She didn't need a translator. How many more people knew about their little jaunt? She was beginning to regret her impulse.

"Guten Abend! Guten Abend!" Gunter all about shouted over his hearty handshakes to them both. He sat. The pints arrived. Three. And Guinness took time to pour. She might be a Yank, but even she knew that.

She looked at Freddie, trying to raise her own eyebrow.

"What?" he asked innocently.

Whatever.

She shrugged. Then surveyed them, each taking a hearty gulp of their thick, dark brews. Her tongue was tied.

"Mein Gott, this is nasty!" Gunter put his pint down with a hearty thunk.

Which made them all laugh. Even as she heard the nervous twitter in her own.

"Ma chére?" Freddie was gesturing at her glass.

She nodded and a bit self-conscious, took a sip. It was good. Thick, dark stout, with a sweet note. She hadn't had one since...law school, probably.

Direct.

"Hamat Allah," she said, looking them both in the eye.

"You bloody...was ist?" Gunter was sputtering. "Wanker!" Pronouncing the 'w' as a 'v.'

"Pay up! Next round's on you, mate." Freddie was chortling.

Her left index finger had begun tapping a rhythm on the table.

"Oh, Toni, there's a good lass. Let the lads have some fun now. We've been in session all day."

Well...

"Okay, but this means a great deal to me," she resumed, throwing caution to the wind. "I want the Taliban to rejoin the talks."

Freddie caught Gunter's eye, then took another sip. "We hear from Kabul that your man there, Herati, told you to shoot them all, the HA."

She nodded. Not really knowing what to say.

"Will you?" Gunter was asking her. She didn't know him all that well. He was the leader of the Christian Democratic Union – a sort of big tent party, in the style of the GOP or the Dems. Her briefing book on him said that as a conservative, he typically favored property rights over the people, was scrupulously honest, and took delight in hunting, his children and his mistress – a blonde cabaret singer with creamy white breasts the size of the Alps. His headache in politics? Alternativ für Deutschland, or AFD, the new, tony, if a bit shrink-wrapped, incarnation of Hitler's National Socialist Party. Motivated in many of the same ways as her own Garnet Gap crowd – hating the migration of the peoples.

His eyes upon her, she answered, "I don't want to."

They looked at each other.

"Toni," Freddie was beginning. Her heart sank.

He caught it immediately, however.

"Right, then. Tell us what you have in mind."

She nodded, began gathering her thoughts.

"And, might I ask, my dear," he lightly touched her on the arm, "being that this is the first such bargain, let's not be too tight-fisted with the till, yeah?"

Buy them off. Perky's voice filled her mind. Then, she abruptly realized that Freddie meant for the UK and Germany.

A trade deal of some sort? Solar panels floated before her eyes. She wondered what Mac would say. No, AI Tech of some sort. That was better. Since, from the morning's session, she could see they were still way behind the supporting infrastructure the US enjoyed. She had been paying attention, for obvious reasons.

And so they had talked.

Feeling her way, she told them everything she could of her phone call with Herati, emphasizing that he was decidedly not her man.

Freddie had smiled at that. That's when she realized that he had been teasing her. Of course, he would know about Foster's connection to...Ricketts, wasn't it? Freddie's speechwriter.

He had quite a gift, she saw now. Freddie kept things light, even when they were discussing meting out death and destruction. It made it all less maddening, somehow. Gunter, too, from his reactions to what she was saying, she could see was clearly on board for...something. He certainly took her seriously. Or the Oval seriously. Or maybe just the US GDP. In the end, did it matter?

She was even honest enough to confess to them that her first reaction had been to hunt Hamat Allah down.

Freddie nodded, vigorously.

"But...!" she was starting to object, when he cut her off.

"Lass, lass! I know what you're going to say, next. That it's not the humanitarian thing to do. Well, those blokes let slip the bonds of humanity long ago, if you take my meaning."

Gunter was now nodding. And ordering their next round, a faraway look in his eyes. Quiet. Troubled.

"And us?" She looked at them, hard.

They both cleared their throats, looking down at the table. Gunter was toying with the drink coaster.

"And the men who are tasked with capturing them?" She remembered suddenly that her briefing said his English was spoken with a Bavarian accent, whatever that meant. Now she knew. It was pleasing to the ear.

"Aye, what about that then, eh?" Freddie was joining in. "Shooting them at a distance is one thing, particularly with a

drone, if you were to get so lucky. Capturing them, though?"
His eyebrow was arching. "A bunch of bloody tossers?"

"Who will pray for their blood, these men we send?" Gunter's
eyes were earnest. Searching hers.

She felt the power of his gaze. She felt tears prick the corners
of her eyes. No! Not now. She blinked.

"I will pray for them." She said it softly.

The second round arrived.

Rod was approaching.

Goddammit.

She harshly threw out a hand at him. He stopped. But did not
retreat.

A corner of Freddie's lips twitched. "Toni, they won't last the
night in whatever jail you throw them into."

She shook her head in exasperation at the thought.

"No, listen, please." Freddie stopped her. "Put them at a
forward operating base and you'll only make it a target. So, it's
a local jail, then. In Kandahar City. They'll die by the hand of
Taliban, that night, if not by their own."

She chuffed. Angry, just as she realized that he was right.

"Then, they make that decision. Not us." Despising herself
for sounding so weak.

They all took a long, meditative gulp of their dark, almost
black stout. The head on Toni's was particularly thick. A tawny
color.

The rest came far more easily: Operation to run through NATO command. British assets on the ground to find Hamat Allah, US special forces to capture them, German Kommandos providing support in case things got difficult, also transport in/out. Artie would have complained about that last arrangement, but then, she smiled grimly, Artie didn't have her job. She needed political cover from their Allies after Chad.

In return, $10B each to grow their respective AI institutes. Who knew? They might even share the fruits of their research someday.

But tonight? She took a last sip, stood, nodded to Rod who was looking like he would like to throw her over his shoulder and run out the door. She shook hands with Freddie and Gunter, slowly, feeling a bit sheepish at this last dig at Rod, particularly when she could see from her companions' eyes that they were also getting the "it's time to go" from their own teams.

From what threat? She never learned.

On the way back to her hotel, Rod didn't say a word. Neither did she.

***

It was Thanksgiving. No, too early. Maybe it was the 4th of July.

Connor was standing at the end of a long table. It was a beautiful, western red cedar surface, polished to a high sheen. A lovely lace spread ran the length of it, draping off the ends.

Brightly sparkling Lalique crystal adorned this festive affair, in the form of wine glasses, three to a setting, for water, red, and white in their traditional, classic shapes. Beneath, just before each of the smiling faces gathered around the feast, were full place settings of Meissen porcelain, dating to the 1700s, surely costing in the tens of thousands. Surrounding the porcelain were scrupulously polished Robbe & Berking sterling silver flatware, several knives, forks and spoons, each with its appointed purpose, a collection dating to the middle 1870s. Not a fixture out of place.

His thirty odd guests, Whiter than White, were equally appropriate to the time, circumstance, and tone of the occasion. The shining faces befitting the four generations of Raines, all dressed in their finest. His father, taking his honored place opposite his son at the far end of the table. His mother, seated at his father's right side. Just as Connor's wife was seated at his. Opposite the two wives were also seated wives – one, Connor's sister, the other, a sister -in-law – of the second generation with their husbands accompanying them. And so on. The third generation filled in the seats found along the middle edges of the cedar dining table, right down to the two darling tykes, a boy and a girl, both grandchildren of Connor, held in the arms of their mothers. The women and the girls all wore delightful dresses with ribbons in their hair. The men and boys squeezed, reluctantly, into formal dinner suits, complete with bowties. Even the two babies wore jumpsuits with matching bibs, inevitably, one a soft blue, the other, a gentle pink. All were smiles. All were happiness, bright laughter. All were joy incarnate at this wonderful gathering of the family on this blessed day of Thanksgiving.

All went silent now, in one beat, full of expectation. All had their eyes on the man, giving him their undivided attention.

The new patriarch of the family – since his father clearly understood that his son, according to every doting father's wish, had surpassed him – stood, solemnly, at his end of the long affair. Ready to perform the ceremony with all due pomp. The table groaned with the weight of an array of porcelain bowls and plates heaped with candied squash, whole wheat rolls, mashed potatoes, green beans with toasted almonds, corn on the cob sprinkled with cayenne, brussel sprouts ladled with cheddar sauce, spiced cranberry sauce, several fruit and green salads of varying ingredients, rounded off with several gravy tureens holding sauces bechamel or espagnole.

The centerpiece sat proudly before him. Likely thirty pounds or more of pure delight, the expected large golden brown, steaming with succulent juices, turkey, stuffed to the gills with salpicon, an old family stuffing recipe that went back generations, and took days to create, right down to the homemade stock and the home-baked croutons that provided the foundational ingredients.

My god, Toni thought, he's outdone Norman Rockwell.

Connor took up a long knife in one hand and a honer in the other and, expertly, ran the blade of the knife along the honing rod, from heel up to the point, traveling diagonally along the tool. And with a reverse-stroke on the underside of the rod, ran the blade right back to the beginning. After a few strokes on either side, the edge of the blade was happily re-aligned – she was certain that there was a metaphor in there, somewhere.

Nevertheless, her opponent – since it had become quite clear as the GOP primary season wound down who would get the nomination – handed off the honing rod to some unnamed assistant, who evidently didn't merit more than a walk-on role and, with a flourish, sliced masterfully into a leg while holding its end just so. The work of a moment and the son lifted it aloft, for his beaming father to admire from the far end.

"Dad?" Connor offered with a just a hint of majesty.

"Of course, of course, son! Brilliant."

The standard bearer of the Republican Party, party of Lincoln, adroitly laid the severed leg on the dark meat platter, held aloft at his side by another, equally nameless, faceless assistant. On his other flank, stood an assistant holding another platter, this one evidently for the white meat. Since Connor was now slicing into the breast of the bird, lifting out one hefty, juicy, tranche after another to serve to his large family.

The entire nation.

Everything was as it should be. At last.

Daddy was calling them.

After their long nightmare stumbling around in the scary forest. It was time to Return Home.

She got the messaging. It was about as subtle as a two by four to the head.

He was a man. She was a woman. A girl, by comparison.

He was White. She was a Blatina, a mutt even.

He was a husband. She hadn't had so much as a date since Artie got shipped out.

He was eminently straight. Her lack of a love life had yielded the inevitable rumors that she was a closeted dyke. There was a string of articles – that would show up from time to time, like a rash – that purported to know who her secret lover was. Sometimes she, and it always was a she, was White. Sometimes Black. Sometimes Latina. Never Asian or Native, though. Which always amused her. Not clickable enough? Perhaps.

He was a father, three times over. Her womb, as dry as dust.

He was a grandfather, twice over, so far. He would found his own twelve tribes of Israel, given time. Or something like it. She was...well...her womb was...you get it.

The Ship of State had been listing, even sinking after Chad. The Captain would now right it and see it safe home to harbor at last. She doubted that Connor was much of a Philosopher *King – as Plato had demanded the Captain must be in his ancient metaphor – but she had no doubt whatsoever that her opponent saw himself as a monarch.*

Besides it wasn't like those shouting "Let It Rain!" had ever read Plato, anyway.

Or maybe he saw himself as Hercules – to trot out another Classical metaphor – and it was time to clean out the Augean Stables that she had mucked up.

Whatever he saw, it was clear that he thought himself the man for the job, and she a class A fuckup.

The marketing was beautiful. Extraordinary. As masterful as the adroit way in which he had handled the honing rod.

Returning Home.

Without a word about her gender, her ethnicity, her marital status, he pointed out that the incumbent and likely nominee of the Democratic Party was...

Different.

Not us.

The Other.

Strange.

Foreign.

Not us. Most definitely not us.

She didn't think like us. She didn't act like us.

Look at Chad.

Look at her cap and trade bill.

Look at her wacky AI jobs training idea.

Look at South Carolina.

And, if you can stomach it, look at Garnet Gap.

That's what happens when you let a woman run things.
Particularly a woman of color.

(Ooops! Can't say that! Well...)

Returning Home.

(They'll understand anyway.)

After all this craziness of the last three and a half years, it's time to Return Home. Return Home with Connor Raines.

Hell, even she was half convinced.

Wasn't she?

What was she doing here? Couldn't, wouldn't have Connor done better in Chad? Maybe those twelve SEALS and that Green Beret would be alive now.

Maybe all his years in Big Tech would have prepared him to ask the questions that she hadn't. Faced with the unsatisfactory answers she had been given, he would have known to reach outside the system for new blood, fresh ideas.

As she had with Garnet Gap.

He would have probably handled that one better, too. With much less loss of life. Or, better yet, Garnet Gap likely wouldn't have happened at all.

She felt herself sinking. Turning.

Yes, it wouldn't have happened at all. Connor was no Black Jezebel to rebel against.

She was whirling, getting sick. Swirling a drain.

Garnet Gap was her fault. Not Gideon Browne's. It was her presumption. Her foolishness.

She was about to vomit.

Her idiocy. That ever thought she could do this job. That ever thought a bitch from the streets of ABQ could sit at the Resolute Desk in the Oval.

She spotted a doorknob.

On the table. A wife had brushed against the lace spread, moved it, exposing the doorknob. Then, had hurriedly covered it up.

A doorknob? In the middle of the table?

Her swirling slowed as she fought the tide. Fought to duck her head down enough to look under the table.

There! She saw it. Dirty egg crates! Disgustingly, filthy egg crates. Stacked as small pillars holding up the table. Which was little more than three doors laid end to end, their doorknobs and hinges hidden from the world.

Beatie was laughing.

Who was *Connor Raines!?*

***

It began with a cough. Or so they told her later.

A farmer cleaning out a local commune's corn shed on the edge of Nueva Concepcion scraped up some dirt on the floor, coughed at the dust and continued on with his work.

By nightfall, he was dead, drowning in his own blood as his lungs collapsed. His wife, horrified at the sight of her husband spitting up large quantities of blood, had grabbed her children and ran to her sister's. By morning, all four were dead.

And the death toll was rising.

Quickly.

Truckers, it was thought, had brought the bug when transporting sugar cane to processing plants in San Salvador, a metro area of 2.5M.

Dr. Ralph Mung, her director of the Centers for Disease Control, had brought her the news. Her Secretary of State being in Moscow, she had to make do with the Assistant Secretary for Western Hemisphere who told her that the new junta was not returning calls.

El Salvador – both the smallest and most densely populated country of Central America – had enjoyed a democratically elected government for decades. Before it abruptly got chucked out by a group of generals backed by the old aristocracy. Something about the new income taxes leveled on the highest bracket.

In any case, the country whose name meant "The Savior" had just unleashed Mother Nature's new superbug and she couldn't get anybody on the goddamn phone to talk with her about it. She asked Dr. Mung if he had any contacts down there. He did, at the Hospital Militar, facilities that served military personnel, which is where what cases they did know about were being treated. But the staff were strictly forbidden to discuss the bug.

Officially, as far as the El Salvador junta was concerned, the bug didn't exist.

Inquiries at the World Health Organization showed that the CDC knew more than the UN did.

What to do?

She thanked them and let them go, with the typical reminder to keep her informed via Warren.

What to do?

As she wandered through the Rose Garden, she found herself meditating on the legacy of Pericles. Oddly. Well, he did die of a VHF. So the guess went, since the archeological record was scant. Back in the days when she was considering pursuing anthropology, she had looked it up. Medieval historians had called it the Plague of Athens, for lack of a better term. Being a true man of the people – outside daily, mixing with the crowds, shaking hands, listening to the stale Dumb Blonde jokes of his era – he had been one of the first to die.

What a way to go.

The greatest mayor – though they called him a stratego – of Classical Athens. The radical bringer of democracy for the first time in human history. So far as anyone knew. Of course, his version of one man, one vote meant that the man possessed both property and a penis. Even so, it was radical in those days. Athens boasted an assembly of fifty thousand citizens who could vote, whereas other cities, such as Sparta, had only two or three thousand.

Being a citizen in Athens meant having to attend city council meetings whether you were in the mood or not. It was a public duty. Pericles also made it a public duty for all citizens to study rhetoric, or speech-making. It was a duty to learn how to be persuasive so that you could fight for your ideas, mounting the speaker's stone in the Pnyx, the assembly area, and argue why you thought the library's parking lot should be zoned with, say, twenty rather than thirty parking spots to make room for the Dodge Rams of those days.

Of course, Pericles wasn't all hero. In true classical fashion, he had a bit of the rogue in him. The NATO of that time, the Delian League, was organized against the Persians who insisted on invading every decade or so. And just as with NATO, the member states all contributed annually to a common fund. The treasury house, with its bank vault, was sited on Delos Island, hence the name of the league.

One day, Pericles was staring at the acropolis, the hill behind the city which every Greek city state had. His acropolis had a bunch of burned buildings on it, though, left over from the last visit by the Persians. He abruptly decided to announce to the world that, in his judgment, the Delian Treasury was not safe on the island and should therefore be kept in Athens. And he mounted a fleet to go seize it, then waited to see who would complain. No one did. Not really. Not enough to mount an army to get it back, anyway.

So, he declared Athens the new home for the Delian League's fund and used the money to rebuild their acropolis into The Acropolis.

Temples to the city's patron saint Athena. Including two colossal statues of the goddess. The first, a colossal bronze called Athena Promachos (Athena of The Front Line – or as Toni liked to think of it, Athena, First One Through The Door No Matter What's Waiting On The Other Side) stood under the sky in the elements with a spear polished so brightly that sailors out at sea could see it at sunset. The second colossal, worked in ivory and gold, Athena Parthenos, stood deep within the newly constructed temple, the Parthenon.

Just as the Eiffel Tower would inspire la Belle Epoque, the Acropolis defined Athens, even if it was funded by a smash and grab. She had to admire Pericles' daring. All too soon, the sculptor who had carved the Athenas, Phidias, would find his name known round the world and through the ages. As would the budding playwrights of that day, competing with each other during the annual Feast of Dionysus – Sophocles, Aeschylus, Aristophanes – finding lasting fame in the newly carved (into the hillside) Theatre of Dionysus that seated seventeen thousand fans.

Then, too, the great schools of philosophy would make their home in Athens when Socrates settled there. His pupil Plato (with whom he fell out) built his Academy there. And Plato's pupil Aristotle (with whom he fell out) built his Lyceum there.

As did many other thinkers, attracted to the bright light that Athens had become.

History, medicine, architecture, theatre, sculpture, painting, pottery and the arts, democratic thought, as well as public affairs, the machinery of good government itself – practically all the great achievements for which Classical Greece is celebrated, all found their zenith in this one city, during this one forty-year period when this one guy was mayor.

And when he died, it all came to an end. Just as la Belle Epoque died in the ghastly trenches of Verdun. The Golden Age of Athens died in the horrifically wasting Peloponnesian War with Sparta.

And how did Pericles die?

The best guess was a VHF – or viral hemorrhagic fever – much like Ebola. Mother Nature, it appeared, liked to throw up a new fright every couple of decades or so just to see if humanity was paying attention.

Toni was. She took it as a matter of faith that part of the challenge of humanity was to gather together and defeat whatever new bug showed up when it showed up. Those who argued that a virus was God's punishment should be locked up. And those like the junta – who could do something about it instead of just sitting on their fat asses? They should be taken out and shot.

Well.

Not really.

But, tugging at her sweater collar because it was making her hot on this early summer day, jokers like the junta made her really angry.

What to do?

As she sat there, honestly perplexed, she spotted Warren approaching. About the Democratic Convention schedule again? Her enthusiasm gap problem?

She found herself tensing until she saw that he was looking relaxed, even a bit jubilant.

Kandahar had proven a success. Mostly. Two Green Berets had died with six wounded, but none mortally. All had come home and were presently getting treated on the aircraft carrier Nimitz, named after the World War II admiral and known, inevitably, by its crew as the "Old Salt."

Those Hamat Allah that had survived the shooting... well...Freddie had been proven wrong. They didn't last until nightfall in the jail.

Still, an all around success. She asked Warren to schedule the calls with the families who were grieving and asked to see the Joint Chiefs.

She had some thinking to do.

Entering the Situation Room later, she asked everyone to sit while remaining standing. Which made them unhappy, so stifling her curse, she sat.

She wanted three plans – better ones than Chad this time, she said – to invade and hold San Salvador, the capital of El Salvador...

The four chiefs – army, navy, air force, marines – four stars all, were blinking, shaking heads, glancing at one another or looking down. The marine, oddly, was grinning, grimly. Warren alone kept his eyes on hers, listening.

...knowing full well that a new superbug, a VHF that had yet to be named, was spreading rapidly, killing hundreds and that the ruling junta refused to acknowledge that fact.

...knowing full well that it was only a matter of days before the bug hit the shores of the USA.

That got them. The blinking, eye-rolling stopped. They straightened in their chairs, quietly, self-consciously.

Three plans that interfaced with the CDC. Three good plans. By midnight.

Someone coughed. In disbelief? Did she care?

She stood. Warren stood. They stood.

Yes, Madam President.

***

Mr. Secretary, the great state of Alabama, home to the fabled Crimson Tide, land of diversity unknown among other states of this great Union, the Rocket Capital of the World, casts its sixty votes for Toni Madison!

***

Cleveland Convention Center. The Democratic National
Convention. Ohio.

Odd.

Like so much of her life these days, the Convention was
topsy-turvy. What was a Blatina incumbent doing in the
conservative Buckeye State asking to be nominated as President?
Drunk with her own delusions?

Levi had assured her that the optics were excellent. She was
President of all the nation, not just half.

She was no expert but the GOP's optics seemed very similar
and far more effective.

Connor's coronation had gone first, a week earlier, and though
it had taken place in his ultra-liberal hometown of San Francisco,
the Republican Convention was very much a coronation. Her
favorite moments of the footage included a short mini-
documentary featuring gay Log Cabin Republicans for Raines.

Watching it with her, Beatie had smirked, putting on her best
drag queen lisp: "I'll take it up the ass for Connor!" Toni had
had to shush her. Sometimes, her friend simply went too far.

Like her Billy the Kid mania. The new tv and web spots were
bad enough as it was. To be fair, it wasn't like she wanted Toni
to dress up in gunslinger garb again. But, she had asked for a
wardrobe change. She wanted outfits with epaulettes. On dress
shirts, on trench coats, on sweaters even. (Who put an epaulette

on a sweater, Toni had wondered?) Inevitable answer, the
military. She supposed that was the point.

They had had that particular wardrobe argument the day they
had invaded El Salvador. For her prime-time announcement to
the world, Toni had opted for a gentle white blouse – to
emphasize the humanitarian aspect to the mission – to emphasize
the support she had marshalled from surrounding countries in
Central America who were understandably freaked out by NCV,
as it became known. Nuevo Concepcion Virus, a cousin of the
hantavirus pulmonary syndrome family. As well as the wary
support from the Security Council, particularly the UN Secretary
General who was still asking for guarantees that the US forces
would withdraw once the crisis was over.

Her plan had been to scare the hell out of the junta. She had
gambled that they, for all their bluster, would prove to be
cowards and wind up preferring exile on Grand Cayman to
fighting for their perch in a rapidly growing diseased home
country.

She had been proven correct. They had fled without a shot at
the arrival of US Special Forces. With the Army's 82nd and
101st Airborne Divisions, supported by the light infantry 10th
Mountain Division, holding down all points, the healers moved
in.

The CDC, assisted by the WHO rapid response team, Doctors
Without Borders and the Red Cross, took over, flooding the area
with doctors, nurses, and support staff wearing hazmat outfits.

Setting up quarantines, deciding triage, experimenting with cures and trying to slow the spread. They were also looking for ground zero to better determine the cause and prevent future outbreaks.

***

Mr. Secretary, the great state of Colorado, defender of the freedoms of this Great Nation, ceaselessly vigilant in its protection of our skies, home to Pikes Peak and the Rocky Mountain Bighorn, unanimously and with great pride casts its 78 votes for the next President of the United States Toni Madison!

***

Odd.

The world had screamed out in fear as the news broke.

Then, as the rash of new cases slowed over the first days, and went into a decline as cocktails of preventive drugs were mixed up and distributed throughout the region, the world had shrugged and moved on.

A number of Republican speakers at their Convention had even felt comfortable going so far as to question the wisdom, if not the legality, of their gun-slinging President's foreign policy. "That's what happens when you let a girl play with guns!" had been the applause line. Again and again and again.

They were getting more out of Billy the Kid than she was.

As for the wardrobe squabble, she had shut Beatie up by agreeing to religiously wear a series of trench coats with epaulettes from now on to Election Day.

***

Mr. Secretary, the great state of Illinois, home to the greatest President of all, Abraham Lincoln, who transcended partisanship to reunite and to heal this fractured nation, home to the tallest building in North America that dares us all to dream big, home to the greatest sports teams this nation fields that remind us all to fight for what we believe in, the Prairie State salutes another fighter in Toni Madison, casting all its 183 votes for her!

***

Odd.

After weeks of wooing her to be chosen as her veep, Bobby Tinder suddenly developed a case of the enthusiasm gap.

Prompting Beatie's tart remark that maybe they should send the good Congressman to San Salvador.

All those long heartfelt speeches about "the extraordinary historical significance" of her administration and what "you, Madam President, have come to mean, to symbolize to little girls everywhere all over this great Earth" and tendering his "hearty applause for your newly formulated, muscular foreign policy that brings the greatest days of Teddy Roosevelt to mind"...

Eeep!

...After all these and many other flowery sentiments, her former mentor in those early days of Congress had suddenly, right on the eve of the Convention, dried up.

Why? Who knew?

Utterly exasperated, she put her Texan on it. And noisily began interviewing other candidates for veep. It was late. It made her look disorganized. In over her head.

She didn't care.

Three days before the convention, Foster came to her in her private study just off the Oval.

"Well, ma'am, a worm's the only critter that can't get any lower."

Okay.

She tried to remember one of her favorite tags of his, but couldn't. Instead, she gave up and, patting the seat next to her desk, tried to paraphrase. "How about less sizzle and more bacon?"

That delighted smile of his, sure to have dropped many a pair of panties, broke out all over his cheeks. He even blushed a bit. "Yes, ma'am."

He sat. "I talked to the good Congressman and, ma'am, that boy is slicker than a slop jar."

Yes, well.

"I mean to say, I know he's been around since Noah, but that man knows more ways of taking your money than a courtroom full of lawyers."

Which was why he was such a star performer on Appropriations.

Growing impatient enough to start "a varmint fight over a crow's nest" – another of Foster's favorites – she, nevertheless, settled down and decided to enjoy the conversation. He would get to it in time. Besides, what was the rush? Really?

She nodded at him, thoughtfully.

"Yes, ma'am, slicker than a Texas interstate after a spring rain."

She nodded again, repressing the urge of her left index finger to start tapping on her desk. She had been working on the latest draft of her Convention speech.

"Ma'am, I know you two go back. But, ma'am, do you happen to know how many nooses there are in the Tinder family tree?"

She had to smile at that one.

"A few, I suppose. Can we get down to it?"

Rhodes won over at last. The good Congressman from Connecticut wanted a co-equal presidency. Not in name, of course. That would be unconstitutional. But, in fact. Wide-ranging powers on all domestic policy questions.

Used to Bobby's negotiating style from their years in the Capitol building together – demand the moon so they're honestly relieved when you finally settle for the corner lot – she shook her head.

"And what does he really want?"

"That."

That?

"Foster…"

"No ma'am. I'm serious. I played along. Had drinks with his chief of staff t'other night. Listened to the moonshine. Met with his domestic policy team the next morning. Laughed, slapped their backs. And, honestly, ma'am, some of his boys are so crooked that if they swallowed a nail, they'd shit a corkscrew." Then, realizing what he had just said to the President of the United States, he blushed, started to rise and apologize all at the same time.

She waved him back down, asking him to continue.

"I talked to 'em. Told 'em you didn't come to town, two to a brokeback mule. That all their wildcatting was getting 'em nothing but dry holes. Even once, near the end, that they were looking a mite few pickles short of the barrel." He paused. "That one didn't go over so well."

She waited. She realized she was growing angry.

"I finally met with the man hisself. Nothing, ma'am. No movement. None at all. Tight as a Methodist's fiddle string. The man wants a porch swing for two in the throne room. 'Bout it."

She swallowed. Her mind awash in the memories of her early days. When he had so generously reached out to her. Helping her. Explaining which Representatives were easy marks and why. Which were stone cold indifferent and why. Which were hellbent on running any woman of color out of the House.

Why wait so long to tell her, though? He couldn't possibly expect her to agree.

"How did you leave it with them?"

"Well," Foster beamed that darling smile of his, teasing a reluctant grin to her own lips. "I did manage to stop myself from telling him to go skin his own buffalo."

"Good."

"Told 'im, I'd go back to you."

"When was this?"

"Fifteen minutes ago."

She paused. Bobby waits until Day Minus Three, guessing that we want to announce the ticket on Day One, well before the roll call on Day Two, leading to his speech on Day Three, and her own, hopefully triumphant, speech on Day Four.

How did he know that he was her favorite? Who leaked it?

She sighed, shaking her head. Where was safe?

"Ma'am?"

Abruptly tired of Foster's homespun pith, she thrust out a hand.

Her old mentor expected her to fold. That much was clear. He was proud of his ability to read people. What politician wasn't? After South Carolina, though, Warren had swept the West Wing with a wide broom. Ruthlessly cutting anyone, everyone who wasn't a Maddie. There were no leaks.

Bobby expected her to fold.

So much for friendship.

"Fuck him."

Yes, Madam President.

***

Mr. Secretary, the Commonwealth of Pennsylvania, memorial to the brave defenders of this great nation at freezing Valley Forge, bloody Brandywine Battlefield, and hallowed Gettysburg, home, too, to the illustrious Liberty Bell which rings forth the freedom of humankind to all the corners of this great Earth, delighting in the great honor given us, unanimously casts its 208 votes for the next President of the United States Toni Madison!

***

Odd.

Happily fat on Malcolm's triple cream brie omelet with homemade biscuits and a blueberry salad – he had insisted she eat all of it – she decided on the spur of the moment to visit Warren the last few minutes before Marine One's liftoff.

Knocking on the doorframe of his office, she spotted Rod hastily closing a file to Warren's curt nod.

Her Praetorian left without so much as a meeting of her eyes.

She turned her own to Warren, who looked down at his desk for a long moment, then, straightening his back, he returned her gaze.

"It's not a problem, Madam President."

Not sure what to say to that, she paused, then deciding that she was only as good a President as those she trusted most, let it go.

Besides, she wanted happy thoughts on her way out.

"Will you walk with me?"

He flushed and almost grunted as he clipped his thigh coming around the desk in his eagerness.

"Now, Warren," she deadpanned, "I do want the West Wing in one piece when we return."

He chuckled at that. "Yes, Madam President."

She took his arm, Victorian style, and let him walk her out to the helicopter.

"Any last words of advice before the jump?"

His jaw was working as they stepped outside into the colonnade bordering the South Lawn. Apparently, he hadn't expected this.

Rod, his team, Beatie and Foster were all waiting for her on the steps of the bird. The gaggle of press were shooting photos, ducking around each other to find that one, iconic picture that captured this moment. It was quintessentially presidential. Even sweet, given that Warren was escorting her. Something they had never done before.

He paused. Far enough out of reach of the sound booms. Though the news crews were clearly trying anyway.

"Madam President?" He was facing her. He had gone white. Which, for Warren, meant that he was greatly moved. One step short of tears.

"Never forget that you have grown to become one of the greatest of those who have occupied the highest office of the land."

She cocked her head. She had to or she would have started crying herself. Grown to become? Probably the most beautiful thing he could have said. It was what she hoped for herself.

"Also."

She came back to him, nodding.

"Given where you're going now, ma'am...Never forget that those who disagree do so out of jealousy."

She patted him on the arm, promising, "I won't."

And she floated up the steps. The helo lifted and, looking down, she saw Warren watching her fly away.

***

Mr. Secretary, the Lone Star State of the Alamo, this cradle to three great Presidents, this home both to the fabled Texas Longhorn and the lowly armadillo, this land of large hats, large appetites and even larger ambition that will take this Great

*Nation to the far reaches of the Solar System, solemnly responds
to the call of duty to help send our neighbor from New Mexico to
the White House, casting its 251 votes for Toni Madison!*

***

It was surprisingly fun watching the floor action of the roll
call. She had loved it last time, too. Ordinarily not one given to
the drudgery of committee work, a national party's convention
alphabetical roll call vote of the states was the apex of committee
work. Fifty thousand delegates, visitors, guests, members of the
media, security personnel, and others, all gathered together over
these tumultuous four days. The shouts, the screams, the
applause, the colorful hats and costumes, particularly the
inevitable gunslingers with cartoonish, oversize Peacemakers in
day-glo colors – since the Toni the gunslinger campaign had
done its damage – the waving signs, the state signs, the feverish
clapping, the chants – "Toni! Toni! Toni!" – "Four More Years!
Four More Years!" – the all around silliness, the preening, the
hoopla, the deafening ruckus that rocked the hall after
Minnesota's delegation put her over the top, the Secretary
announcing that "the candidate wishes that the roll call proceed
so that all may hear every voice of this great nation," the happy
applause that responded to this request.

It was magical.

Levi had insisted on the complete roll call. Yes, it was unusual. Yes, it made things longer. Yes, it showed the nation, the world, that all fifty of these great states supported a Blatina for President.

They were still being dogged by the enthusiasm gap. The special elections this spring and summer to fill seats unexpectedly emptied by illness, resignations, politics, all across the country were revealing that.

The Dems may be screaming themselves hoarse at the moment. Whether they bothered to vote for their girl come Election Day was another matter entirely. A full roll call could only help right now. And not hurt.

***

Mr. Secretary, the Old Dominion, the Commonwealth of Virginia, home to the first band of hearty adventurers who crossed the great seas to land at Jamestown, home to the United States Atlantic Fleet who carry that inspiration into the 21st century defending the interests of this great nation on the waterways of this great world, then, too, cradle to eight Presidents, including the greatest one in our country's most illustrious forefather and first General George Washington, including as well the visionary father of the Constitution, James Madison, this state humbly begs the honor of making history by assisting the election of a second President Madison, proudly casting its 108 votes unanimously for her!

***

After a raft of unnerving articles by the major media sources about just what Toni expected to do for a vice president and whether she was up to the task of choosing "the man a heartbeat from the presidency" – it appeared that for the first time since the 80s, a nominee was about to be acclaimed without anyone having a clue who the veep would be.

Bobby's people – or Bobby – let it go until an hour before the roll call began on Day Two. They asked to meet.

Foster was ecstatic. "Ma'am! Ma'am! Let's shoot all the lights out!"

She gave him a twisted grin. Then asked him to let it go.

He stood there, stunned. "Madam President...I..."

She was tired of men dictating to her.

He stood there, his mouth open wide enough to...catch a bottlefly? No. A Texas Longhorn. She grinned at her own Texan saying.

Then, he left.

A few moments later, an aide held out a phone, saying it was her chief of staff.

She sighed, thinking that certainly didn't take long.

"Madam President, I just wanted to let you know UN Secretary General Pharong is offering to replace our units in El Salvador with a peacekeeping mission. The Comms team is preparing a statement. Anything you wish to add?"

She smiled, a tear welling. When did she become such a softy?

"Yes, Warren. 'Bring our boys and girls home!'"

"Yes, ma'am," the happiness in his voice its own accolade for her gamble, her risk, her win.

Then, he paused.

Well, why not? She was happy enough. "Foster call you?"

"Yes, ma'am. I told him that I stand by your decision. Further, if scraping barnacles off the President's yacht isn't his idea of an inspiring pastime, he might consider doing the same."

"I see."

In the wee hours of the morning after the roll call celebration of the evening before, Bobby came to her, himself. Full of apologies. Explained that he had been misled by his staff, had fired the two responsible. Was horribly embarrassed. Only wished to serve. And a number of other mellifluous meanderings.

She thanked him and said that the news of his earlier disinterest – while wholly misrepresented to her – had regrettably moved her hand in a few other directions.

And, in truth, it had. She no longer cared who was her veep. The position wasn't worth a bucket of warm spit anyway. She should know.

Bobby was very understanding. He was careful not to leave the door closed, suggesting they meet for coffee later in the morning? He might have some insight into her prospective choices?

She nodded.

After a sleepless night, she remembered that her pettiness was beneath her oath to defend the Constitution. Like it or not, no matter how she may feel, the veep *was* one heartbeat away. Whomever she picked had better be worthy of the nation.

Bobby, then.

Even so, she let him wait.

***

Before we announce the final tally, pursuant to the rules of the convention, the Chair has moved to suspend the procedures of voting and declare by universal acclamation Toni Madison as nominee of the Democratic Party for the office of President of the United States. Is there a second?

(loud roar) Aye!

All those in favor?

(even louder) AYE!

IV

Toni stepped out of the campaign bus and stretched. It was a beautiful scene. A rest spot on a state road in Wisconsin, just outside the small town of Rhinelander. Quiet. A gentle breeze kissed her cheek. The road was bounded by two charming lakes and thick clumps of birch trees, the bark peeling off in many places, as it did so naturally, just waiting for a Hiawatha to come along and turn them into a canoe. Birdsong surrounded her. Everywhere. So joyful, so cacophonous, she couldn't identify any more than the occasional robin or wren.

In the distance, on either side, she could see houses dotting the lake shore. Small boats were plying back and forth, carrying hobby fishermen with their catches of the day, going home in the afternoon to clean their lake trout and smallmouth bass for dinner.

It was as far from ABQ as she could get. The painful memory of Mama's funeral interceded just for a moment. Reminding her of how the Soldados and their chicas had looked at her. Even back then. The one who got away. The girl who broke free of the streets. Because of moments like this. The rigors of retail campaigning might get her down from time to time – such as when she had to deal with a bozo or even an outright racist – but she never tired of seeing new places.

Following the hoopla of the Convention, her triumphant speech asking the Dems to help her Fight For A New Tomorrow – Bobby at her side, hands raised together in clenched fists – the army of balloons dropping on cue – the screams so loud they seemed to lift the roof off the convention center – they had hit the road with thirteen weeks until Election Day.

Bobby was hitting the Northeast. She was visiting the Midwest. Both were focusing on swing states – those states that could swing the election either way. Bobby had on his list states such New Hampshire, Pennsylvania, Virginia, North Carolina. She had Colorado, Indiana, Iowa, Wisconsin, Michigan. It went without saying that being so close to Illinois made one or two stops in Chicago mandatory. It was the anchor of the Midwest for the Dems.

The speeches had gone well, at first. All were minor recaps of her acceptance speech with plenty of room to thank the local celebrity Dems standing on the stage with her. She learned to speak of Hap in a new way, focusing on his dreams rather than the man. Her New Tomorrow envisaged a country without gun violence, without income inequality, where gender or race did not determine opportunity, that tamed carbon emissions and prepared workers for the Age of AI, that reached out to the stars and made its home in the solar system. Bobby echoed her themes, as well as telling folksy stories about serving with her in Congress.

The opposing ticket barely mentioned issues at all, all through the month of August. Buck Jones, a former Senator from Louisiana now running with Connor, made hit speeches. One after another, in classic veep as pitbull formulation. He mocked her as "a little girl who liked to play with guns." Who massacred the good people of Garnet Gap with her inexperience. As a cowgirl who liked "to risk the lives of our brave boys and girls in uniform." (At least he remembered that women served in combat roles now, too, she reminded herself.) Buck damned her for "the reckless loss of twelve brave SEALS, throwing their lives, their futures away on her childish whims." He even derided her collaboration with the UK and Germany in Afghanistan, skipping over entirely their success in bringing Hamat Allah to ground, merely stating that "Connor would never trust our boys to foreign powers not worthy of such grave responsibility." He ridiculed her adventures invading helpless countries like El Salvador, conveniently deleting all references to the threat CNV had posed. On and on, one hate-filled diatribe after another.

Levi had asked to go negative on Connor in return. She held back. Bobby asked after one particularly virulent Buck speech about "the crying children who lost their daddies in Chad, a place no one could point out on a map." Again, she resisted. She wasn't sure why. Maybe it was because Beatie had some sort of plan in mind. She thought. She wasn't certain. She simply saw that her chief strategist was calling her "chica" again and had this Cheshire cat smile on her face as if she were enjoying some private joke.

In any case, Toni noticed that for all his vitriol, Buck was not daring to poke at her skin color. Not yet.

Connor, on the other hand, did so. Daily. Without ever using the words. His speeches were folksy, warm, references to God, to his savior Jesus, spring roundups and riding the horse to church, to square dances and barn raisings, hay wagon Christmas caroling, family dinners where everyone got along, where everyone felt at home. To listen to him, Toni might have thought that he had grown up in a hut in some Georgia cotton field instead of scootering down the steep hills of liberalized San Francisco with his grunge band LGBT friends and their Peacenik no-nukes neighbors.

And it was working. Poll after poll showed her trailing him 51 to 49. He was getting the lion's share of the Independent vote. (The rule of thumb she had taught herself last time around appeared to be holding for this time, as well: Both parties got 43% of the vote, totaling 86%, leaving 14% of the voters up for grabs.)

Connor had gotten his post-convention bounce. As had she. It didn't matter. Ever since Super Tuesday, those numbers 51/49 had shown up and, no matter what Team Madison did, that ratio remained the same.

Then, too, the enthusiasm gap persisted. Pew Research had released some truly frightening numbers just a few days ago – which was why she had agreed to this Rhinelander trip – 75% of Dems planned to vote in November, 90% of Republicans.

This was shaping up to be a losing campaign. Not since her first run for Congress had she been so embattled.

Hence their trip north to Hodag Country, after paired speeches in Chicago. Senator Brian Sorenson, retired, was an old Badger State Democrat of the Scoop Jackson variety – never met a nuclear weapon he didn't like. He was also the Grand Poobah of middle and northern Wisconsin. Outside of Madison and Milwaukee in the south, the rest of Wisconsin was Sorenson country. Whomever got his nod, got his territory.

Toni had been skeptical. She honestly didn't think she had anything in common with him. But Levi had insisted, saying that Sorenson had asked for her personally. That he had some feud with Raines that went back a couple of decades and that it was "absolutely insane not to pluck fruit hanging as low as this!" She was still chewing her lip over it when he mentioned that Sorenson's family friend had been the one to give a hodag to Senator John F. Kennedy during his run for the presidency. Way back when.

Well. If hodags were involved... She nodded, much to Beatie's bemused expression. Which would have infuriated her, except Beatie was happy these days, and Toni wanted her to remain that way.

Hodags. Hodags were an invention of a local wit in the late 1800s. Originally a fixture of Paul Bunyan legends, this mythological creature – resembling a small dragon with the face of a frog, fierce red eyes, large teeth and claws and a row of spikes along its back and tail – became a source of local fun. The local prankster had gussied up some sort of stuffed animal that looked vaguely like the one from the tall tales and gathered his friends around it out in the woods for a photograph – the hunters celebrating their kill – and gotten it put in the local paper.

Soon, the hodag became the local celebrity, much like the World's Largest Ball of Yarn or World's Largest Cable Spool did in other towns, giving locals something to visit on a summer day and something to gossip about with their neighbors.

The local Chamber of Commerce had a large statue of a hodag, crafted by a local artist, mounted outside its offices. She had spotted it on their drive in. Inevitably, the hodag became the local high school mascot. Even the school itself was informally known as Hodag High. There was a summer music festival built entirely around the creature, bringing tourist dollars to a section of Wisconsin that had little else to offer other than hunting and fishing.

Regardless, whether Sorenson planned to give her a toy hodag or not, she was ready to meet him. And there he, apparently, was. Just pulling up now in a battered old Ford pickup. He got out. Scandinavian red cheeks, wispy white hair and a hearty handshake over his flanneled pot belly.

"Madam President."

"Please, Senator, call me Toni."

"If you call me Brian."

And that was that. To Rod, she had only thrown out a hand, stopping him. Brian noticed. Instead, she bundled into the passenger side of the senator's pickup and off they went, just the two of them. The campaign bus and all her staff left to toodle around aimlessly in their wake. Her Praetorian, she noticed in the side mirror, was motioning up a following car and getting in.

After a few moments of silence down the road, she began to feel around. Levi had been cagey about what Sorenson was expecting, only replying, "Take him as he comes. We need this, Toni." She asked him how retirement was coming along. She had never worked with him while in Congress, but she had certainly heard of him, his work on the Senate Armed Services Committee and in foreign affairs generally.

His answers were mundane. Accompanied by the typical jokes of a local hunter or fisherman poking fun at "the yahoos from Chicago" who came up each fall "to shoot their foot off."

She nodded. Thoughtfully.

She made a half-hearted attempt at climate change but, as expected, he shot it down, saying, "That math has yet to be determined."

Ah, well. She decided to wait on events, and took to complimenting the natural beauty all around them. That seemed to warm him up a little more. Where he was taking her, she could not say, at all. They had quickly turned off the state road after leaving the lakes behind and were now bumping around on some dirt road heading somewhat west onto higher ground. Rod and his team were out of sight. Freedom.

It was early September. She had just flown back out to the Midwest from DC, catching up with the bus in Chicago. Her speeches had gone well, though there were those disturbing comments afterward from state and city party leaders about how she had better "catch Raines." As if she hadn't noticed she was behind.

The leaves were turning. Maple red. Oak brown. Birch everywhere, of course, their leaves turning a bright yellow. It was magical. She said so. And got his first real smile as a reward.

Behind her head, she noticed two rifles. Two long, heavy rifles. That looked capable of stopping a lion.

Brian was just pulling off the dirt road into a small copse. He got out, after casting an approving glance at her hiking boots, which she had thrown on as a lucky guess. His door squelched open, he got out, shaking his hip a bit. She wondered if it ached.

Turning, he reached behind the seat and grabbed out two hunter orange vests for them to don. As well as two cruddy, rumpled baseball caps that used to be hunter orange. No matter, she put them on and waited with a smile.

"I'm sure you'll have noticed the Marlin." She was about to look around for the bird – a marlin was some kind of...hawk? – when she realized that he was nodding at one of the rifles. She smiled deeper. What else to do?

"Annie Oakley favored them, but I'm sure you knew that." There was the lightest emphasis on the word 'sure.'

He reached in for the rifle, while she frantically scanned her mind for any reference to...oh, the sharpshooter from Buffalo Bill's Wild West Show of Gilded Age America. Annie Oakley used to shoot the middles out of playing cards and other tricks. Or something like that.

"Course, she was firing a .22." He was clearing the chamber, then loading it for her.

Toni tried to nod knowingly and reached out for the rifle as he handed it to her. "That's a .450."

Okay, she had just run up against her first obstacle. Long experience had taught her, though, that people, in their own bailiwick, were forgiving of others who didn't know the particulars, so long as they didn't pretend.

"And yours?" She nodded at his rifle.

He looked surprised. "Winchester 70."

"Ah," she smiled again, as he loaded his own.

"Oh, I know. Takes a fast hand to operate a Marlin when a black bear is charging you, but I figure with your gunslinger reputation, you're plenty quick."

He smiled back.

Men. Always whipping it out to measure.

She kept her voice low. Decided to move in an opposite direction, entirely. "Black bears are falling in number where I'm from."

He snorted. "Not here. DNR boys counted well over thirty thousand this year. Biggest number since the 80s. We've got plenty to choose from. Might have us a couple of bear steaks for dinner, I figure."

This was surreal.

He had to be joking.

But he was turning away, heading toward some foot trail, she could see now.

Okay, not a joke. A test?

In any case, she wasn't having it.

"Brian."

He stopped, turned to look at her. He had a smirk on his lips. She saw it now. It *was* a test. And she was about to fail it.

"I'm not shooting a bear, Senator. I'm sorry."

He nodded. "Not so Billy the Kid, after all."

"Oh, no," she was surprised at how quickly the anger was building. "I'm hell when it comes to facing down armed gangers in the street. Done it many times. How about you?"

His smirk deepened, incredulous. "Armed gangers?"

"Oh, yes. I'm guessing, though, that you are better off with defenseless bears. More your style."

He looked like she had slapped him. His mouth opened to retort.

"Don't bother," she snapped. Spinning on a heel, she walked back to his truck and laid his rifle carefully in the bed.

Then, she started back up the dirt road by herself.

His pickup roared past her a few minutes later, not bothering to stop as she got out of the way.

It was okay, she thought. It was probably only a couple hours until she came across Rod. In the meantime, she had birdsong for company.

*****

In fact, he found her moments later. He had been running, gun out. Two of his team were following. The fourth, presumably, left with the car. Spotting her, he paused, heaving for breath, looking out into the woods. Angry. Really angry.

She didn't care.

She strode right past him.

They didn't say a word to each other. The other two of her bodyguard immediately turned around forming a secure perimeter while leading her back down the dirt road to the state one.

A half hour later, and she was climbing back onto the campaign bus. One glance told her everything. Levi was looking out the window, his ever-present cellphone clenched in his hand. Foster was looking at his feet as were the rest of the traveling staff. Beatie was positively amused. Which really pissed her off.

Stopping by her campaign manager, seeing the spots of red dotting his pudgy cheeks, she snarled, "Next time you want to send me to a gun show, why not dress me in a bikini?"

***

The Islamic Center for America. The largest masjid – or mosque – in America. She had a speech scheduled later in the day in Detroit.

Well, the Center was just a few clicks down the road, down Ford Road, in fact, lying just west of Detroit, in Dearborn, hometown of Ford Motor Company.

It tickled her to know that this strangest of strange (to some), oddest of odd, least familiar of all cultures in America would be sited right smack in the middle of the most apple pie of all American industries. Ford engineering, stamping, manufacturing and assembly plants lay a few blocks to the west of the mosque. Ford Motor Company HQ, even Ford Motor Company Worldwide and many other sprawling arms of the sales side of the business lay just a few blocks east. The mosque had even been built, in part, with Ford money.

Yet, Levi resisted. Because he was Jewish?

She didn't care. She was still angry about Hodag Hell as she called it. They were early for Detroit. It was a visit to the mosque or a trip to Dairy Queen.

No media, he made her promise.

She smiled right back. His jaw working furiously, she stepped past him. She knew better than to invite him outside with her.

And got out. Alone. Rod was there, of course. But he was keeping his distance.

It was a large park. Here and there, she could see that he had placed his team in discrete locations, making her perimeter as secure as she would let him.

The massive dome of the masjid dominated the skyline, as did the twin, very tall minarets. There were young and old wandering around. Taking photos, visiting as tourists, their family members who lived locally walking with them, pointing out different aspects to the building. It was striking. White stone, bronze colored domes both large and small. Large stretches of green grass surrounding it. The whole assembly made one feel...peaceful, she decided. She wandered over to a park bench and sat down.

The tourists had noticed her campaign bus immediately, of course. Several guests were pointing at it, the large Fighting For A New Tomorrow and Toni Madison for President letters dwarfing them as they walked by it, asking questions of each other.

No one seemed to notice her, however. There was a metaphor in this, she was certain.

Eventually, however, a girl came over to her. Toni tugged nervously at her headscarf, regretting that she hadn't checked it in a mirror before leaving the bus. She had been too busy sticking it to Levi at the time.

The girl's name was Farrah. She asked Toni if it really was her. Toni smiled. And that broke the spell, for several girls came over now, all wearing hijabs over their hair and under their chins.

They wanted to know if this was her first time visiting and she replied that it was. Farrah wondered if she could go inside and ask if one of the sheikhs could come out to say hello to her. Toni had doubts about whether they would welcome an unscheduled stop, but she agreed. Farrah went off with a friend in tow and a happy smile on her face.

The other girls quickly ran through the typical questions and comments – they had seen her on tv, of course – what was campaigning like – was it difficult to be President and a woman – where had she been – did she expect to win. The smiles, shy at first, had grown broader, bolder. The laughter, hidden behind hands at first, became more open.

Particularly when someone asked why she wasn't married.

She only smiled and turned it on them. Where were their boyfriends?

Oh, my! So many gasps and moans, even muted shouts of dismay. Blushing cheeks. Eyes turning demurely downward, hands clasped up to lips. Toni felt like she was back in junior high.

Farrah returned just then, looking a little put out. Sheikh Raza had said that it was not permitted. And that was that.

Toni didn't mind. She wasn't surprised in the slightest. Even today, the premier gentlemen's clubs of London went into a tizzy whenever a woman was elected PM, because they knew they would have to open their doors to her at some point. Freddie loved to joke about it.

Toni did mind, though, that Farrah was unhappy, maybe even a bit embarrassed.

So, she asked the girl about her boyfriend.

Now, the clucks and the cries became louder, the teasing more pronounced. The laughter, loudest yet.

Farrah, something of a leader, Toni surmised, smiled quietly and said, "Abdul is just over there, with his friends." And she pointed at the eastern minaret.

"May I meet him?"

Farrah's eyes got really big, then she nodded and immediately bent her head to start texting. Her friend was giggling, then began texting as well. As did several of the girls.

Before long, Farrah looked up, over Toni's shoulder. She waited, watching the effect on the girl. Farrah might be strong, in this group, in front of her friends, but as her boyfriend approached, she tucked all that strength inside.

Toni didn't know what to think about that – other than it takes all kinds to make this world the wondrous place that it is.

A very thin, very handsome youth, with a very thick head of hair approached, flanked by his friends. Ah. If Farrah led her friends, Abdul led his. It made sense. It almost seemed entirely expected. Not ceding him the initiative, however, Toni immediately asked the boy when he planned on proposing to Farrah.

Who shrieked in dismay. And joy. For days afterward, Toni asked herself how the girl managed to combine the two in one. She never could have. Not at any age.

Abdul looked like fireworks had just been set off. As did pretty much everyone else. He stood there, in the center of all the jokes, the shouts, the guffaws, pretty much stunned. His friends were slugging him on the shoulder, trying to get him to come around.

At that point, Farrah asked him something sweetly, in Arabic? Persian, maybe? She knew the mosque was Shia.

He answered, a bit tersely.

She persisted, batting her eyes at him.

He swallowed. Then, turned to his friends looking at one, then another. They both shrugged.

And they set off.

Farrah asked her to wait. Someone was reaching up to her headscarf. Adjusting it. Into some kind of more ornate fashion.

A few moments later, Farrah received a text.

"Please, Madam President, will you enter the masjid with us?"

"I would be honored to."

A stirring conversation later with Shiekh Naqvi – the youngest, so she gathered, of the three sheikhs who ran the mosque – about why women were not allowed to teach the Quran, and she was leaving. She felt, rather than saw, Rod just at her shoulder. How he got there anybody could say. Foster was waiting for her in the lobby. "Thick as fleas on a honeyed up bloodhound ma'am." She didn't have to ask to what he was referring.

Farrah and her friend had disappeared, she was sorry to see. No matter, there were several more girls and their mothers now looking at her with great interest. They accompanied her to and outside the great door at the front.

Right into a sea of flashing light bulbs, large cameras and a thicket of sound booms. Even though mosque staff were holding them back, it was with some difficulty. The shouted questions, at any rate, reached her easily enough.

"Madam President! Madam President! Buck Jones says that you are consorting with known terrorists here. Do you have any comment?"

She waited until she had cleared the front courtyard of the mosque, so that the people could have their sacred building back, at least. Rod's team had already fanned out around her, as she moved through the media.

"Buck wouldn't know a terrorist if he tripped over one," she smiled, feeling a glint enter her eye and hearing, even at this distance, Levi's sigh.

"Connor Raines says that's it's a shame that you're not President of all Americans, just the ones who refuse to fit in. Any comment?"

She stopped. The bodyguard stopped with her.

"Say that again."

The reporter repeated the remark.

She waited. They waited with her. Sensing the dramatic splash about to come.

"Since Connor believes that," she heard her voice crackle with fury, "our first debate will be held in a mosque. It'll be a good experience for him."

***

Late that night. After the shreds of the Detroit speech – ruined by the mosque visit and her comments afterward – had been safely tucked into the miles behind the campaign bus. They were circling back to Ohio. To Cincinnati.

Levi came to her.

He sat next to her in the small chair next to her bed. The only bed on the bus, ceded by universal agreement, to the candidate.

His eyes on the floor, he said, "Madam President, I am sorry. You were right. I was wrong. I am sorry."

That preamble over, she waited.

He took a deep breath, then said, very slowly. "Please Madam President, please do not let your anger at my mistake in Rhinelander allow this schmuck to more easily paint you as The Other."

She heaved her own sigh. Then nodded.

***

Of course, it was too late. The following weeks after her mosque visit, Connor's campaign played her comments endlessly. They bought extra ad time, at the astronomical rates that media markets charged for last minute purchases, just so they could play it, infinitely. FOX News, not to be outdone, devoted whole segments to the visit. Replaying, in myriad detail, the visit, the comments, various experts free to extrapolate all kinds of wacky explanations for why she did what she did.

One would have thought she had robbed a bank. Or blown her head off.

Buck was all over it, venting that "permissive attitudes" like hers about Muslim terrorists were "downright dangerous" and "this is what happens when you let a girl play with matches!"

Connor joined in, declaring that he was proud never to have entered a mosque. That he wasn't about to start now. "It's clear that my opponent is afraid to cross ideas with me in honorable debate for the future of this great nation. She's running, hiding behind such empty parlor tricks."

Their polling gap widened. The following weeks revealed it for all to see. Now she was trailing him by ten points, 55 to 45. The battleground state polls were not quite in agreement. But, then, they never were. All the pros cared about, however, was that, largely, the swing state polls were hovering around the same ratio of 55/45. It was looking grim.

While the World Council of Churches praised her actions at the mosque, not to mention her statements, her team began to see the whole affair as presaging the end, summarized in one word: Dearborn.

Levi was apoplectic. Not around her, of course. She heard about his raging infernos from others.

Perhaps not surprisingly, donors began pulling back from their commitments, diverting their money to Senate and House races.

Which triggered Foster's wit. "It's so dry now that Baptists are sprinkling, Methodists spitting, and Catholics handing out rain checks," he joked. Then, too, "It's Armageddon in the fruit cellar when your friends send postcards from three states over."

Warren looked drawn to the point of breaking.

Malcolm began serving her a small single malt, followed by a large chamomile tea each night, standing by her bed, chatting nervously about the weather and Broadway musicals until she drank it all.

Only Beatie seemed happy. Oddly happy. Serene.

One afternoon, tiring of everyone's angst, she decided to take in the blooms of the Rose Garden. Its height, of course, had occurred in June. She seemed to have missed it this year. She might have walked through its delightfully fragrant pathways, but her mind had clearly been somewhere else. Now, in late September, the Election just over a month away, the gems of the garden were the soft pinks and peaches, the gentle whites of chrysanthemums. Adorned by the sweet purples and blues of flowering kale. Those would stay with her for quite a while she knew.

Not that she would have many chances to visit the Rose Garden in the future. This visit – sobering thought – might well prove one of her last.

The ten-point gap was truly difficult to swallow, mostly because it was a self-inflicted wound. One of pique, not of planning. Of carelessness, not of calculation. She had brought it

on herself. And her staff was extremely disgusted with her for
doing so. She should have known better, they told themselves.

She wondered about that.

What price an Oval Office? Denying good Americans their
place at the table simply because they look, they sound different?

Or, worse, becoming the agent provocateur who separates
them out? Setting them aside into their own cultural
concentration camp. Shoot, why not just shut them up in a
modern-day Manzanar, like the Japanese Americans of World
War II?

She knew Connor was guilty of that. She was growing to
despise him and his choices. His daily actions that showed just
how low he was willing to go to gain an Oval Office.

He reminded her of America's villains. The turncoats. For, as
much as she loved her country, as much as she esteemed the
country's heroes, she took time to study its scoundrels.

Aaron Burr. A machine politician – before the name had been
invented – of New York City. Jefferson's veep in the race
against John Adams. At the time, the Constitution stipulated that
the guy with the most votes won the presidency. Jefferson's
supporters were worried that no one would vote for Burr – only
on the ticket to convey some sort of national feeling – because
even then, he was widely considered a knave. Well, their
fieldwork had proven excellent, as everyone who voted for
Jefferson also conscientiously voted for Burr. Thus, they tied,
the two top vote-getters in that election, with Adams and his

veep left in the dust. While everyone assumed Burr would do the honorable thing and step back in favor of Jefferson, the enterprising New Yorker merely claimed that "the People have spoken." Driving everyone mad with fury. The resulting election between Jefferson and Burr was then thrown into the House of Representatives where, in a moment of extreme electoral irony, Adams supporters had to hold their nose voting for Jefferson. Anything was better than Burr.

Who happily went on to serve as veep. Then got into his infamous duel with Alexander Hamilton on a ledge twenty paces long above the Hudson River at Deas' Point, New Jersey. Which effectively ended his political career.

To what did his entrepreneurial eye turn next? Why, starting his own country! Shortly after the Louisiana Purchase, he assembled his own private army, moved to the Southwest (of those days), and laid plans to separate out the great port New Orleans from the new nation, cobbled together with lands in Texas that would do nicely for his own kingdom. Andrew Jackson and a number of other US military officers stood by ready to help. Nevertheless, betrayed in the end, Jefferson had him arrested and tried for treason. While Burr escaped conviction, he fled thereafter to Europe.

A second villain that she was thinking of today was Clement Vallandigham, Lincoln's bête noire, though Toni knew few had heard of him. An Ohio Democrat, he started off simply enough, as one of the first Copperhead leaders – Democrats who favored peace at any price during the Civil War, including the resumption of slavery or, even, letting the southern states go their own way. The carnage at Fredericksburg moved him to take it up a notch. He mounted a stage in a small town in Ohio and delivered a fiery speech a few months later in which he demanded 'King Lincoln' be removed from the presidency and declared that the war – being fought to free Blacks and enslave Whites – be brought to an end, saying that "defeat, debt, taxation, sepulchers, there are your trophies."

His inflammatory speech, and he, might have ended as historical footnotes, except that the local military governor, Burnside (coincidentally responsible for that carnage at Fredericksburg), ham-handedly threw him in jail for sedition. At a stroke, Vallandigham became a national hero to anyone fed up with the war. New York City's mayor proudly took up his cause, no small potato given that the new military draft laws were wildly unpopular and could easily, and did that summer, lead to riots in Manhattan. Vallandigham's plight soon became one of the first test cases before the Supreme Court, questioning whether a President truly had the power to suspend habeas corpus – one of the few black marks attributed to Lincoln during the war years. As Lincoln put it in a letter to Vallandigham's supporters...

Must I shoot a simple-minded soldier boy who deserts, while I must not touch a hair of the wily agitator who induces him to desert?

In any case, exasperated beyond endurance and certainly not wanting to turn Vallandigham into a martyr, Lincoln commuted his sentence and had him escorted to the front lines. Which seriously freaked out Jefferson Davis who recognized a shyster on sight who would provoke a rebellion within the Rebellion within the week. Davis promptly had him thrown in jail until he could figure out what to do with him, eventually sending him north to Canada.

Where Vallandigham rested. Ran unsuccessfully for Governor of Ohio (in absentia). Then, realizing that Lincoln would not move against him, he cheerfully came south just in time for the 1864 Democratic National Convention. Where he hammered out a peace at any price plank to the party platform that even the party nominee – retired General George McClellan – rejected outright.

Shortly afterward, it became known that this self-proclaimed patriot of the Union had also spent his time in Canada laying plans with the Knights of the Golden Circle – a secret society complete with a secret handshake – to split off the northwestern states (of those days) – Aaron Burr style – and create a new country, with himself as President, no doubt. Broken by the revelations, he retired into obscurity – also Aaron Burr style – and died shortly thereafter.

A third villain on her mind – because of Connor's magnetism – was a rogue of a different sort. Father Coughlin, a Catholic priest in Detroit, of all places, was one of the first radio personalities. He began, admirably, standing up to the Ku Klux Klan that had resurfaced as the dire grip of the Great Depression began to take hold of the country in the 1930s and simple people began looking for scapegoats to blame for their suffering. From there, having discovered his talent, and his audience, Coughlin went on to become a champion of social justice. Indeed, the newspaper he soon founded was titled just that, *Social Justice*. He was one of the first to support FDR and the New Deal. He lent his growing radio audience, national now, and his growing newspaper, also national, to the cause. He was ascendant. Then, just as Burr and Vallandigham were seduced by the power of their own feverish dreams, celebrating themselves as the arbiter of all things, Coughlin went awry. He decided that FDR wasn't going far enough in fighting for social justice. His radio addresses became more strident. More martial in tone. More pugilistic. He convinced himself that the true evils of the age, oddly, were Joe Stalin and Communists worldwide, aided and abetted by the treacherous Jews, and that the President was being duped by them all. It was only one or two steps further looking for another leader to anoint as the new Messiah. He embraced Hitler, then Mussolini, and Tojo. After Pearl Harbor, this was going too far. All too soon, Coughlin ended up where he had begun, a simple parish priest just outside Detroit without a radio license or a newspaper to carry his views to the nation.

Toni knew the country's villains, these and others. She didn't believe for a second that Connor was one of them. Even as, she had to admit, all had started off at a very different place before growing drunk with their own brilliance, their own ambitions.

Nevertheless, as she contemplated her ten point gap in the polls, what fascinated her was not the villains but their followers. For, as each rogue had turned from fighting for the Cause (whatever it was at the time) to fighting for his own Castle (as it were), his followers were left with a choice. Did they follow? Even when the new cause, the Castle, seemed entirely at odds with what had attracted them to their leader in the first place?

That they did so was historical fact. Most, if not almost all, of their supporters made the leap with them. How? Did they turn off their minds? Did they cease all critical thinking?

Take Connor. A Silicon Valley self-made billionaire. Which was truly impressive all on its own. How many – in the history of the nation – could claim such a feat? Few.

Why not run on that, then? Well, there you have it. Politics had their say, too. For reasons that she still didn't really understand, he had decided to run as a Republican. Indeed, a New Republican (at least in the early days before gaining his party's nomination) who could bridge the gap between Democrat and Republican. Who could be President for all Americans. Thus, the rhetoric. In the early days.

But then, he had gotten the nod. What had happened? The 21st century big tent GOP was split hopelessly between Wall

Street bankers (Connor's natural home) and Main Street Evangelicals. That Raines had brought on a conservative Christian in Buck Jones to balance his ticket, she had been wholly expecting. Anybody could have predicted that. She had done precisely the same in her own way with Bobby and unions.

But, that Connor himself had decided to embrace that same folksy, rural, Bible-thumping persona (at least to a degree) had taken her completely by surprise.

Why? Had internal polling told him that he needed to?

It was so odd.

Even more surreal was the fact that his supporters – and if enviros were her bedrock, Evangelicals were his – had completely whitewashed his past of any of his playboy, cocaine-snorting, party-all-night, hang with the rockers, fuck your way through the groupies because you can days. Anybody who had known him these last decades knew that Connor was work hard, play hard. This new, shrink-wrapped Connor had the second part completely deleted.

Fair enough. She had problems with her own Billy the Kid persona.

But his followers? The fact that they willingly tuned it out? That everything about his life right up to the moment that he had gotten the nomination was in direct opposition to everything that they stood for, everything that they fought for, everything they taught their children to hold dear. And they simply ignored that. As if they had turned off the critical thinking part of their brains.

Did they approach buying a new car in the same way? Oh, the salesman says such and such, so it must be true. Of course not. Or, even more importantly, how did they approach buying a house? Or choosing the right school for their children? Well, the real estate agent says it's just fine, so…

Of course not. Nobody would. That was insane.

With Connor they did.

Hell, what did they do about the weather, she wondered? Did they look outside the window for themselves, or did they turn off their brains and ask Connor whether it was raining? It amounted to the same thing.

Unless they didn't practice what they – often all too loudly – proclaimed.

Apparently, heated rhetoric notwithstanding, choosing the next President was nowhere near as important a choice as which church they attended. Or nursing home they trusted with their parents. Or what hedge funds they trusted with their retirement. Or any of a sundry of mundane, yet vital, choices made in a lifetime.

Fingering a fading bloom, she wondered if she were simply missing the point. Somewhere.

Perky's voice floated into her mind. *The threat that your dark skin, your boobs present to them.*

Her eye caught Merry, one of Rod's best, standing near the wall of the colonnade where Rod usually was. Odd. Meredith, a black man, was a former running back for UCLA who had spent years with the FBI. Beatie, loving his fine biceps and backside, had told her that he still taught Criminal Justice part-time at Georgetown.

She had no doubt that Merry would take a bullet for the President. Whatever the skin color.

Nevertheless, could it be as simple as that?

Ten years of politics had taught her that identity trounced issues. And why not? Issues were complex. They changed daily. Unless you were getting paid to follow their labyrinth-like evolutions, sometimes even if you were, political questions got mind-numbingly complex. That's why leaders had staff. It was impossible to do the job otherwise.

Identity was all. For some. *He's my guy! He's just like me.*

What if your candidate pretended to be who he was not?

What would it take for you to overlook that falsehood? That deception?

Slowly the answer appeared. Shocking. Yet, all too familiar.

What would it take to look past the lie?

The knowledge that the alternative was so much worse.

***

It was cold. She saw her breath. Foggy. The kind that seeped into your bones. Dark. Overhead a cloudy sky, no stars. She could see a darker shape looming ahead out of the black wetness.

Wet. She was at sea.

What?!

She heard cackling.

Beatie's cackling. God, she hated that sound.

It was unearthly, scary. Frightening. Like her friend had become a ghoul of some sort.

She heard a ghostly bell tolling. Not a large one, a small one. Like those used to call the watch on...

She was on a man-of-war. Looking up, she spotted now the sails, neatly coiled about their booms overhead. Just the top ones – top gallants? – were hanging down – sheeted home? – catching what little breeze there was. Like Old Ironsides, the USS Constitution of War of 1812 fame, that she had seen once visiting Boston, on whose deck she had walked. Imagining the old days when the Royal Navy had ruled the world's waterways in that era of wood and canvas sailing. Until the iron and coal days had bankrupted their might. And turned that weighty responsibility over, much to his glee, to T-Rex and his Great White Fleet.

The United States Navy had the charge now.

And she was its Commander-in-Chief.

Beatie was cackling again, overhead, making the hairs rise on the back of her neck. Dammit! Toni looked up. She couldn't see her strategist. Or maybe there she was. A lump, a frumpy lump, way, way up the mainmast, sitting on the cross-trees. Muttering to herself.

Looking down, Toni again saw that looming darkness ahead, over the waters. On the right. Threatening. The closer they got, the larger it towered over the sea. What was it?

It couldn't be an iceberg. Could it? And now there was another on the left. Closing them in.

Beatie was speaking aloud now. Maybe? Moaning. Sighing. What was she saying?

Then suddenly shrieking.

"There it is! I done told you, bitch! I done told you!"

Great. Back to bitch, again.

Well, of course it was there. They were there. She could see them herself.

They were huge. Icy. Frightening. Their mountains unforgiving. Their boulders pitiless. Their jagged edges, stretching out into the water, on both flanks, only too eager to pierce the sides of her ship. Severe. Heartless. Uncaring. The icy death they represented remorselessly cruel.

And her ship was headed straight for them.

Do something!

She was the Commander-in-Chief. Order somebody! Where were the Joint Chiefs!?

Don't panic, she chided herself. Calm. Take stock.

Her ship was stout. That was right. It was named Old Ironsides for a reason. It was an heroic ship. It had taken on the best shellacking that the Royal Navy had had to offer back then and come out just fine. Even better than fine.

They were okay.

But where the hell was her crew?

What kind of Commander-in-Chief didn't have a crew?!

She looked down and saw the spokes of the wheel between her fingers. Christ! She wasn't the C-in-C. She was the pilot.

Seeing the glittering letters painted onto the wheel – USS New Tomorrow. Oh, fuck! This wasn't Old Ironsides.

This was the Ship of State. And she was plowing it straight into a pair of icebergs!

She heaved on the wheel. It didn't move. Frozen.

Beatie's cackles, her harshly rasping guffaws, were growing louder now. Terrifying Toni.

"Do something!" she cried, her voice breaking.

"Why?" her would-be friend was asking, incredulous.

"Why?!"

"Bitch, don't you see it?"

"YES, I fucking see them, now...!"

Panic was making it difficult to speak. The icebergs were almost upon them, forming a wall of death. Together. No escape. Coming to claim them.

She abruptly found her voice. "You're my crew, dammit, so get your fat ass down here and...!"

"There!" Beatie whooped, pointing. "I done told you! There she is! Just like I said!"

Frantic to the point of freezing herself, Toni watched in horror as her friend pointed out a fissure that was now appearing between the two menaces.

***

Deciding that enough was enough, upon waking, Toni resolved to ask her friend what her plan was.

It was a bucolic autumn day, early October. The sun coming through the lunette, softer. Gentler. The election itself, a mere four weeks away. The debates, as yet, unsettled. Connor's campaign had dallied, objected, obfuscated for weeks about the Dearborn moment. Using her mosque challenge as an excuse.

And why not? He was ahead. She was behind. She needed the debates. He did not.

All he had to do at this point was play it safe and the Oval would be his. Like a prudent QB taking a knee the last few plays of a winning game, running out the clock. The fans might be disgusted, but a win was a win. The fans would forget by the next game anyway.

This election was over.

Or?

Beatie was reaching down to pluck up one of her namesake cakes. Eagerly snatching a large bite with her hungry teeth.

Malcolm was pouring Toni a cup of coffee. She waited until he had finished, then laying a hand on his arm, she merely asked, "A moment."

He had nodded, nervously.

She looked down the hall and saw Merry. Again. No Rod. Vacation? It must be. He certainly deserved it. She wondered if she could ask Warren. She shook her head. Unseemly.

She refocused.

On her friend.

"Tell me."

Beatie swallowed. That same Cheshire cat grin suffusing her cheeks. The cat who had just swallowed the canary. This cat, however, had a streak of milky sugared cream at the corner of her lips, not the proverbial yellow feather.

"Stacy Halpers, 21. Erickson House, a private clinic for the silver-spooned in the Fillmore District of San Fran. A stone's throw from Grace Cathedral. January 21st, 10 am, five years ago. Here's the photo from security tapes. Cost a pretty penny."

Toni found herself choking on her fury. "This is your plan?!"

"Hold on, bitch."

"No. We are not doing this."

"Ratfucker pretends to be what he ain't. Well, all those Evangels going to have make up they minds, now ain't they?"

"No."

"Listen, bitch. We be past the point of – !"

"NO!" She was up, running. Where? How the hell should she know? Where did one run? How did one hide when one is the President of the United States?

She stopped. She was at the east lunette. The companion to hers at the opposite end of the White House. Merry was right at her shoulder, barely breathing. Like Rod would have been. Barely breathing.

She was panting.

"Where's Rod?" she heard her voice. Curt.

"Madam President, I am instructed to direct your query to your chief of staff."

She turned to look at him. And saw his eyes falter, then look away. Back to Praetorian. Checking the perimeter.

Of course.

Men. Their goddamn egos. So fucking fragile.

Beatie was coming to her. Slowly. Panting herself.

Toni smiled. What else could she do?

Her strategist sat opposite her.

Before long, Malcom had appeared with a tray of fresh coffee, fresh cakes for Beatie. This time, not willing to leave.

"Bitch, they won't debate you."

Whatever.

Wow. It was just hitting her.

For the first time since, well, whenever, there would be no presidential debate going into the election.

"Tell him he's a coward."

"Him?" Beatie beamed.

Fine.

"Tell the world."

And Beatie did. She huddled with Comms – within minutes – within the hour, news flashed all over the world, begun by Bobby, that Connor was too chicken to take a debate with the Blatina chica.

Day Two was the same. Beatie, Bobby, Levi, Foster and/or somebody, lined up a number of friends on Capitol Hill who questioned the historicity of a challenger to an incumbent not consenting to a single debate. Would the mandate of the winner be legitimate?

Day Three was the same, with a new spin. Someone, somewhere had found a flaccid stalk of celery costume. Maybe it was from a health store. Maybe it was a celery costume that somebody had adapted to look flaccid. Either way. It made its appearance at a Connor rally – wearing a sign that said "Limp Stalk" – a video of which quickly went viral. All over the world.

Day Four saw thirty such Limp Stalk costumes around the country at various rallies. Buck even tried to punch one. He couldn't help himself. Maybe. The camera shot was inconclusive. Nevertheless, a Buck Makes War on Limp Stalk meme took hold among pundits just dying to have something to talk about now that the election was well nigh decided. Endless speculation about what a vigorous Raines foreign policy would look like, how aggressive, how collaborative, where permissive, if at all, and other questions in that vein.

Which triggered a round of comedians asking the question of just what Buck was compensating for. After all, they, too, were just dying for new material now that the election was a done deal. Several featured a cage match between actors playing Buck and Limp Stalk.

The meme dominated the news for several days, almost a week.

Which triggered a new round of process stories – presumably set by Beatie since it had her scent all over them – about just how incompetent a Raines administration would prove. After all, they lost control of several news cycles during the campaign. Wait until they were governing.

It went on and on. Toni was beginning to think it was going to extend into a second week. Until Connor called, ending it. They had their debate. Just one.

The Commission on Presidential Debates called, asking that, given the late notice, the debate be held at Hofstra University on Long Island, scene of many past presidential debates. Apparently, they had a good system in place there – particularly when it came to logistics and security for the candidates.

Somebody agreed.

The debate was set for the last Wednesday in October. Around ten days before the election. Toni could hardly have cared less.

She had a bigger fight on her mind.

***

She cornered Warren in his lair.

From the look on his face when she entered, he knew what was coming. He looked down at his desk for a long moment. He appeared old. Exhausted.

He spoke. "He asked to be transferred, Madam President."

What?! She inwardly raged. Did everyone in this goddamn fishbowl know that she dreamed about fucking him?!

Nevertheless, she smiled. "I see."

Warren's secretary stepped in, apologizing, set some papers on his desk then fled.

"Where?"

His eyes snapped to hers. "Rowley. He said that he wanted to retool."

"Retool."

They looked at each for a very long moment.

His hands started reaching upward in helplessness. "Ma'am...!'

"Don't bother." She turned to leave.

"Ma'am, please! He only left when he was certain that..."

She turned back, very slowly.

Waiting.

Warren sighed, giving in. "When he was certain that 3G was a myth. Just good old boys talking big on barstools. He said."

"3G?"

Warren paused again, surveying her face. Not liking what he was seeing there.

"Warren, we can do this all day if – "

3G was shorthand for Garnet Gap Guerillas. After the assault on the compound, the FBI had watched chat sites very carefully for weeks, looking for signs of resurgence. There was nothing. Finally, just before the Paris Summit in June, they found the first indications that someone, going by the codename of Red Wolf, was starting up a group of like-minded souls in Eastern Washington State to take revenge on the Black Jezebel for the massacre. The FBI had informed the Secret Service immediately, of course. Security was tightened a few notches until more intel could be gathered.

Toni had a brief memory of the Irish pub in Montmartre. Rod's exasperation with her. She felt a flicker of shame, but cast it aside.

"And?"

They had kept tabs. There had been a lot of chatter just before the Convention which was expected since everybody in the world knew where the President would be on that fourth night. They had pulled in several suspects over the course of the Convention. Quietly. But it all led to nothing.

The interrogations took time. Lawyers had pressed their suits, freeing the suspects, one by one. It had largely been a frustrating affair. Even attempts to infiltrate the 3G had failed, four times. It was shortly after her return from...

"Dearborn." She said it.

"Yes, ma'am. That they realized that it was nothing more than a few boozers in a bar. More or less. A compound or two. But barely worthy of the name, other than to talk smack, Roderick said, and shoot paintball. Dreaming delusions that they would never truly attempt. 3G suddenly became three guys. Or so the joke went."

It was shortly after that that he had requested transfer, been denied, requested again, then was accepted. Then the final weeks were spent evaluating his replacement options. He had chosen Merry.

"Ma'am, I want to assure you, Meredith has Agent Bergen's and my highest – "

"I get it."

She stalked out.

Briskly walked the colonnade back to the White House, went upstairs and cried.

The Child. The One Who Got Away.

Guess even Leaders Of The Free World don't get the guy, now do they?

***

They were using the press briefing room for debate prep. After the Comms team had cleared it, of course.

She played along, even though she hated it. Nothing ever really prepared a candidate for debate. Not that she had had a great deal of experience at it. Her one debate as veep candidate had been far more a genteel roundtable discussion than anything else. Apparently Hap's boys had thought she couldn't handle any more than that.

No, she just remembered from her courtroom days. She might pace back and forth at her apartment rehearsing her lines the night before a case or, after Artie had died, at Mama's. Yes, it helped. Of course, it did. But there was nothing like the thrill of crossing verbal swords in the wink of an eye with an opposing attorney in front of a judge.

In any case, she played along. Foster was playing the role of Connor. And, true to form, as soon as he realized that Madam President's heart wasn't in it, the Rhodes scholar got tucked away in favor of the Texan.

It had been during a hit question. Connor's software firm That Moment had had to let a vice president go recently because of charges of malfeasance. The point being, of course, given that Connor had hired a guy who turned out to be a crook, how honest could the nation expect his cabinet to be?

Toni had braced herself for a long diatribe how personally let down her opponent had felt, how he had trusted the man, yet, when presented with the evidence, he had moved immediately to have him fired.

Foster merely crowed in a magnified twang, "Listen, my guy? He's so honest Girl Scouts give him their cookie money for safekeeping!" Which had broken them all up into laughter.

Except for Beatie. Who scowled. As she had been for days.

Later, during another hit question about whether Buck's "assaulting" the Limp Stalk had cost him in confidence at all in the eyes of her opponent – her Texan had cried, "Buck's so brave he'd charge Hell with a bucket of ice water!"

More laughter. From Beatie, more scowling.

Then, a bitter question from her strategist about whether they'd still be laughing in three days when they got their asses kicked.

Toni had raised her hand, looked straight at her friend. "I'm not doing it."

"Bitch! I done told you! We be past that point!"

The room had gone still. Everyone, frozen in place, in time.

"Find another way!"

"What way, bitch?"

Toni struggled to find the words.

"This ain't no campaign about issues. He done made sure of that!"

Toni crossed her arms.

"Ratfucker's goin' all MLK on ya! Claiming that it's about character, not the color of anybody's skin. Except he ain't!"

279

Now is he? No, with every one of his fucked up stories, it's all nudge, nudge, wink, wink. It's all Norman Rockwell bullshit with a bunch of Whities sitting around the turkey. They the only ones who belong around that table. Certainly no Blatina bitch pretending to be President be welcome!"

Foster raised a hand.

"Shut the fuck up!" Beatie shouted him down. "You don't get it, do you? None of ya!" She flung a stack of papers up at the ceiling. "This debate is it! We expose him for the ratfucker he is or we pack up!"

The last papers were just settling on the ground all around them. Like shrapnel.

"Then get me anecdotes about him in his youth. What he was really like. In his playboy days."

Beatie snorted. "Won't work, bitch. His Evangels will just croon that he changed when he met Jesus."

The room breathed. A moment. Then, two.

"I'm not...using...her."

Her strategist chuffed. "Her?! That what you worried about?! Cracker bitch'll have a modeling contract before the debate's finished."

Toni stared in disbelief at her friend. Not seeing her. Seeing the warped mind that she had become.

What price an Oval Office?

"Not by my hand. Find another way."

Yes, Madam President.

***

Two sleepless nights later and Warren was escorting her out to Marine One. Beatie and Foster were waiting on the steps.

Both looked pinched, haggard. Particularly Beatie. She hadn't seen her chief strategist since the blowup during what turned out to be their last debate prep session. Well, it wasn't like this debate was going to turn on the issues, anyway.

Beatie looked her in the eye, then glanced away.

One great thing about Beatie, after she had had her say about the trainwreck that was impending, she stopped bitching, sat down and buckled up for the ride. It was one of the many reasons that – difficult as it honestly was to work with her all these years – Toni had never split with her.

Warren was starting to look skeletal.

She thought about ordering him to let Malcolm stuff him, worry over him, spoil him a bit. Then, rethought it. She honestly wasn't certain how her patrician chief of staff would handle a gay man clucking over him.

"Last words?" The helo's blades were starting to whirl, a sign that they were running late. Beatie's head was already ducking down, even if she was on the steps. Another good sign. Toni had once explained to her that because the blades are flexible, the wind sometimes made them bend down. It was rare to bend that far down, but ever since, Beatie had bent over almost double if entering a bird when the blades were whirling.

Warren was watching the blades turn.

"Madam President, do you mind if I quote a Republican?"

She giggled. It felt nice. "Please do."

"You can fool all the people some of the time, some of the people all the time, but you cannot fool all the people all the time."

Ah. Lincoln.

"Ma'am. He's not right for this nation, and he never will be. Find that tonight, ma'am. Explain it to the people."

Entering the helicopter, she walked up to Merry. "I need to talk with Rod."

His mouth dropped open in confusion.

"No, I'm *not* messing with your procedures. You lead this team. Nevertheless, I need to talk with Rod. Now."

Yes, Madam President.

***

The James J Rowley Training Center – the Secret Service's Quantico – was tucked away in the forests of Maryland, just a few clicks northeast of DC. Marine One made it there in minutes.

Rod was waiting at the helipad, wearing heavily stained sweats and sneakers. He looked like he had just come off an obstacle course. He also looked better. Fitter, more heavily muscled. More relaxed, except around the eyes.

"Madam President."

"Walk with me."

He did.

She led them far enough away from the helo that she could see the details in the leaves of some nearby trees. She wasn't hoping for birdsong. She knew better. Not with a massive helo making them all dive for cover as if it were a falcon looking for its dinner.

"How's the retooling coming?"

He blushed. His eyes flickered away, almost. Then came right back to hers.

God, she missed the sight of those liquid gray eyes. She turned slightly away from them.

"Madam President...I..."

"I have a question that I need to ask you. That I need to ask someone who takes a bullet..."

She paused. Slowed down. She wanted to get this right.

"Someone who trains continuously for that day that hopefully may never come."

He nodded. His brow furrowed. Drops of sweat beading it. From his obstacle course? Had to be. He was never nervous enough around her to actually sweat. She had to restrain her hand. She wanted to wipe away those drops so badly.

"Someone that I trust."

He nodded again.

"If you came across intel that the President was lying to the American people, would that impact your mission?"

Without hesitating, he replied. "No, ma'am."

"Why not?"

"That's the job." His answer came just as briskly.

She nodded, thoughtfully.

"Ma'am?"

She quickly raised her hand to stop him then, realizing whom she had done that to, she closed it in a gentle fist and slowly lowered it.

His eyes widened.

"Ma'am, what...? Is Merry...?"

"Merry is everything he should be," she replied, firmly. "I wasn't surprised in the slightest at his quality. I knew that you would be very careful with my security."

He stiffened to attention. "Thank you, Madam President."

She briefly considered teasing him with the thought that "a goodbye would have been nice" but tossed that out almost as quickly as the thought had formed.

"What if the lie entailed the President misrepresenting...himself...as a person...to the American people?"

"No change, ma'am. It's the job."

Now they were at the crux.

She turned to face him. To face those gray eyes full on.

"What would you think of him, personally?"

For the first time, he was hesitating.

"I...Ma'am?"

"Would you be disgusted?"

His eyebrow flicked.

She lowered her voice, made it gentler. "Why?"

He looked away. She saw his jaw working. Boy, did she miss provoking *that* reaction in him! She shushed that thought. And waited.

Finally, he looked back at her. "Because...well...ma'am..."

"Because?"

He abruptly firmed up. "Because he's the President."

***

She guilted him into coming along, of course. She knew that she would. Swore up and down that it was "a girl thing" which she immediately regretted because it positively alarmed him.

Then, instead, she lied through her teeth. Said that Warren had asked what she needed to deliver her best debate performance tonight and that she immediately had responded, "Rod at my shoulder" surprising them both. She was guessing that it was merely a habit.

Rod had nodded, then disappeared. It had to be the fastest shower and dressing job she had ever witnessed. There he was, bounding up the steps just like old times. A handful of mano-a-mano words between him and Merry and both looked satisfied.

Men.

One would think that they could have fought over her, at least a little.

The flight up to NYC was uneventful. She felt happy, at peace. Martin Luther's words came back to her, just as he went into his darkest days...

Hier stehe Ich. Ich kann nicht anders.

Here I stand. I can do no other.

Foster cued off her, claiming that he felt like he "had a thumping ol' Christmas ham all to himself!" Even Beatie was looking more tranquil.

Maybe Rod *was* lucky for them all.

The drive over was equally undisturbed. There were the usual security procedures. She wouldn't exit out front. The SUV convoy was taking a roundabout way in the back end of the campus to drop her at the service entrance of the building's rear. Yet one more walk through another kitchen or loading dock or storerooms or whatever. She always had the disconcerting thought that all those action adventure movies with assassinations or bombs going off – or not going off, since the muscular Rod-like hero swooped in at the end to defuse everything – none of it captured the mundane, prosaic boredom of being a chief executive transported to her next gig.

As always, her mind skipped free and she focused on the people. The crowds were already lining the sidewalks in advance. Even at the back of the campus. Walking along, chatting, looking excited, expectant. It was a nice evening. A hunter's moon was just beginning to make its presence known. A great night for a stroll. A night out with friends. To take in a show. Or a dinner. Or drinks. Or all three. Fun. This election might already be over, but the happy people she saw certainly hadn't gotten the memo.

All too soon the convoy was stopping, she was out, and Merry was leading her through various poorly lit, dusty hallways to a modified green room.

Where she sat. And waited.

And thought happy thoughts. Rod was at her shoulder.

When did she get so girly?

And then it was time.

***

The lights were dazzling. On the eyes. She couldn't see beyond the moderator, Frank Hobart, a journalist and pundit of the old school, sitting at his desk, facing them at their podiums.

Connor looked much the same. Fighting trim. His hair, that gorgeous mane of white, sat on his head like a florid crown. Or maybe a rococo one.

She used to think him handsome. Maybe that was before she had learned about his hush money payment to a twenty-one year old.

She growled. Or maybe it was before he began using her as a pinup girl for terrorists the world over.

Either way, not attractive. Just pathetic.

He was gleaming. Looking attractive in his dark blue suit, with its bright red and white and blue tie. A signal, like so much of him. Symbology. Let other GOPers wear their red ties, their red pantsuits. He was a President for both parties, for all Americans. Just look at the polling.

Connor was sagely nodding along with the moderator's welcoming speech, his explanation of the rules, his reminder to set all cellphones to vibrate, his admonition not to applaud or cry out during the debate, his welcome to the audience to applaud both candidates now, this one time.

It was glorious. She was singing inside. She remembered this tune. She hadn't heard it in a very long time. Not since the days of her first Congressional win. Or before that, of going after Reyes Latino. She was singing the song of the happy warrior. Who delights in battle itself.

The moderator was flipping a coin. The first question was to go to her.

He was asking her about her cap and trade bill.

She cut him off, assuring him that she would be delighted to talk cap and trade and saving the planet for our grandchildren, but first...

"We have had such a splendid campaign these last months. Not to get all girly on anyone, but I can't help but feel a bit sentimental now that it's coming to an end. If Connor has his way, I'll be returning to my hometown soon, Albuquerque."

She turned to him, saw his "well, shucks" smile adorning his cheeks.

Feeling the glint coming into her eye, she made her smile even broader. "And if I have mine, he'll be returning to his hometown of San Francisco. So, Frank, before we jump into the fray, how about if we each take a human moment and say hello to our respective hometowns?"

Without waiting for his answer, she smiled straight into the camera.

"I wanted to say a big hello to Albuquerque, home of the best Tex-Mex I have been able to find on this planet. Home of all those hardy prosecutors who helped me make war on the Reyes Latino, breaking that street gang that was trying to enslave the city and sell their drugs to our children, breaking it all to pieces. Hello ABQ, I miss you!" And she waved for effect.

The moderator, chuckling, was turning to Connor. "Mr. Raines?"

Who paused a moment. Smiled that gorgeous smile. Then, a bit stiffly began, "Well, Frank, I believe I stand here for all Americans—"

She pounced. "What? And not say hello to San Francisco? Connor! That's not nice. I mean, I get it. Some might say that San Francisco is too liberalized. And maybe it's party all night attitude goes a bit too far at times. You would know, right? I mean, the stories."

Frank was cutting in. "Madam President."

She overrode him. "But to turn your back on all your grunge band, peacenik, LGBT friends? Don't you want to say hello to them?"

She smiled.

Waiting.

He was running his hand through his hair. She had rattled him, that was certain.

Frank prodded him. "Mr. Raines, did you have a hello for your hometown? For San Francisco?"

Connor smiled back. A tight smile.

"Hello to the Golden City! And, maybe my opponent is right, San Francisco can be a little liberalized at times. Yet I am proud to be from there. I am even prouder to have met so many of this great country. This nation that inspires me to be a President for all Americans."

"Not just the White ones?" She cut in with a grin.

Connor looked to the moderator. His hands turning up in a gesture of "What gives?"

Who took his cue. "Madam President, I'm going to have to ask you—"

Who cut right in. "Of course, Frank, of course. I'm just so excited to finally have a debate with Connor. He does say all the time, practically quoting Dr. King from memory – it's not about the color of my skin—"

Someone in the audience gasped.

"—it's about character. So what does it say about a man who turns on his hometown friends, refuses to recognize his gay and dyke friends with whom he snorted cocaine all night, night after night—"

Connor broke in, his voice raised. "I never—"

To have her take it right back. "The photos say otherwise." And almost winced – hoping that Beatie actually had some – before plunging on. "What does it say about a man who deserts his gay and dyke friends, refusing to recognize them publically when their sexuality stands between him and an Oval Office?"

Frank was gesturing, raising his voice. "Madam President! Please, you must—"

Connor was shouting. "That's not true. That's not me! I never!"

She pirouetted. "Never had gay friends?"

In the brief gap that ensued, she winked in the camera. "Well, when the going gets tough, I guess we know how long it'll take

Connor to dump" she mimicked his stentorian tones "all of
America."

"Frank, either this debate will follow rules, in a fair and
honorable fashion or…!"

"Madam President!"

"My bad!" she beamed.

Everyone paused. A moment. Connor was taking a sip of
water. She could see a slight tremor in his hand. Frank was
adjusting some papers on his desk, then clearing his throat.

"Mr. Raines, during your campaign, you have consistently
critiqued the current Medicare system. What changes would you
make to this program that cares for our elderly?"

She listened with one ear for Connor's measured, polished
response. Was not surprised in the slightest that it was heavy on
promises "to fix the broken system" and light on the specific
ways in which he intended to do it. That's all right. It was
Congress' job, anyway. The President could lead, could
cheerlead, could threaten, but it was their job, not his.

Asked the same question, she responded. "I'm sorry, I'm still
stuck on San Francisco."

She heard rather than saw Connor's chuff.

"If Connor won't defend his hometown, extolling its virtues, I
guess I'll have to. When it comes to healthcare, I think of the
Erickson House in the Fillmore neighborhood, just a stone's
throw from Grace Cathedral. Now some might say that it's a
private clinic, attending only to the secretive…" – and she

paused just a moment, not looking at him – "needs of the uber-wealthy, but, hey, I say that's what makes San Francisco great. They take care of the poor. They take care of the wealthy. Everybody needs a doctor at some point."

Frank was moving on. "Next quest—"

She zinged it. "Did you know that Erickson House is even open in January? *Late* January?"

She saw it. They all saw it. Connor broke, just for an instant. He swallowed nervously. Then again.

Then, he rallied. "Frank, I must insist—"

She cooed. "Of course, Connor, of course."

Frank was staring at her, incredulous.

So, her happy warrior in full swing, she went on. "Frank, could we take a break so Connor can lie down? The pressure's getting to—"

"That's enough!" Gone was the smiling, avuncular, everybody's favorite daddy, leading the family into a golden age. Connor looked angry, ugly angry.

She couldn't stop. "Or you'll punch me like Buck did Limp Stalk?"

Where was she going with all this? As Connor paused, frozen, in frustration, then turned his ire on the moderator, half of her mind asked herself. What was she doing? Showing off in front of Rod? She hoped not. Proving to Beatie that she could do it? Her way? Maybe.

A dream that she had had last night suddenly hit her. Just now remembering it.

They were on a mountaintop. Beatie next to her, surveying all the lands in sight, like some kind of mad Alexander the Great, plotting her next conquests.

Toni was exhausted, crying.

"Why's it so hard?"

"Bitch, what?"

"It used to be so quiet. So peaceful. Now it's so hard. So many struggles. So much pain."

Beatie had snorted. "That cuz you stopped being they doormat, Chica."

And that's when she saw it. She saw what she was after. No, she was not here to out him, and certainly not the girl.

Far from it.

She simply wanted him to know that she knew. And that she despised him for it.

Time to play nice for real.

And she did.

The rest of the debate proceeded amiably enough. It was, likely, her last public appearance. At least for a long time. She wondered what life would be like as ex-president. Maybe Beatie and she would open that ABQ coffee shop, after all.

With a clinic in the back? For girls on the street. Definitely a
domestic violence shelter. She couldn't see any less than that.
Maybe have anger management classes in the evenings for
Soldados?

Her mind tripped along. The debate went on all around her.
Connor was pontificating about getting the youth involved in
politics.

"Particularly twenty-one year old cute girls?"

She didn't say it. It was on the tip of her tongue. But she
didn't.

Instead, she saw herself visiting Freddie, maybe getting some
help from some sort of sister organization in London. Maybe
some sort of international domestic violence agency? Focused
on Africa and Latin America, since the numbers showed that
those areas of the globe specialized in domestic violence to the
point that it was practically institutionalized. Besides, as Mama
would say, she looked the part. A Blatina hell on wheels.

At some point, right at the end, when she was summing up,
making her last statement, she heard a flurry in the audience.
Several people seemed to be pulling out their cellphones, she
couldn't be sure. It was too difficult to see with the lights in her
eyes. Frank was talking with someone on his earpiece. Arguing.

Oh, well.

She finished up, thanking everyone for the chance to have
served them as their President. An honor she never dreamed
would lay within her grasp when young. Then, as if she could

hear Beatie's hiss in her ear, she went on to say, gamely, even if she didn't feel it, that she looked forward to serving them with honor four more years.

And that was it. The crowd was applauding. Connor's team was gesturing at him to get off the stage. She looked off left, saw that Rod and Merry were waiting for her, Foster holding her trench coat on his arm. She turned back to shake Connor's hand, but saw that he was leaving. She shook Frank's instead. He looked a bit frazzled. She thanked him for a wonderful debate, even kissed him on the cheek. Which frazzled him even more.

Out in front of the stage, the auditorium teemed with people, talking, chattering excitedly. Several were reading their phones. Probably looking for the early reviews. She wondered if she had "won." Did anybody win these debates? She looked longingly at them. The people. Her people. She wanted to join them.

And then she did it. She gave Rod a quizzical smile. Saw his "oh shit!" look, then bounded off the stage into the crowd.

Why not? She wasn't going to be President much longer anyway.

She was surrounded by outstretched hands, smiles, grins, beams. Red cheeks, blushing exhilaration, shyness, joy, excitement. Nobody saying anything other than the typical, "Hello, Madam President! Great debate, Madam President! I voted for you, Madam President! I'm going to vote for you!" And so on.

Rod appeared by magic at her shoulder. Merry was in front, his team surrounding them. Checking hands reaching out to her for guns, knives, machetes, dirty bombs. The usual drill.

Well, she sighed. She did get to have one moment of freedom. At least.

Merry was moving them along, out of the auditorium, into the lobby. Crowds thick, throngs, bottlenecks appearing that Merry sliced straight through, mobs, masses. Shouts, chatter, laughter. What a feeling!

Through the lobby, out the doors, the convoy approaching, half a moment away.

"Gun!"

Rod was diving in front of her. Something hit her shoulder like a brick, but she was already spinning, twirling, like a little girl doing a ballet, Rod's arm around her waist, throwing her in the SUV on the back seat.

Glass was shattering.

He was throwing himself on top of her.

Someone was firing a gun. Somebody should do something about that.

She heard someone throwing up, then realized it was herself. The SUV was charging through the streets, its lights and siren wailing out loud. Too loud.

She felt herself sliding off the seat from the harshness of a turn, just to feel Rod grab her and pull her back on it, under him.

She looked down and saw that there was blood on the floor.

What?! Her shoulder. She looked back and saw only a torn epaulette. Then she spotted it.

"You're bleeding!"

"Madam President! Stay down!" His hand went up to his neck.

"But you're bleeding!"

"We don't know what we're facing! Stay down!" He checked his hand, then put it back on his neck.

"But—"

"Toni, please. Just stay down."

More in shock from him using her name, at last, than anything else, she did as he ordered. She lay there. Watching blood pulse out from between his fingers, running down his wrist, to plop on the floor. One drop after another.

Her own pulse beating, not quite, in time.

Epilogue

It was a beautifully moving funeral. Everyone said so. She didn't trust herself with the eulogy. She asked Warren.

She met his wife. His two darling, ice cream blonde girls. If they hadn't been crying so hard, she would have hated them. She knew that she shouldn't. She couldn't help herself.

A rapid, and furious, investigation showed that far from being an ideologue like the supposed 3G guys, the assassin was an out of work coal miner whose wife had just left him, taking the kids with her. Blaming Toni's cap and trade idea for the layoffs at his mine, he had loaded his pickup and his AR15 to the gills and driven north to the one place he knew where she would be and when. The debate.

The fact that he managed to go through thirty some bullets had more to do with his high capacity magazine than anything else.

That, and he had jacked himself up on enough painkillers that he could sustain seventeen gunshot wounds, still firing, until an agent had finally shot him in the head, ending it.

The bullet that had creased Rod's artery and ended his life just before they reached the hospital had also torn her left epaulette. She didn't know what to make of that, other than to cry, Malcolm's hand on her shoulder.

Given the eccentricity of the assassin, the fact that she had not been hit, and the GOP's desire to talk about anything other than Connor's embarrassment, the House Oversight Committee declared hearings days later to inquire into whether the "assassination" was staged.

Which made a young woman in Manhattan so angry that she went out, bought a trench coat with epaulettes, just so she could rip the left one and wear it as her own private protest.

Within days, trench coats across the nation were sold out, torn epaulettes on left shoulders seen everywhere.

Perhaps not surprisingly, the enthusiasm gap among Democrats disappeared almost overnight.

At the same time, a Miss Halpers of San Francisco broke her non-disclosure agreement and began talking to the media because, as she put it, "the debate showed me that Connor was not someone I needed to fear, after all."

In any case, while the Evangelicals didn't publically break with Connor, they did stay home on Election Day in such large numbers that his lead dissolved right before his eyes.

In the Rose Garden, Toni planted a row of blue hyacinths. The groundskeeper helped her, every step of the way, explaining that the flower was recognized as a symbol of fidelity.

She smiled at them. Rod's blooms.

It was a bittersweet thought knowing she would be able to enjoy them for four years.

Toni's Smile
By Jeff Stilwell

Book Club Questions

What answer does Toni offer to her question asked at the beginning of the novel: What *is* left after we die?

This novel is primarily about power. What power dynamics do you detect? Which dynamics affect you most poignantly?

How do men use specific language and imagery to discredit Toni throughout the novel? How does she respond?

How do Toni's dreams inform the story line? What is your favorite dream of hers? Why?

How does Toni draw upon her childhood experiences to sustain her?

How do Toni's mental sojourns in the Rose Garden inform the story line?

How do Toni's fantasies regarding Rod sustain her?

During the debate, Toni dreams about life as ex-President, almost as if she is relieved. Do her musings reflect how she has changed over the course of the year? Explain.

How does Toni answer her own question: "What price an Oval Office?"

Does Toni win the election on her own account or because of the assassination attempt?

Throughout the story, Toni smiles at various points. Explore the reasons for her smiling, and whether those reasons change over time.

Author Bio

Jeff Stilwell excels at the unexpected. Not content with his Midwestern roots, he found ways on the cheap to explore the wider world including selling gummy bears in high school to visit the Alps of central Europe. To pay for college, he worked a slime line as a head chopper in the clammy tundra of Alaska.

His thirst for adventure next took him to Asia where he studied Asian philosophy and the martial arts while exploring exotic locales including the Himalayas and the lands of *Lord Jim*, even surviving a squall in the Gulf of Siam.

An abiding love of people throughout history, as well as his years in Asia deeply influenced his lifelong search for meaning, culminating later in his magnum opus - *Here and Now: A Whimsical Take On God*. In this illustrated work, his adorable cartoon character Thrashin' Jack leads the reader on the skateboard journey of humanity's creation of God. Readers find *Here and Now* "simple yet profound" and "something that can be read in minutes, and thought about for a lifetime."

In Asia, Stilwell also met and wooed his wife, jewelry designer Manya Vee, winning her heart by following her to Java. She taught him to gallop bareback at the family farm in the storied Yakima Valley, the inspiration for his first novel *Fighting for Eden* – where readers found "a heartfelt story" in which "one finds their own Eden and their own truth."

Ever restless, he once completed a solitary 750-mile hike from Stevens Pass in Western Washington to end, a Biblical-sounding forty days later, at Old Faithful Geyser in Yellowstone National Park.

These days, Stilwell lazily daydreams about a meadow of several billion flowers reaching up to the sun, each celebrating its distinctive hue, without a single groundskeeper choosing which is a weed. Sound like humanity? He thinks so, the cheeky sod.

If it's big, Stilwell has dreamt it, attempted it, or achieved it.

* * * * *

More Books by Jeff Stilwell

Fighting for Eden

Are your dreams worth fighting for?

Meet Jake. He wants to be a soldier hero. Meet Andrew. He's a Pacifist with a brilliant mind. How can they ever become friends?

Enter Jessie, Jake's little sister. She wants to run the family ranch – an impossibility in the patriarchal world of her rural home.

For Andrew and Jessie, their dreams don't fit in with the world they were born into.

Along comes Jake, the most unlikely of all people to understand Andrew. In addition to Andrew's brilliant mind, he is a Pacifist, while Jake is in ROTC and about to become a soldier. Somehow, these two opposites find a way to become friends.

Jake's tragic death in the opening days of the Iraq War leaves Jessie and Andrew reeling.

Jessie suddenly finds herself all alone in the fight to save their family cattle ranch, even as the patriarchy of the Valley seeks to crush her.

Andrew's questing mind is driven to the brink of madness as he seeks to balance his pacifist convictions with his friend's sacrifice. Andrew wrestles with various religious answers to war and life in a classroom setting as his beliefs are challenged by other more conventional religious structures.

Drawn together, this unlikely pair of Jessie and Andrew struggle to find meaning in their loss while they help each other fight for their dreams.

Now available on Amazon with this link:
getbook.at/fightingforeden

Here and Now: A Whimsical Take On God

In the beginning meets kindergarten story time

Philosopher Jeff Stilwell takes us on a journey that begins in ancient history, in the land of Ur, where God making was all the rage. Pursuing that thread through the Abrahamic religions of Judaism, Christianity and Islam to the present day, we discover that we don't need to make up gods to explain things anymore.

Since we all come accessorized with an expiration date, Stilwell encourages us all to make the most of this life we have to live, here and now.

Starring Stilwell's freethinking alter-ego Thrashin' Jack and his friend Lotus, *Here and Now* features over one hundred delightful and charming comics illuminating the story.

Available on Amazon with this link: getbook.at/hereandnow

Enjoy Jeff Stilwell's cheeky political thoughts on his YouTube channel:

Https://www.YouTube.com/c/jeffstilwellsthisisit

Find Jeff Stilwell's political commentary and cartoons on Facebook/stilwellwrites or Twitter/stilwellwrites.

Visit Jeff's website: JeffStilwell.com or send him an email at info@jeffstilwell.com.

www.ingramcontent.com/pod-product-compliance
Lightning Source LLC
Chambersburg PA
CBHW022019240626
47154CB00007B/2170